BLIND CORNER

BARRIE TAYLOR

Black Rose Writing | Texas

ISBN: 978-1-68513-503-4
PUBLISHED BY BLACK ROSE WRITING
www.blackrosewriting.com

Printed in the United States of America
Suggested Retail Price (SRP) $21.95

Blind Corner is printed in Minion Pro

*As a planet-friendly publisher, Black Rose Writing does its best to eliminate unnecessary waste to reduce paper usage and energy costs, while never compromising the reading experience. As a result, the final word count vs. page count may not meet common expectations.

This story came about because I was challenged to come up with something a little deeper and more twisty than my first effort. I thought about it and decided to take up the task.

Generally, I'm not a fan of crime procedurals. I wouldn't dare to criticize Agatha Christie, Colin Dexter or the people who created *Columbo* and the like, and I certainly wouldn't compare my effort with giants like those, but I knew what I wanted to avoid. There are a lot of clever mysteries that I've enjoyed but I couldn't think of one that really grabbed me and didn't let up. To be honest, I found them a bit plodding, and I wasn't interested in plod. I wanted something with raw energy. That was my starting point.

I'd be either naive or delusional if I said this plot is perfect. I did however, enjoy creating the central story and how the whole narrative ties together. It takes a lot of planning to put something like this in action, and I take my hat off to people such as Sir Arthur Conan Doyle who seemed to be able to come up with these plots in his sleep. It was good to step out of my comfort zone and try something a bit different, hence a whodunit with a romantic B-story.

But there's still plenty of car chases, shootouts and all the other lovely stuff that a growing lad needs!

Thanks to all those at the RAF Museum Cosford, Vulcan to the Sky, East Midlands Aeropark, all those at Barksdale AFB in Louisiana and Bruntingthorpe museum.

For Karen, Gin, Phreddd and Hoss. You told me I could do anything I wanted. Here's the proof.

BLIND CORNER

PROLOGUE

"This signal is blocking anything with a digital computer interface, Jack. Whoever is doing this has taken down everything. Communications, the internet. We can't scramble any of our aircraft! None of their systems will operate!" Simpson's filtered voice stated on the old- fashioned dial telephone's tinny speaker. "We're completely open to attack with no way of countermanding this digital block."

The President of the United States was meeting with the Prime Minister. All security measures which could be taken had, of course, been done, but it was still a tempting target.

Too tempting.

With the President and First Lady on the way to Downing Street, a sudden blackout of all communications had occurred. Cars ground to a halt on Whitehall, no computer or mobile phone could be switched on and it was the same story across the whole of the south of England.

It had to be something planted in the mobile phone towers that had cropped up all over the land for the situation to be so widespread, Colin Haltwhistle surmised.

No messages had been received from anyone issuing demands and there had been no warning of any threat.

Air Vice Marshal John Cartwright took the news in sagely. "I understand sir. We'll work on it from this end."

His senior officers faced him from the other side of the desk. Haltwhistle was already thinking of a strategy, while James McCleland must have been looking for a way around the problem.

"We need to jam this transmission long enough for the police and SAS to find this lunatic. He'd have to have a controller, probably a mobile phone on him. If we could shut down the jamming signal, we'd find him in a heartbeat," said Colin.

"That's all well and good, Haltwhistle, but how do we jam this thing?" Cartwright replied. "We can't rig any equipment up because it relies on the tech that this blackout... well, blacks out!"

"Couldn't we use an older aeroplane?" asked Colin. "A Tornado or a Sentry? They have radar jammers, and this signal is just another radar-type transmission."

"No," Jim told him. "They were all updated with digital computers and stuff years ago. They'd never start up, let alone get off the ground and I don't fancy a Sentry suddenly dropping out of the sky on Trafalgar Square, do you?"

Cartwright drummed his fingers on the desk. There seemed to be no answer to this. The situation was desperate. The early warning radar stations would be running on backup generators but their effectiveness would be limited. The whole of southern England was currently vulnerable to an attack with no way to strike back or defend against whatever would come.

"We need another answer, people."

Jim and Colin exchanged a look. Even Haltwhistle's detective senses were failing him. McCleland looked around the room hoping for inspiration. The pictures of aircraft on the far wall got his attention.

He moved toward the framed prints, a smile starting to cross his handsome features.

"Would she still fly?" he asked, turning to his colleagues beaming from ear to ear.

Cartwright saw what his pilot leader had spotted. "Now wait a bloody minute! She hasn't flown in 30 years, McCleland! She's not airworthy."

Haltwhistle picked up on Jim's idea immediately. "But she is kept in perfect working order, sir. And the jammers are still in place."

The CAA would have a field day with the investigation if the aircraft got off the tarmac, not to mention the questioned asked in the halls of the Ministry of Defence and the House of Commons. The plan was crazy, irresponsible and totally illegal, but it was also the answer.

Black Jack, as the only qualified pilot of the type went to his filing cabinet. Opening the top draw, his bone dome and oxygen mask were fished out.

"Come on!"

Colin looked between them. "You're really going to do this, aren't you?" He got up and ran after them as Casey Matthews looked on in confusion.

***

Cartwright's MG ZT screeched to a stop outside the hangar building. Joined by his two colleagues, he showed his pass to the confused concierge.

"We're requisitioning your aircraft for official government business," Black Jack informed him, marching into the building as he spoke.

"This is a retired, grounded airframe!" was the protest.

"Not any more, it isn't. Get it fueled, and get on to the tower," Cartwright commanded. "I want the runway kept clear of all aircraft."

The cockpit door swung down on its pistons and the yellow ladder so familiar to Cartwright was folded into place. Climbing it, the familiar smell of the foreboding black cockpit, the aviation fuel, hydraulic fluid and Bakelite scent wafted down to his younger subordinates.

McCleland followed him up, his helmet already in place. "It's been a while since I sat in one of these."

Cartwright squeezed through the gap between the front seats and settled himself in the pilot's chair on the left. Yes, still just as cramped as ever. With difficulty, Jim somehow got his burly frame in place and twisted into the right-hand seat. The dials festooning the flight deck were identical to those he had seen on the Battle of Britain Memorial Flight's Lancaster, which came as a surprise. A layman would be baffled but McCleland understood it all in seconds and smiled to himself how simplistic it was. The layout of the controls reminded him of the VC10. His head bumped on the low curved canopy.

"Bloody hell," he grumbled. "This wasn't built for someone my size!"

"Get used to it," Black Jack told him as he reached for the intercom button. He paused. "If this amazing plan of yours goes wrong we're all in the shit."

"If it goes right, we probably will be too," Haltwhistle said darkly from down the back of the cockpit.

Cartwright looked over the controls so familiar to him. It felt good to be back, but he didn't have time for nostalgia.

"Alright, we haven't got time for a checklist, this is gonna be a QRA start... if the rapid starter still works. Colin, are you with me?"

"Yes sir." Haltwhistle, seated at the Air Electronics Officer position was already uncomfortable.

The cockpit was hot, cramped and far too dark. The sea of dials and switches in front of him was incomprehensible and the exposed wires around his feet made the oppressive atmosphere even more claustrophobic. "I've seen newer stuff in an antique shop!"

"Well, it's all we've got to work with." Cartwright reached down to his left and pressed the fast starter control. The four giant engines began spooling, emitting a low whistle.

The hangar doors were already open and the fuel lines disconnected. The crew chief began waving his arms, ushering the huge aircraft into the open air beyond.

The ground crew watched as the graceful Avro Vulcan, its engines humming rolled out of the safety of the building, turned and trundled up the taxiway. The huge triangular bird turned onto the runway on the far side of the airfield.

"Request permission for takeoff," Cartwright said over the intercom.

There was a reluctant pause before the clearance came.

Holding the brakes on, Cartwright pushed the levers controlling the Bristol Olympus 202 engines forward to the stops. The infamous howl that the Vulcan was famous for filled the air and the aircraft surged forward, a huge cloud of unburned fuel in its wake.

"Call out the speed, Jim," Cartwright ordered, knowing McCleland had never flown as a co-pilot before. As a fast jet pilot, he'd been trained as a flyer only, and his experience meant that he was fast tracked into the captain's seat of the VC-10 straight away.

"I need to rotate at 180," the pilot explained.

Watching the analog gauge closely, Jim called out the appropriate speed. It had been 34 years since Black Jack had flown the Vulcan, but it was all coming back to him now. The flight stick was pulled back, and the giant wings did the rest as the aircraft almost jumped off the ground with a roar of power. The huge triangular aircraft climbed steeply over Southend and banked hard over, turning right and heading up the Thames Estuary, leaving hundreds of people on the beach below in awe of the sight and sound.

At the top of the takeoff climb, Cartwright leveled out and checked his dials. Airspeed and altitude were right. Adjusting his flaps, he pushed the rudder pedals and turned XL426 toward London, the lights of the capital and the tall skyscrapers of Canary Wharf could be seen over to their right, and following the course of the Thames made navigation easy.

Cartwright keyed a couple of the switches on the roll-out panel by his right knee.

"Fuel flow is good, all four engines are fine," Jim said, looking at the pressure and temperature dials. He paused. "I think... See? I told you she'd fly, sir."

"Indeed," was the pilot's wry remark. "Keep an eye on the fuel tanks. You need to keep her balanced."

"Are they these buttons down here?" McCleland pointed to the sliding tray between them. He had once had a tour of a cockpit when he was young and he was dredging his memory for what everything did.

"You learn fast." Cartwright nodded.

"Looks like they've kept this in really good nick," Jim said looking over the dials. Retro nostalgic did not even begin to describe how antiquated the cockpit was. By comparison, the Tornado had seemed quaint but it was light years ahead in terms of how dated it was.

"They used to really throw this around in the day at airshows," said Colin. He could remember seeing a display at RAF Finningley in the early 1990s. The Vulcan's remarkable ability to turn quickly had stuck with him.

"This really will be the final flight!" Jim said darkly. He could see the brass and the air crash investigators sticking their noses in after this.

"Colin, it's all on you. You need to switch on the countermeasures and jammers if this is going to work."

Looking over the vast wall of controls at his disposal, Haltwhistle was baffled. This technology was beyond him. The switchgear seemed endless and the dim light didn't help matters. At the other end of the desk, a radar screen came to life, throwing off an eerie green glow. Whoever had last used it had clearly left the unit switched on. The image looked like an old 1970s video game but it seemed to Haltwhistle that the ground below them was being scanned. He could make out the land either side of the river.

"Which one is it?" He was hesitant to touch something. He had visions of the priceless aircraft blowing apart if he pressed the wrong button.

"It's the controls on the panel in front of you," Cartwright told him.

"Yeah... but which one?"

Black Jack rolled his eyes. "I didn't look after that, I was up front. There should be a label saying War Use or something like that on it. I think there are a set of red lights on it. Press them all if you're not sure!"

Randomly pressing buttons and flicking switches, Colin had no idea if what he was doing was accomplishing anything. The dials did not give anything away.

"I have no idea if I'm doing anything, sir."

From below the Vulcan's underside, flashes of light dropped away. The flares used to counteract incoming missiles were of no use, but they made for a pretty firework display for anyone watching.

Black Jack reached for a set of buttons in the middle of the console framed by yellow paint and pressed something.

"What's that, sir?" Jim asked.

"Ram air turbine. More electrical power. We'll need every ounce of electricity for this."

Cartwright brought the fearsome aircraft in low over the center of London still following the river.

Below he could make out the Houses of Parliament and Big Ben through the Vulcan's tiny windows.

"Alright, here we go."

Those on the ground saw the giant triangle swoop in following the river and instantly their mobile phones began beeping with incoming texts and notifications. The equipment in the tail of the aircraft may be obsolete but it was still effective. McCleland's plan was working.

Phones began ringing on the desk of the office the Prime Minister and the President were holed up in. Out of the windows backing onto the garden, they saw the strange delta shape as it overflew them.

An aide rushed into the office. "Sir, we have telecoms back."

"I want whoever sent that jamming signal found, now!" he ordered.

"We're on it."

"And find out who's in that plane up there!"

Overhead, the bomber circled, the transmission from its Red Shrimp and Red Steer jammers playing havoc with the person responsible for this crisis' phone signal.

From his hiding place within Embankment tube station's stairwell, he tried desperately to send the ping again, but the airborne menace had put paid to him. In frustration, he slammed the keys of his phone. Using their own units to locate his signal, the police were soon with him.

"Excuse me, what are you doing?" asked a gentleman, suspicious of his actions.

"None of your damn business!"

A nearby police officer spotted the culprit and moved to investigate. The crazed man pulled a gun, pointing it at everyone close by.

"Keep back!"

Radioing for assistance, the officer was soon joined by his colleagues.

"It's over chum, put the gun down, now!"

Before he could react or flee, a brave security guard rugby tackled him to the ground. The gun and the phone was kicked away from him.

Picking up the offending phone, the officer examined it.

"No, don't touch it!" the man begged. "You can't stop what's coming!"

"Oh yes I bloody well can!" The phone's battery was snapped out of the case.

Almost instantly, the interference ceased. Computers and electronic equipment came back to life as if by magic. Bootup screens appeared on every monitor that had been active, TV pictures returned, and anyone watching the news was surprised to see an Avro Vulcan soaring over the capital.

From his office, Air Marshal Simpson looked up at the magnificent aircraft. "Jack, you crazy bastard, you did it!" he muttered to himself. He went to his desk and flicked a switch on his radio set.

"Air Vice Marshal Cartwright, come in," he said.

In the cockpit, Black Jack was not looking forward to this. He toggled the intercom switch.

"Cartwright here."

Simpson went out on the balcony of his office. "Jack. I know it's you in that tin triangle, don't try to deny it. You'd best beat a hasty retreat before people start asking questions. We'll talk later."

He rang off, shaking his head but secretly loving the solution his man had come up with.

The AVM looked at Jim, who shrugged. He pushed the controls and turned for Southend, but he couldn't resist a parting gesture.

Sweeping past Big Ben on his left, he opened the throttles of the enormous engines. Thousands of people watched as the old bomber howled past, its wingtips waggling in salute.

Crowds clapped and cheered in acknowledgment at the Vulcan. The enforced flight came to an end, signing off its flying career in style, doing the job it had been originally designed for back in 1947.

***

The formidable form of Air Marshal Andrew Simpson, head of the RAF was making his way toward the office. Greeted by Cartwright and Casey Matthews, Black Jack ushered him onward. Simpson's expression was as uncompromising as his body language.

"God, it's like seeing a heart attack roll toward you," McCleland murmured.

Colin stifled a chuckle and punched his friend on the arm. The last thing he wanted was a severe bollocking, which he was sure was coming. In fact, he could see the end of his career flashing before his eyes. The two older men came into the office where Jim and Colin quickly threw a salute and stood to attention.

"I'll keep this short. Well done, Jack," Simpson said, addressing the officer. "A rather... unorthodox answer to the situation, but problem solved anyway."

It was rare for the head of the service to personally visit the AID bunker, but the circumstances warranted the brass treatment.

"We had to improvise, sir. It is why the department was put in place." The AVM took in Jim and Colin, both still trying to look as innocent as possible.

"Yes, an unorthodox but well executed plan, Cartwright. I am curious, though." He paused for effect.

"Whose idea was it to take a grounded, unregistered aircraft for a joyride?" Simpson eyed them all suspiciously. He suspected he knew the answer.

"Erm... mine sir," Jim said, looking straight ahead.

The senior officer admired the honesty. "McCleland, you are impetuous, incorrigible and willful, traits I admire personally." He looked them all over. "Professionally, I should drum you all out but your actions, as unusual as they may be, get the results we need. The relevant authorities will be fobbed off, as usual." He paused and smiled. "That little farewell display you pulled off? The head of the CAA himself had steam pouring from his ears!"

"It seemed a more worthy sendoff than what 558 was forced to do, sir," Cartwright said lightly.

That was a point that Simpson had to agree with, even if what they had done to resolve the situation was preposterous on several levels.

"Do we know what the suspect's motives were, sir?" Haltwhistle asked, hoping to change the subject and wishing the senior officer would just get out of their hair.

"Yes, he was just another lunatic who hated the world. A computer programmer who decided he could bring the country down for money." Simpson shook his head. "We don't know if it was political or ideological or whatever yet."

"I wouldn't fancy the technology he had falling into the wrong hands," Colin said. "If it was adapted somehow, it'd make an awful weapon for someone."

Simpson thought for a moment. The white cap was right. All it would take was some adaptation and a means of delivering the signal, but in the right hands, it could be an effective deterrent.

"Again, good work people," he said. He saluted them and turned and left briskly. Once he was gone, the three looked at each other.

"I don't like the sound of that," Cartwright said. "I don't know if our intervention prevented a disaster or just delayed it."

"Probably best not to think too much and move on to the next job, sir," Colin replied. "You said yourself we're here to clean up the mess that people try to leave on our doorstep."

There was a thin smile on Black Jack's lips. "Yes, and it's a full time job!"

"At least we gave the Vulcan the sendoff it should have had," McCleland grinned, looking at the picture on the office wall again.

Cartwright smiled. "Always a silver lining with you, isn't there McCleland? And don't bother to try to look innocent, that cheeky grin of yours will get you into trouble faster than anything!"

He wondered if some of his old colleagues would agree with Jim's sentiment.

ONE

The Cessna 182 clawed its way into the twilight sky and turned towards the east, leaving the grassy airstrip behind. At the controls, Chris Woodley knew for him to get away with what he had been tasked to do, he had to keep under three hundred feet or risk being picked up by radar trackers.

That would make the Cessna, even as small as it was stand out like an illuminated Christmas ornament.

It also meant being hit by a bird could shred the propeller and would make this a very short and costly trip.

He could not believe that he had allowed himself to be forced into doing this, but under the threat of being exposed, he had agreed. He had the training and most importantly the means of transport to carry out his task. Checking his altimeter, Woodley leveled out at 280 feet.

That would give him a nice cushion - just high enough to clear treetops and telegraph poles and anything else which might creep out of gathering gloom to potentially end his journey early. It would also preclude the possibility of his being detected, which was good as the last thing he wanted was to be found out. Pointing the Cessna towards the east coast, Woodley knew he had about an hour until he reached that point with the course he had in mind. He was hoping this was a one-and-done deal. If he was discovered with what he had stowed away on board, he would be up the creek without a paddle.

He reflected on what the voice, accented in Spanish had said before he took off. "Deliver the package, or I will make you wish you'd not failed me."

It was a decision that he was coming to regret, and if his father found out, there'd be hell to pay. He'd come up with excuse for the difference between the hours on the airframe and what the logbook said.

But his life in the RAF would be over if he did not go through with this. It was a calculated risk, he had made this run before and there was only one other flight after this one to go.

A quick look over his shoulder showed his payload was secure and most importantly, nicely hidden.

Woodley sat back in the reasonably comfortable confines of the pilot's seat and continued his unspectacular progress towards the east edge of the British Isles. If he had been higher, the villages he was passing over would have appeared as pinpricks of light on a velvet background, but at this low altitude, he could make out individual houses. He was maintaining a discreet distance from settlements, hoping he was far enough away that he would not be heard.

Spots of rain splattered on the windscreen. Big splodges sat on the glass like vast bubbles floating up from a bowl of kitchenware being washed. This was not a good sign: he was flying straight into a thunderstorm. If he climbed to get over the cloud tops, which in a Cessna was unlikely he would most certainly be picked up on radar. If he stayed low, he pretty much doubled the risk of hitting something in the terrible visibility. The rain grew steadily worse as sheets of lightning and St. Elmo's fire danced around his cockpit windows and even over the nose which housed the engine, the thunder was overwhelmingly loud. At least no one would hear him now, he mused. As he got further into the storm, the visibility continued to decrease to where he could barely make out the engine cowling ahead of him.

Hopefully, this wouldn't continue for much longer. He checked his GPS.

Fortunately, he wasn't near any towns or villages or any large aerial masts which could take him by surprise, so he could at least continue to keep low and hopefully out of trouble.

The rain continued to batter the little Cessna, and it buffeted violently in the turbulent air, swaying and bucking while Woodley strained to keep the thing flying in a straight line. Finally, mercifully stars began to appear through the wisps of cloud and the thunder and lightning eased.

He was nearly clear of this mess, fortunately.

As the Cessna broke free from the roiling mass of the storm, Woodley checked his instruments again. He had dropped to 200 feet and had drifted a few miles south of his ideal flight path. Giving himself a break, he brought the machine up to just under 300 feet again.

Ahead through the wisps of cloud, the land gave way to a large, black vastness. The occasional light away in the darkness gave away ships on the dark expanse of the North Sea that was now dead ahead. He was nearly clear of the confines of merry old England and so he could relax a little. He still had the problem of getting to Holland, landing and coming back, but at least the first part of his journey was done with.

There were just a few more miles to run out before he was over the coastline and out of Dear Old Blighty's jurisdiction.

Anyone on the ground a few miles south of Lowestoft, Suffolk would have looked up to see a flash of light not far above the ground. A tremendous boom echoed across the peaceful, open fields. A mass of twisted, flaming metal and fiberglass fell from the sky and crashed into an unpleasant mess in an unsuspecting farmer's potato field. The remains of the Cessna eventually burned themselves out as the sullen rain lashed down on the wreckage.

Chris Woodley's final flight would never reach its destination.

At first light, the owner of the potato field brought his tractor to his property, intending to harvest his crop for the upcoming Farmers' Market. The elderly man had hoped to be done by midday and then head off to the local pub and enjoy a game of dominoes with his friends over a few pints. The smoldering remains of the Cessna piled in the northern corner of his land meant his day was going to be rather different than he had planned for himself.

***

The phone's insistent ring tone awoke Jim McCleland from his slumber. Next to him, he felt something warm move across him trying to reach for his mobile.

"It's too early," the girl's voice mumbled. "Turn it off."

But the phone kept calling. Jim groaned and stretched and pulled himself upright.

"Hello?"

"Jim? I'm very sorry to interrupt you but you're needed." The sarcasm Flt. Lt. Colin Haltwhistle was employing virtually dripped down the phone line.

"Yeah? What is it?" McCleland rubbed his eyes.

"You'll need to get to the office, now." Colin's smile was obvious. "Sorry to tear you away from your lady friend, whoever she is this morning."

Lily was now awake enough to hear and understand. "Whoever she is…? How dare you?"

"You cheeky...!" was all he could respond with. In short order, he found himself abruptly thrown out of Lily's apartment, just as his commanding officer hailed him.

"Report to me at once," was the simple command.

The Mustang started and the disgruntled driver began the short drive into central London.

Arriving at the archway under Waterloo East station, the Squadron Leader headed underground to the meeting he had been summoned to. Entering the bunker, he was led straight into Cartwright's office by Casey Matthews.

"Took your time, didn't you, McCleland?" was Matthews terse comment.

"Bit like you doing anything. I hope you don't keep your missus waiting," was the blunt reply.

Their relationship was still testy at best. Matthews led Jim into Cartwright's office and went back to his work. He so wanted to wipe the smile from McCleland's face somehow.

Seated in Black Jack's office, the Squadron Leader was quickly filled in on the details of what had happened overnight.

"As far as we can tell it was an unscheduled flight and it came to an equally abrupt end. I want to know what's going on," Black Jack insisted. "Go and assist Haltwhistle in whatever way you can."

Why Colin was already on the scene was something that puzzled McCleland.

"Because this is an investigative matter, he had to go straight there, Jim," was Black Jack's only comment.

"Yes sir." Jim still wasn't sure about the logic, but his was not to reason why, he supposed.

"You and Haltwhistle are to take over whatever investigation is already going on. Doesn't matter if it's forensics, our dear friends from Farnborough or Dirty Harry, this job is an RAF priority and I want to know what happened," Cartwright stated simply.

"I'm sorry sir, but why us? A private plane crash doesn't exactly fall under our remit, surely?" McCleland asked.

Black Jack simply looked at his subordinate with a mixture of pity and impatience.

"The aircraft is believed to belong to the base commander of RAF Sutton Donington," the matter-of-fact tone of the AID chief meant this was not open to negotiation. "That's why. So yes, it falls to us and that's why there's a connection to our section."

Jim groaned inwardly. He was hoping to wriggle out of it by this thing being a wrinkle of CAA authority. But no. Added to that, the air crash people would be crawling all over the site and slow them down. But the small print in the AID's writ meant they took precedence, which was a comfort.

"The Air Accidents people are going to love being told to piss off, sir," Jim smiled. He had no love for that agency.

"Then you'll have to be your good, diplomatic self and be nice about getting rid of them, won't you?"

Cartwright shared his lack of respect or time for them, but they also had their own job to do.

"I'll do my best, sir." He frowned.

"Good luck to you both and report progress." Black Jack smiled just a touch.

With that, Jim saluted and was out of the office. Checking his trusty Ruger .357 out of the armory, he picked out a Sig Sauer P226 X5 .40 for his partner and headed back to street level where he knew his 5.0 Ford Mustang was waiting for him. A nosy traffic warden was checking around the big American machine and was pulling his writing pad to give McCleland a ticket, when Jim got back to his vehicle.

"Is this your car sir?" was the typical introduction.

"No, it's the invisible man's," was the sarcastic reply. "Yes, it's my car."

"Well if you don't want to pay the £25 fine I'm going to give you, this vehicle will be towed and then it will be invisible," the traffic warden said in an especially officious manner.

Jim pointed to the sign affixed to the wall behind them. "This is private property mate, so you're trespassing. I suggest you move on."

The traffic warden continued jotting down the Mustang's details, and tore off the counterfoil, handing it to McCleland. Jim simply tore it in half and dropped it.

"Take it and stick it, pal. You're on private land, so jog on," was the blunt comment as he climbed into the Ford and started it up.

"I'll be writing this up!" the aggrieved warden protested.

"Make sure you sign it 'courtesy of Mr. R. Sole," Jim shot back. The engine roared into life, and he shot off.

Heading north out of the city McCleland put in a call to Haltwhistle on the hands-free phone.

"Col, you out there?"

"Yes mate. Where are you?"

Jim swerved through the traffic, heading for the M11 which would put him in roughly the right direction while the phone reception cut in and out, causing Colin to fade in and out.

"I'm heading to Norfolk now. The old man filled me in."

"Alright. I'll see you when you get here."

Jim knew nothing about crime scenes, but he knew the deceased would have had to be removed.

"Has the bloke who croaked been spirited away? Do we know how he snuffed it?"

There was an audible sigh from the other end of the line. "What a charming turn of phrase,"

Colin chided him. "Yes, the deceased has been removed. I haven't worked out how he was killed yet, but beware though, the jokers from the Air Crash Investigation are already on the scene."

McCleland made a face. "Oh lovely. I'll be there as quickly as I can. Just hang tight, okay?" He gunned the Mustang along the dual carriageway making good time for his destination. He had no love for the CAA's crash scene investigation unit, having first-hand experience of having been cross-examined by them when giving evidence on a crash of a Tucano, a type he had passed his basic flight training on. The investigation had been a tedious and overly long-winded process.

An hour later, McCleland screeched to a stop by the field he had been told to report to.

Colin's Mondeo parked on the opposite side of the road meant he was in the right place. A little green MG ZR hatchback was similarly parked just ahead of him. Changing into a set of Wellington boots he hooked from the boot, Jim clomped across the muddy field. He flashed his pass at the local constabulary who had set up a cordon around the scene and found his partner in the middle of a very loud argument with his opposite number from the CAA Crash Board.

"This is a crime scene! If you keep moving stuff around, you'll ruin any evidence!" His loud protestations were not without merit, but the first of two investigators who had been sent by their unit didn't see it that way.

"Look, you're in the way of some very delicate work. How would you like to be thrown off the site?"

"This is bullshit!" Colin shouted angrily. It was unlike him to swear on duty, but he was becoming stressed. He presented his identification again. "What does that say? Read the small print, you ignorant bellend! We have the authority, so you can piss off!"

While the argument went on, the smaller of the two plastic-clad figures ignored the two squabbling men and continued to take measurements and jotted those down on a notepad which Haltwhistle, despite the inconvenience presented by the CAA official, noticed was covered in facts and figures.

McCleland could hear the yelling from halfway across the field as clear as day. He couldn't help but smile a bit at his friend's exasperation. He got worked up far too easily. Probably why Col hadn't made it as a pilot. Being hot-headed while at the controls was not smart. He reached the tarpaulin-covered crash scene and ducked down to get in. The smell of fuel and scorched fiberglass hung in the air.

"What's going on here?" he asked, although he didn't need to. He showed his identification.

Colin saw him and sighed with relief. "Thank Christ you're here. I've been trying to tell these arseholes that they're messing up the evidence that's here. I could do with a bit of backup."

Haltwhistle was feeling punchy. He took his duties seriously, especially with this kind of situation and he intended to carry out a thorough investigation. The two air investigators were getting in his way, and he didn't like it at all.

For their part, they didn't want some upstart from the RAF thinking he had carte blanche to do pretty much whatever the hell he liked screwing up their evidence-gathering exercise. Jim could see both sides of the argument.

"I'm sure we can find a way to work together," he said soothingly.

That was not what Haltwhistle had expected or indeed wanted to hear at all.

"Yeah, sure we can. You can get your boy here and both of you can bugger off while we do our job," said the first investigator, clad in a plain white forensic suit.

"'Boy?'" Colin spluttered. "You sanctimonious prick!" He squared up to the man and said through gritted teeth "Take this hanger-on of yours and get the hell out of here! Military priority!"

"Col, cool it," Jim warned him warily.

Colin's hotheaded temperament was showing itself graphically. He grabbed his shoulder and pulled him away out of earshot, making it clear he wanted a word in private and for no one else to hear.

"I need to check this place over. This is an RAF-related crime scene and I need to investigate. I can't do that with those two wankers screwing everything up. Give me an hour and get them out of my hair."

Jim simply looked at his friend with a 'Who, me?' look on his face. "How am I supposed to do that?"

"Do what you do best, take them to the pub or something," Colin spat.

"And suppose they're teetotal?"

Christ, Jim could be petulant at times. Haltwhistle was in no mood to tolerate his friend's sarcasm.

"Then find a massage parlor and get them laid! I don't care. Just get them out of here, okay?"

Colin was getting ever more exasperated by the second. Jim nodded and opened his jacket.

"Your little joke got me thrown out this morning. I'm not sure insults are in your remit as my partner."

"Sorry." The white cap certainly didn't sound apologetic. "It's not likely to stop you from picking up another girlfriend, is it? Now could you please get those morons out of my sight?"

Instead, Jim showed Haltwhistle the Sig P226 Elite .40 and holster.

"What's that?" It was not so much a question of what the gun was but more of what his friend was trying to accomplish.

"It's a feather duster," was the sarcastic response. "It's your new piece. I want to be well tooled up and after our last jaunt, I thought you should take this. It's legit and hits anything like a hammer," he explained.

"Do you think that's a good idea to bring it here with those two watching?"

"Now's as good a time as any, mate." Jim handed him the functional, silver automatic.

"I'm not checked out on this thing. I always use a Glock," Haltwhistle protested.

McCleland raised a skeptical eyebrow. "If you think my wingman or I are going into the lion's den without some hardware, you're very much mistaken."

"But I was certified with the 17. It's a good weapon," Colin protested.

"Yeah, I know all about you winning the pistol competition, and I've seen you shoot."

Haltwhistle had won the annual RAF pistol shooting competition three years running. His reputation as a marksman with a handgun or rifle was known throughout the service, and Jim, having first-hand experience of how devastating his friend could be with a gun, knew a formidable shot needed a sidearm to suit.

"I'd rather go with the Glock." Colin turned the weapon over in his hands.

McCleland shook his head. "I've got a bad feeling about this and I want something hardcore. Do me a favor, skip the water pistol and have this."

Haltwhistle took the pistol. The .40 round had a decided edge in stopping power over the 9mm Glock, so it was a shoe-in as far as Jim was concerned. Haltwhistle reluctantly agreed. The weapon was fitted with wood grips which felt good in the hand.

"Trust me, you'll thank me," Jim assured him.

Colin noticed a non-standard sidearm was placed into McCleland's shoulder holster.

"Don't worry, I got them from the armory." Jim's face was a picture of wryly amused satisfaction.

He'd rubbed off on his friend and he was enjoying every minutet. He nodded to the two people working the crash. "I'll get rid of our friends over there and get you the time."

Becoming more irritable by the minute, Haltwhistle said "I'd very much appreciate that. It doesn't do to work within the law when we don't have to. And time isn't on our side."

"Watch a master at work." Jim headed back to where the two white-clad figures were hunched over some wreckage that the tarpaulin was not covering up. They were taking pictures and making measurements of the carnage when he approached them.

He smiled as he decided on his course of action.

"It looks like the two of you could do with a break. How about something to eat? My treat," he offered hopefully. He looked from one to the other. The first man shook his head.

"No thanks, we're fine." He continued with his work but the other looked at their wristwatch.

"Actually," a pleasant feminine voice came from under the white cape of the other suit, "We could probably do with a break. Alright."

The first figure looked a little dejected from his body language. McCleland smiled, knowing his job had just become considerably easier.

"I know a nice pub nearby which does a very good carvery. Interested?" It was a white lie as he didn't know any pubs in this area, but being the countryside, there was bound to be one around.

"I don't know. I'm a vegetarian," said the feminine voice who was obviously looking at him.

Despite that, McCleland knew he was on to a winner here.

"I'm sure we could find something to your liking," he told her. Apparently, he had as she gestured for him to lead on.

Jim started heading across the field, while Colin appeared to head off toward the line of trees at the other end of the square section of land. He crossed a stile and went into the next field, heading for the lane from the other direction.

"Is that mouthy bastard not coming? You'd best not be-" the man said testily, thumbing to Colin.

"I wouldn't dream of it," Jim assured him. "And neither would he."

Fortunately, Colin was making his way back to his car as well.

"He'd better not interfere with the crime scene. Why isn't he coming to the pub?"

"He's teetotal. And with guards everywhere, I doubt he can do anything," said Jim with a grin.

He could feel his partner's eyes boring into the back of his head. Colin wasn't so far away he couldn't hear Jim talking. The girl giggled at his joke.

Haltwhistle got in to the Mondeo and appeared to drive away. McCleland led them back to the Mustang, and changed out of his wellies. The two investigators got rid of their unflattering full length suits. Having offered them a lift which was accepted, he held the passenger door open for them. The gentleman was middle-aged and was testy of temperament, and scrambled into the back of the muscle car.

By contrast, the young lady was in her late 20's, attractive in a cute way with dirty blonde hair which she had styled in a long bob parted on the left and large, round brown eyes. Her face had an unblemished complexion. She was a little on the petite side, Jim thought, maybe about 5'3".

He took in a discreet view and found himself checking her out.

She was certainly a pleasant person to be around too, just from the brief conversation so far. He snapped out of it before he was caught window shopping. Colin had asked for an hour for them out of the way. He was sure he could get him two if he could get one or both of them talking.

"Very nice car," the girl said as she got comfortable in the leather bucket seat.

"Thanks." Jim started up, the stereo blaring AC/DC as he headed off up the road in search of the pub. He noticed out of the corner of his eye that she was giving him a good look over in return.

The attraction seemed to go both ways and apparently, she liked what she was seeing.

"I don't see why I should be cooped up in the back of this thing," grumbled the man as he hit his head on the low curved roof.

***

Now that Jim had got those two arseholes out of the way, Haltwhistle could get to work. He pulled up beside the field again and traversed the muddy ground. Finishing his half-empty bottle of soda, he pocketed it. There was no point looking for a black box as light aircraft didn't carry them. No, the evidence he needed was right here in front of him. All he had to do was look for it and find it.

The tailplane of the Cessna was intact, as was the engine compartment. The registry numbers were emblazoned just fore of the stabilizers. No wonder Black Jack had been able to tell them who the plane belonged to. The fuel tanks had not been destroyed, which meant this was not an engine or fuel explosion. The aircraft's wing boom was mostly in one piece if a bit singed and melted in places. But the cockpit and passenger compartment had been completely blown apart, and from the state of the fuselage's blast damage, it had been destroyed from the inside out. So, whatever had caused this must have been stored in the cockpit area.

Among the crumbling plastic of the cockpit's dashboard, a set of dog tags dangled forlornly.

Colin grimly understood that the owner of them had been immolated along with most of the aircraft and his remains, if they hadn't already been removed, were probably under his feet. It was a notion he did not want to entertain. He was not squeamish by nature, but his one experience of witnessing an autopsy had not been pleasant.

Fortunately, the dog tags still had the basic details of their wearer legible. That meant only one thing: the pilot had been RAF. And with the owner of the plane being an RAF officer, no wonder Cartwright had wanted to keep this an internal investigation and for him and

McCleland to get to the scene as fast as possible. With the service number printed on the tag as well, it would be easy to track down who the unfortunate soul at the controls had been.

Looking at the remains of what was left of the rest of the cockpit, the charred remnants of the seats sat like ghastly effigies, upright but grisly. There was nothing else really of note to be found in the forward part, so Colin switched his focus to the rear and worked his way backward.

The blackened tatters of what used to be a kit bag blew around. Even under the tarpaulin there was an annoying breeze. The kit bag had piqued his curiosity. What had been in it?

A check of where the storage compartment should have been revealed, just like the cockpit, it had been completely blown apart by a blast made from an internal space. That confirmed the idea whatever had been stored on board had destroyed the Cessna.

But what?

Under the rags that had once been the kit bag, a small silver switch lay burned and scorched. The legend *No.7 Mk 1* was just about readable, along with some other, numerical script. At that moment, Colin knew what had destroyed the plane. A quick check of the registry showed the Cessna had been kept at a private airfield in southern Leicestershire. The best place to check for a flight plan was there. Pulling out his notebook, Haltwhistle jotted down his findings and took some photos of what he'd discovered.

Making his way back across the mud got Colin's mind whirring. They of course needed to notify the next of kin, find out the flight plan and why he was carrying military weapons on a civilian private aircraft. Who were they delivering them to? And why? And was this an accident, or was it deliberate? If it was the latter, they were looking at a murder investigation.

He headed back to the Mondeo, satisfied there was nothing else to be gained at the moment.

Anything else would be detailed in the forensics report. Getting into the car, Haltwhistle took the receiver from the armrest, the secure and direct channel to Cartwright back at base.

"Rapier 2 to Wren's Nest. Rapier 2 to Wren's Nest. Come in."

"Wren's Nest," came Cartwright's deep, gravelly voice.

Colin turned the dog tag over in his fingers. "Request you get a next of kin check on C. Woodley, Serial number 17013745607."

After a few moments, Cartwright's voice filtered back.

"Christopher Woodley, Corporal. RAF Sutton Donington. Next of kin: Group Captain Frank Woodley and Mrs. Jennifer Woodley." Colin was about to reply when Cartwright cut in.

"Additional information: Frank Woodley is the active base commander of Sutton Donington and the owner of the aircraft. I should have informed you of that earlier. I had the serial number of the aircraft checked. It was Woodley senior's."

That complicated things somewhat. There could be conflicts of interest and accusations of favoritism as possible motives.

"Corporal Woodley appears to be the pilot of the Cessna sir. And he's dead," Colin said quietly.

"Are you sure? I need to be sure before we go any further," Black Jack told him.

"I have got his dog tags which I just pulled from the wreckage, sir. I'm certain that it's him. I need to make sure that the Air Accident Board doesn't know what we know, and I need to know the home base of this aircraft."

Black Jack snorted. "You don't want much, do you? What else did you find?"

Colin looked at the detonator. "I think it was a Dingbat mine that caused this plane to go down."

There was an intake of breath at the other end of the line. "Are you sure? If that's the case it changes everything."

"I've got the detonator pin in my hand, sir." The Dingbat, an anti-personnel mine was now restricted under new legislation and the MoD was in the process of disposing of its stocks. There were only handful of places where such a thing could be got. A munitions store on the military base being the most likely.

There was a brief pause while Cartwright typed something, which Colin assumed was a gagging restriction to be sent off.

"Alright. The registered aerodrome is Melbourne Airfield. It's a light aircraft strip in north Leicestershire. I'll take care of the air crash Wombles."

Haltwhistle nodded. He always appreciated his boss's help. "Thanks. Rapier 2 out."

TWO

While his partner was busy gathering evidence, Jim McCleland was finishing tucking into steak and chips and a pint of creamy, dark ale which tasted smooth but stout. A good wholesome pub lunch.

And it was as well. The pub was a typical, warm, cozy English country pub with a roaring log fire and oak beams supporting the ceiling and lining the walls. Pictures of the local countryside and the sea which wasn't far away adorned the walls. It had a real down-home feel and the smell of the wood hung in the air.

Behind the bar, an aging couple who owned the place kept a watchful eye on the patrons, not that there were many of those at this time of day. The carpet was sticky, a legacy of dozens of pints that had not found the thirsty lips of the local or the traveler who had bought it, which was frankly heresy.

Jim regarded his two guests. While Phil, the lead investigator was a bit of a bore, he was also pretty unfriendly. He also liked jazz music and crosswords. Erm…ok. As Colin had said, he needed a visit to a massage parlor and the salubrious delights they offered. It may have lightened his mood. The mention of jazz made Jim think of *The Fast Show,* and Phil reminded him of Louis Balfour, even vaguely resembling the tone-deaf musical host played by Jon Thomson.

The girl, however, was another matter entirely. Her name was Sophie and, to McCleland at least, was much more interesting. Aside from her obvious physical attributes, as a person she had got Jim's rapt attention. It was her eyes that were the most striking thing about her, being dark brown.

"I have a degree as well," she said as he snapped back to attention. "In criminal law and forensic science."

It fit. If she was a crime scene investigator, intelligence was a requirement for the job.

"That's pretty impressive. I have a few A-Levels but never got that far. Too busy learning to fly."

"That sounds like it was hard work." She looked at him, clearly expecting more details.

"The actual flying part is pretty easy, it's all the other stuff you have to do with the instruments and managing the fuel tanks, that's the hard bit," he explained.

Her taste in music leaned towards pop rather than rock and metal. "Metallica is too heavy for me. I do like Nirvana though," Sophie admitted, to a broad grin from her host. If he had to pick a favorite band, Motorhead would surely be it, but Nirvana ran them close. She was a *Star Trek* fan, but he'd let that one slide. He didn't have the heart to tell her what his preferences leaned toward, especially if word got back to his best friend. Colin would have a field day with that! He stuck to sports.

"I guess you have a lot of girlfriends in your line of work," she said. After catching her looking him over, he was sure it was attraction rather than just idle conversation, but he played along.

He scoffed. Haltwhistle had made sure he was single at the moment! "Nah, I'm always too busy to enjoy that sort of thing." He attempted to be cool. "You?"

"I don't have anyone at the moment." Sophie had picked over a leafy salad meal and drunk her ice water. She was now asking him about his life. "So, you're a pilot?"

McCleland smiled, he had got her attention as much as she had captured his.

"That's right, but not actively at the moment. It's only part of my job."

"And what does the rest of your job involve?" she asked, genuinely interested. She was looking for an angle. The fact he was present at an air crash scene put him on the map.

"Oh. A bit of this and a bit of that," he said, trying to be as vague as possible. *Yeah, I'm sure you'd be interested in knowing about me traveling around the world, blowing shit up and killing people who threaten the security of these green and pleasant lands,* he thought. But he certainly didn't want to let on he and Colin were involved in criminal investigations, although that was probably obvious, based on their very presence.

"Let me guess. You work for the government?" she guessed.

Jim's eyes narrowed. "What makes you say that?"

"To be able to just waltz into a crime scene and give orders like you own the place, and you're not wearing any kind of uniform which just screams government agent." She set her fork down and looked at him. "By the way, if you or your friend had attempted to tamper with anything, that's a serious offense, even for an agent."

Damn, she was good. Very observant, very smart. Jim noticed her partner was keeping quiet, though.

In response, he simply said, "Something like that."

"And your first name is Jim. Is your last name Bond?' Sophie teased.

He laughed. "No. McCleland. James McCleland."

The girl pouted her lips a little. "Is the man an animal?" Was this lady some sort of idealized version of his dream woman, who knew exactly what he enjoyed? Wow.

"It depends on if I'm going for first or not," he winked.

She laughed a little. She had a nice laugh. Her button nose wrinkled and she brushed her hair behind her ear.

"You look surprised I'd know something about that. I love a bit of motor racing. Well, the older stuff. The new stuff leaves me cold." Jesus, this girl was heaven-sent.

He had to agree with the assessment. "You're right about the modern racing. It's rubbish compared to 20-odd years ago. Yeah, I suppose there's a bit of rose-tinted glasses, but I'd much rather watch the older F1 and sportscars and stuff than the newer seasons."

She took a drink of water. "Did you have a favorite driver?"

Jim grinned. The chance to talk racing with a like-minded fan was Too good to pass up. "Yeah. Gilles Villeneuve, and Keke Rosberg. And Senna."

Sophie looked confused. "He was a bit before our time, wasn't he? I liked his son."

"Yeah, but I like James Hunt as well."

"That figures!" she laughed. "I was a big Damon Hill fan. And then Hakkinen." She paused. "And I think Alonso is fit."

"Schumacher was better." McCleland had a big soft spot for the ultra-successful German legend.

She giggled and finished her salad. That was her only downside, Jim decided. But it was her choice to make. She looked at her watch, as did Phil. It hadn't escaped Jim's notice that he had remained almost silent throughout the entire meal.

"Right, Sophie. We need to get back to the site. End of break."

As promised, Jim paid for their lunches and they stepped out into the crisp, damp air. Jim turned his collar up. A fine drizzle was falling, not heavy enough to be rain but more than mist or dew.

Piling back into the Mustang, he set off back to the crash site. His passengers cringed, enduring his enthusiastic driving style.

"Careful, pal, I don't want there to be a scene of a second crash in this area," Phil warned Jim.

A few minutes later and they were back where they had started that morning.

"Well, er... thank you very much for the meal," said Sophie.

"No worries." Jim handed her his card. "Keep in touch." He had noticed Colin's Mondeo had gone when they pulled up and hoped the two investigators wouldn't realize what had happened.

Not too quickly, anyway.

He bid his farewells and drove off. Once he was around a corner and out of sight, he put in a call to Colin.

"What did you find, chief?"

"A lot of interesting stuff. I'm heading down to look at the Cessna's home airfield," Colin replied. Jim reckoned something was coming which he would not enjoy. He was right.

"I've got a job for you, mate," Colin went on. He filled McCleland in on what he wanted him to do. As he had expected, Jim was not relishing this job.

"Erm, mate, I don't feel comfortable doing that," he said, suddenly feeling guilty.

"You have to. I'm sending you something now, so watch your phone."

"Are you sure you don't want to wait and do this together?" Jim didn't want to sound like he was trying to get out of a tough task, but he was.

"I don't know how long I'm going to be checking this thing out. I need you to do this, ok? If you can find out who this Chris Woodley's contacts are, what division he works in and talk to his friends, that'd be a big help. I'll be there as quick as I can," Colin told him.

McCleland sighed. Giving bad news was not something he signed on for, but the most unfortunate task an officer had to perform had fallen to him on this occasion.

"You'll owe me for this, mate."

Signing off, he pointed the Mustang westwards and worked out despite the sat-nav telling him it would take about three hours to get to his destination. Heading across the Norfolk fens, he decided the fastest way to do this was to head for Boston, then go through Sleaford towards Grantham and then head south, avoiding the East Midlands cities of Nottingham and Derby.

RAF Sutton Donington was one of the largest bases the Royal Air Force possessed. Once a home to a section of the V-Force, fielding the Vickers Valiant, it had also been the home to several squadrons of Jaguars before the introduction of the Tornado in the early 1980s had seen the station convert to the new type. It was where a young Flying Officer Jim McCleland had reported after graduating from flight training to begin his career proper as a mud mover on the Tornado GR4.

After various moves and squadron amalgamations, he remembered he had not set foot on this camp in ten years. As he pulled up to the gates, he felt a pang of nostalgia. The gate guard asked for his ID, which he provided.

"Nice car," the guard said appreciatively, taking in the sharp, aggressive lines of the muscle car.

"Thanks." He pulled smoothly through the barrier and took a quick look at the gate guard, a Tonka GR1 in desert pink Gulf War One colors. He had a lot of nice memories of piloting the jet. And some not-so-nice ones, it had to be said.

It was a good thing he was driving slowly as a huge articulated lorry swung wide from his right.

Its driver, apparently not seeing the red and white American car blast it's horn.

Taking quick action, Jim swerved the car to the left, mounting a curb and wiping out several flowers under the wide racing tyres. McCleland stopped, jumped out and discovered the Mustang had not been damaged. For his part, the truck driver continued on his way.

"You fucking twat!" Jim shouted, but to no avail.

A corporal hurried over. "Are you alright, sir?"

Still checking the right side of his car for dings and scratches, Jim replied absently "Yeah I'm fine."

"Those idiots," the corporal went on. "Coming and going all week with new kit. Fortunately, that's the last load. I hope so at least." He seemed genuinely relieved, as if it had been a chore to deal with.

"Last of what?" Jim asked, looking at the young man in his early 20's. Sharp featured and with gray, intelligent eyes. He had a scar over his left eyebrow which aged him somewhat.

"Surplus and old weapons sir. They came last night for them and to drop off new stock."

"Well, that driver needs to be taken out and shot with whatever guns are in the back of that artic. He bloody well nearly wiped me out!" Jim complained.

"I'm very sorry sir," was the earnest comment. "Do you want me to report it?"

Satisfied his car had not been a prime candidate for the knackers yard, Jim got in. "No that's fine. Thanks though."

The corporal stood stiffly to attention as Jim drove off, clearly envious of the car.

He pulled into the car park and stopped near the mess accommodation. Checking the details on his phone which Haltwhistle had sent him, he took a deep breath and went up to the gleaming white painted door. The house was as immaculate as the door was. A neat row of colorful plants lined the front garden and some well-trimmed bushes in large pots sat on either side of the door.

Then a thought struck him. The base commander would be on duty at this time of day surely? He walked along to the main administration building and signed in.

An eager corporal showed him to the office of a short, mustachioed Group Captain, Frank Woodley stood and shook hands with Jim. Woodley had not been at the base when Jim had been there, but they had heard of each other by reputation. The office was a typical MoD room, plain white, with old metal sash windows. A large wooden desk with bookcases and filing cabinets lined the wall and a decrepit old fan spun noisily on its axis above them.

"What can I do for you, Squadron Leader?" He offered Jim a seat.

"Well sir, I think it's something that you and your lady wife should know at the same time," McCleland was serious and quiet.

"Why, what's happened?"

"Do you own a Cessna, registry G-KHNN?"

Woodley leaned forward and rested his hands on the desk. "Yes, I do. What about it?"

"Well sir, there's no easy way to tell you this. Last night your Cessna crashed in Norfolk. We believe your son was killed." Jim was not comfortable, and Woodley picked up on that.

"Are you sure that it was my aircraft?"

Jim produced his phone and showed him the photos that had been taken. The registry of the aircraft was the dead giveaway. At that moment, the phone on Woodley's desk began trilling. A little shakily, he answered it.

"Yes... Yes, darling I know... I have a young man here who is telling me now... Yes... I'll be there in a few minutes. I know." He placed the receiver down. "It looks like you're right, Mr. McCleland. My wife just saw on the news the crash you're talking about."

He got up, took his topcoat from its hanger and slipped it on.

"Come with me. We should visit my wife."

THREE

Haltwhistle arrived at the aerodrome after a cross-country drive similar to Jim's. Unlike Jim he didn't have over 300 horsepower and a need to drive like a racing driver to get somewhere. The field of the aerodrome was littered with light aircraft, parked neatly around the control tower which was based in the portakabin which also passed for the office and coffee shop. The airfield itself, a grass strip sat on the crest of a hill and was overlooked by an ancient church tower to the south and a row of trees to its left which extended to the road which passed the whole site. Colin stopped the car in front of the portakabin and headed inside. A short-haired woman who, from the state of her voice had smoked more than her fair share of cigarettes, her fingers were stained brown from the nicotine and her skin was creased from the drying effects of the tar leaned against the counter. She was short and squat but was friendly enough.

"Can I help you?"

"Yes, I'm interested in seeing the logs from last night and any paperwork you might have filed for an aircraft that's based here," he said politely.

"I'm sorry. I'll need written notice for that," she replied.

Colin produced his ID card. "Good enough?"

She gave him a quizzical look and disappeared into another room. He took a look around the portakabin and out onto the aerodrome through one of the bug-spattered windows. It was a typical small field. It didn't even have a hangar, instead a large piece of canvas was held up by telescopic poles which gave a modicum of protection. The inside of the cabin was dominated by a huge plotting chart of the British Isles which was covered with air flight lanes and pins which denoted other airfields.

The lady returned with a couple of logbooks which she set down on her counter.

"Here they are." She opened one up and slid it across for Haltwhistle to look at. "This one gives all the aircraft which have been signed out, and this one has all the routes flown."

Colin scanned the pages for the last twenty-four hours. There was no sign of the Cessna, and nothing with a serial number remotely similar was listed. He checked the inside spine of the book. No torn out pages, no sign of tampering. The aircraft had simply not been listed as taking off.

"How would you account for this? It's aviation law that every flight has to be recorded. Also, I think you'll find an aircraft is missing from this field and hasn't been accounted for."

She started, her eyes widening. "Which aircraft?"

He looked at her. "Cessna. Registry G-KHNN."

"That's Mr. Woodley's plane! He and his son came down a lot and they would take turns with flying it. What happened?"

Colin shook his head. "I need to know why your paperwork isn't in order first."

She went over the logbooks again and rooted for some card files, which she opened up. "These are where the flight plans are filed."

She went through them, but again there was nothing to be turned up.

"I don't understand it!" wailed the woman. "There's no way this could be."

"Was there any sign of tampering when you arrived this morning? No broken locks, doors, windows or anything?" Colin asked.

She shook her head. "No. Nothing at all."

Haltwhistle scratched his head and ran his fingers through his wavy brown hair.

"Well, we may not know when it took off or where it was going, but we know where it ended up."

She was on edge. "Really, where?"

Colin chose his words carefully. "Its remains are sitting in a field just south of Lowestoft in a burned out wreck."

The woman was visibly upset. She was very fond of both the Woodley men so for something to have happened to one or other was very distressing to her. Colin sat her down with a cup of coffee.

"It seems the pilot was carrying something on board he shouldn't have been. Does either man have a locker here or something?"

The lady looked thoughtful for a second and sipped her drink.

"He brought a couple of big holdall bags in a few days ago, but I've not seen them since."

Haltwhistle was thinking quickly. Could that be what he took with him? Could one or other still be here?

"Where did he leave his things?"

She shrugged. "I think he put them on board the plane. He never left anything in here."

How convenient. So, no trace or anything lying around. He'd make sure for himself, of course but doubted he would turn anything up.

"Could I have a look around?" he asked.

She turned her hand up and swept the room with it. "Be my guest."

She watched as he went through the log books again, then turned his attention to the airfield registry. The Cessna was listed in it, alright, and was active. A look through the draws of the counter revealed old documentation, bills, orders for fuel and requests for spare parts and maintenance, all ordered in slim binders. Colin was about to give up when a small business card caught his eye.

Pulling it out of the draw, he discovered it was a standard RAF card of the type given out to people in case of need to get in touch. It had Chris Woodley's name on it. On the back, in scrappy handwriting, was written: "Meet KJ 11 pm."

"Can I have this?" he asked her.

"'Course. If it helps. He was a good lad. They are both good lads. They both loved to fly What a shame," she said sadly, finishing her drink.

Haltwhistle nodded. "Yes. A shame. Well, thanks for your help." He tucked the card into a clear plastic bag and put it in his pocket. He went back to his car and drove away. Making the short journey to Sutton Donington which wasn't too far away, he was thoughtful. He wanted to meet up with Jim and let him know what he had found so far, and to see what Jim had done.

Arriving at the gate of the base, the guard let him in and pointed him in the direction of the officer's mess.

He found his partner's unmistakable set of wheels parked near the officer's quarters, a row of houses set up like a suburban street, each of which looked very grand and imposing and each of them identical. Immaculately presented gardens adorned each house.

Most RAF stations were impressive and ordered, but this was especially so. There was an almost fastidious tidiness to how well set it was. He parked, walked up the path of the house he needed and knocked at the door. A tearful-looking young lady answered it.

"Hello, I'm looking for Sqn. Ldr. McCleland and Gp. Cpt. Woodley please."

She let him in, and he headed into a plain white living room which was undecorated, but featured comfortable furniture. Gp. Cpt. Woodley led him to a seat opposite Jim who was being shown a photo album by a very upset mother.

"This is Chris when he passed out from basic. And this is when he passed his trade training," she was explaining.

"What trade was he in, ma'am?" asked Colin gently.

She stood up and acknowledged him. "Oh, I'm sorry I'm Jennifer. I'm... I mean I was Chris's mother."

Colin nodded in understanding. "I'm very sorry for your loss Mrs. Woodley. And yours, sir."

Gp. Cpt. Woodley nodded. "Thank you, Mr... Haltwhistle."

God this is like being at a church fete, Jim thought. *Everyone is being so polite and nice and having tea and biscuits while that poor sod is smoking away in that bloody field.*

The young lady, which Colin took for being the younger sister offered him a drink. He asked for a black coffee, sweet which she poured for him.

"Thank you. I was asking what trade Chris was in," Colin pressed on.

"He was a weapons fitter," Gp. Cpt. Woodley said from his winged back chair. "He worked air side, mostly."

Colin looked at Jim in affirmation. That would explain where he got access to Dingbat mines and their fuses. Jim nodded a little, too subtly for the family to pick up on, but enough for Colin to know.

"Would he have access to the weapons stores, do you know?"

The commanding officer of the base shrugged. "I don't honestly know. Usually, that sort of thing is transported from the store and then handed over to the fitters."

Colin finished his coffee. He gestured to Jim that they should head out. He got up from his chair while McCleland collected his coat.

"I'll need Chris's mobile number," Colin said. "Might be worth checking who he was talking to."

"Of course." Mrs. Woodley wrote it down. Colin pocketed the paper, determined to have it checked out.

"I think we've taken up enough of your time for one day. Thanks. We'll head back here tomorrow."

Woodley stood up. "I can have some quarters assigned for you here on the base if you'd like."

Jim shook his head. He had vivid memories of camp accommodation and it wasn't to his liking.

He had got his own place off base as soon as he could afford it. "No thank you, sir. I like the comfort of my own bed. But thanks for the offer."

"Could you let the station's duty police officer know I'll be calling on him, sir?" Colin asked.

"Of course," Woodley countered. "Are you sure I can't prepare rooms for you both?"

Haltwhistle also turned down the offer. "I need to go home and think."

McCleland led his partner towards the front door.

"Thank you. We'll be back in the morning," Colin assured them.

"Thank you to you both," said Mrs. Woodley. "It's not been easy on any of us, and it's never nice to deliver horrible news like that."

They took their leave and headed back to where they had both parked.

"I'll see you in the morning," Jim told his friend.

He and Colin fist-bumped each other and McCleland got into his car. The red Mustang nosed out of the car park for the main gate, its driver wanting to get home quickly. Colin wondered who he had lined up to entertain tonight...

A roar of V8 power filled the air as the car took off from the base's entrance. Colin was about to get in his machine when a voice stopped him.

"Wait. Please." It was the girl. She was upset, and understandably so. She went up to him.

"Please find out what happened to my brother. Please." She hugged him and clutched at his hands becoming almost hysterical.

"I will. I promise," he assured her. She let him go, but she was shaking. "I need to get home. As I said, I need time to think, but I will find out what happened." It seemed to help as she calmed herself and let go of his hands.

He wanted to get home and see Anna. He had a feeling this was going to be rather more complicated than a tragic, if suspicious accident, and that he was going to be spending a fair bit of time away from his wife over the next couple of weeks than he would care to.

FOUR

McCleland got back to his apartment block just as the sun was setting. He rolled the Mustang into his allotted garage, switched off and locked the doors. Noticing the same dark green car he had seen at the crash site earlier, he guessed he had a visitor.

Bounding up the stairs to his top floor apartment, he decided against drawing his weapon. Jim had already decided his guest didn't pose a physical threat. He opened the door to find his lights switched on. It was only to be expected, of course.

Pushing his living room door ajar, his furniture, martial arts wooden dummy and collection of movie posters adorning his walls greeted him. *The Terminator, Robocop, Lethal Weapon, Die Hard, Rambo, Hard Boiled, The Rock* among others. His film collection, not extensive and mostly made up of '80s and '90s action thrillers along with the obligatory *007* and *Indiana Jones* box sets sat neatly in a large bookcase in an alcove, sharing space with well-thumbed thriller novels, books on pilots, racing drivers, aircraft and motorsport history. A complete set of review DVDs on sports cars, saloon racing and open-wheelers sat by his television and stereo, which had a tall rack of CDs with mostly rock and heavy metal bands featured.

A couple of scale models of a Tornado and Vulcan along with a nicely detailed Ferrari F1 car sat on a sideboard under a painting his dad had given him of the sea. The large, panoramic windows went from floor to ceiling and gave a nice view-when it was daylight-of the hills of the home counties surrounding Hemel Hempstead, and if slid aside, gave access to a small balcony.

As he had suspected, Jim did indeed have a visitor.

Standing in the middle of his front room waiting for him, wearing a denim coat with a sheepskin collar, skirt and tall black boots with her arms folded was Sophie.

Her stark facial expression and body language gave a persuasive hint that she was not in the best of moods.

"Oh, hello," he threw his car keys into a glass dish and smiled.

She did not return it.

"You deliberately got me out of the way, didn't you?" The young lady was genuinely upset. "Phil was right. That lovely meal you bought for us was a ruse, wasn't it? To get us away from the crash."

To say she was not pleased was an understatement. Jim immediately regretted deceiving her.

She was clearly highly intelligent and credit where credit was due, had worked out what he and Colin had done rather quickly. Haltwhistle removing the evidence was the dead giveaway.

"Well, that was Col's idea. And I was under orders. I just fancied some dinner. And the company was good too."

Sophie was not mollified. "Your friend tampered with evidence and spoiled a CAA investigation scene and you helped him out! I have a good mind to report you both!" Her eyes were wide and she was pointing at him with an accusing finger. "How dare you disrupt our work just so you can do yours! I warned you it was an offense to tamper with a crime scene!"

Jim sighed. He knew that any report she filed would mysteriously return as unresolved, given the department's power, but he wasn't in the mood for an argument. And to top it off, this girl was taking him to task, in his own home! His plans for the evening were rapidly going for a Burton.

"Look, love. I'm not about to excuse myself or my mate. We had work to do. It looked pretty serious, it was an RAF matter and we needed answers. And besides, I just had to tell a mum and dad that their son wasn't coming home again today, so quite honestly, I can do without the drama."

Intentional or not, Jim's tone was patronizing and if there was one thing that Sophie hated, it was being spoken down to.

"Don't 'Love' me," she shot back. "An RAF matter gives you the right to just steamroller us and do what you like?"

McCleland looked at her. "More or less," was the straight reply. "Don't like it, then the door is over there."

Sophie bristled. She was a very capable examiner and was not used to people waltzing in and waylaying her work. Generally, she got what she wanted and got results, even though it could put people's noses out of joint.

And this charming but completely unscrupulous guy had bulldozed his way in. He had pretty much done to her what she had been accused of doing to other people. The girl decided to have it out with him.

"And that's it? That simple? You just barge in with your friend and take over, and that's good enough for you?" she demanded.

Jim could see why she was upset but this being of AID interest took priority. He pursed his lips.

"If you want to put it like that, yeah. It's how our work rolls."

She let her arms drop. "And who exactly do you work for? It sure isn't the RAF." Jim looked around and then back at his visitor. "I was right, wasn't I? Government work? You did say you were under orders." She clasped her hands behind her back and seemed to puff her chest out, while turning on her right heel, expecting an answer. He had to hand it to her, she was right on the ball.

"You win *Who Wants to be a Millionaire* for tonight," Jim said glibly. Then he got around to thinking. "How did you get in here?"

This time it was her turn to smile, a rather cold one at that.

"You two seem to be detectives who are out to solve everything, you work it out," she quirked an eyebrow at him, mimicking his behavior.

If Sophie wanted to play that game, then that was fine with him. Jim put his best thoughtful expression on his face. Just to go through the motions.

"Well, let's see. I gave you my card. There's a doorman downstairs with a master key. So... I'd say you asked him?" He gave her a cheeky smile, which she was not about to mirror.

"Wow. You're good. Do you practice?" she asked, her voice dripping with sarcasm.

"Elementary, my dear Sophie. I didn't take you to be a locksmith." Whatever shade the girl could throw, Jim could counter.

Dammit, he had an answer for everything. It was infuriating. Sophie stared daggers at him.

"You're not funny. At all!" she snapped. "You've set us back a good day or so's worth of work and now I have to explain to my boss that a couple of self-absorbed tossers pretty much railroaded us, and think they're above the law."

Jim took in her natural slightly curvaceous beauty. He couldn't resist his next comment, despite the fact he risked being slapped.

"You know, you're kind of cute when you're annoyed," he responded. "And for your information, a lot of people think I'm very funny."

Sophie was becoming more irritated by the second. "Are you always this much in love with yourself? I just thought it was for show!"

Jim merely shrugged and smiled. She shook her head and threw her hands up. Either this guy took nothing seriously, or he was overcompensating in a big way. The fact he had just mentioned having to speak to a bereaved parent suggested the latter. The girl paced round his front room, taking in his decor. It was very much a bachelor pad and not to her taste at all.

"You're a big-headed shit," she told him and turned to face him again. "Tell me about this government work. Did you get what you wanted? You ought to have done. Your friend was very choosy about what he took. He must be the smart one out of you two!"

"Well…" he paused. What the hell? "You did kind of… walk straight into it."

She held her hands up to shield her eyes. "Wait, I can't see. I'm blinded by your intelligence!" Sophie fumed. "You are a real piece of work. I now have to build our case based on scraps you two left behind. Thank you very much!"

Jim shook his head. He had underestimated Sophie and was going to have to treat this young lady carefully. She was too intelligent and opinionated to do anything else.

"There are some things I can't tell you about. There's something a lot bigger going on here than a plane crash. As for what we wanted, I'd have to ask Col."

He knew despite the position his work afforded him, what he had done was morally wrong.

McCleland circled her with his hands in his pockets. She was watching his every move. Finally, he looked at her, apologetic.

"You're right, We had to get you out of our way. It was crass but it had to be done. I can't tell you why, just it's something that could be very high risk to the nation."

Sophie was not sure if she believed him, but he sure believed what he was saying.

Jim eyed her, a little sheepish. "And I'm sorry."

The girl seemed to soften a little. She had gotten what she really wanted, an honest apology. His expression looked rather like a little boy who had been chastised by his parents for being bad. It was his turn to look cute.

"That's better," she told him. "I much prefer a humble man over an arrogant prick."

"As a wise man once said: My hypocrisy only goes so far," he admitted.

"I'm your huckleberry," Sophie teased him. Recognizing the quote, he grinned. She moved close to Jim and looked up at him with those big brown magnetic eyes he had first noticed of her.

Even wearing heels, she didn't come up much past his shoulder. There was another shake of her head.

"You are a manipulative, two-faced, flirty arsehole." Her smile was finally genuine.

"You mean I'm a bloke then?" he grinned, as he knew what was about to happen.

"A very handsome, manipulative arsehole," she corrected herself as she got ever closer to him and let her coat drop to the floor.

McCleland looked her up and down and returned her quirked eyebrow. "Looks like I'm going for first!"

Sophie kissed him fiercely and he responded in kind. Looking up at him afterward, she had a lovely glow about her. She poked him in the chest.

"You're still in my bad book. You'd better make it up to me, mister. Right now."

From Jim's perspective, the evening was not a total loss after all.

FIVE

Haltwhistle pulled into the camp gates early the next morning. He was eager to crack on with the job at hand. He hadn't been able to talk to Anna (Official Secrets Act and all that stuff) but she had been understanding enough to know he had a big job to do. She had been horrified when he had come home more than a little worse for wear after the first mission for his new line of work.

She had accepted he may have to be away for extended periods, and her work as a primary school teacher meant she was busy most evenings anyway. But she still missed him. His favorite meal of steak and kidney pudding with mashed potato had also helped getting him to lighten up.

A nice quiet evening together had been a just reward for them both.

Beginning with the records department, Colin sat down at a reading machine with Woodley's personnel file. Being the son of an officer, he seemed to hold himself to a higher standard of excellence and worked himself hard. Nothing remarkable on his record, a few comments from superiors saying he was a good worker and the usual annual reviews, but beyond that there was just the usual stuff about being conscientious and ordered. A thought niggled him. If this guy was the son of an officer, why was he also not on the higher food chain? Interesting.

Something to follow up with the man's parents.

What he wanted to do now was go down to the weapons fitting area where he worked and check it out, but really, he needed Jim. A pilot would know a fair bit more about air-side work than he did.

Unfortunately, Jim had not shown up yet in a typically uncaring fashion. Colin signed in with the duty officer and cursed his partner for being tardy, yet again.

"You'll need a hi-vis to go air-side, sir," the aircraftsman said.

Colin groaned inwardly. He had little love for the Health and Safety Executive. He just wasn't as vocal about it as his partner or boss was. Black Jack labeled that outfit as the Killjoy and Form Filling Brigade, while Jim was just a little bit more direct.

"Bunch of cockwombles," was his comment on the matter.

Reluctantly slipping a hi-vis on, he was led out to a set of missiles on a rack about to be tested and worked on by a group of technicians. The open-air facility had a metal roof but aside from the office, it was open to the elements. A chill wind whipped through the place, and Colin felt himself clenched up in the warmth of his topcoat. They looked like sidewinder heat seekers, but he wasn't a spotter, so he said nothing. Looking over the missiles, he was impressed with their purposeful look and sheer size. He had expected them to be quite small, but these things were at least four feet long. He watched the mechanics fiddling around in the innards of the weapons for a while.

"Can I help you?" a voice from behind him interrupted.

Colin turned to see a severe-looking chief technician who was looking at him with suspicion. He was holding a clipboard. He was a barrel-chested man with a rugged face. Not someone to be trifled with. Colin recognized him but couldn't put a name to the face.

"Yes, are you the senior officer here?" Colin asked.

"Who wants to know? This is a restricted area-"

Haltwhistle cut him off by waving his pass under the man's nose.

"Oh, that AID outfit? Bunch of wannabe secret agents, you lot," he snorted. "Anyway, what do you want?"

"I could do without the attitude for a start," Colin said testily, folding his arms in unimpressed bemusement. He noted the man's NCO rank. "I want to know about one of your men. Chris Woodley."

Noticing the other technicians turn towards the conversation unfolding, the chief barked at them to get back to work. Colin however felt emboldened.

"So how much do you know about him?"

The chief took a step back. "What about him?" he asked warily.

"Is he a good worker, has he been having any problems?"

The grizzled man shook his head. "No nothing really. He kept his head down mostly."

"Did he have any trouble with anyone?"

Again, Colin noticed a lull in activity close by as the technicians were watching. The chief had also noticed this.

"I told you to get back to work!"

Colin watched his body language carefully, his eyes, his demeanor, anything to give anything away. Thoughtful, the techie took a few seconds to answer.

"Not that I heard of. He was pretty friendly with a guy in the stores. We called him Fliplugs. You might want to check with him."

"What's this Fliplugs character's real name?" Colin expected an answer quick time.

"Erm... I think... Joe Smith," was the answer.

Colin's search for body language was paying dividends. This man's eyes were darting about all over the place to any answers he gave.

"Just finally, what's your name? For my records."

"Marinell. Tim Marinell," came the reluctant response.

Colin felt the hair on the back of his neck stand on end. Now he remembered him.

"I believe you forgot to say 'sir' at the end of the statement," Haltwhistle stood with his hands on his hips.

There were muted snickers from the technicians working on the missiles.

"Sir." Marinell almost hissed.

Colin put his hands back in his pockets. Christ, it was cold. "Alright. Thank you for your time. I may call back later."

Checking out of the weapons compound, he could hear Marinell berating his men from inside the office as he signed the log. For his part, Marinell could swear he had met Colin before somewhere, but couldn't remember when.

Colin noticed Jim's Mustang rocking up and heard the strains of Nirvana's *Smells Like Teen Spirit* blaring from the speakers. The music was so loud he could hear it over the growl of the engine, which was normal for his friend. He played his music louder than anyone else he had ever known. Taking a sip of his Mountain Dew, Haltwhistle then stuffed his hands in the pockets of his topcoat.

Once Jim climbed out, his partner looked predictably worse for wear, the legacy of an energetic evening.

"Where are we at, Batman?" was his cheerful greeting, making a half-arsed attempt to straighten his uniform.

"You're late," Haltwhistle observed.

"So sue me," was the predictably nonchalant retort.

Colin was not impressed. "I need you to start taking this seriously, mate," he said testily. "You stuffed your face yesterday and apparently, you stuffed something else last night."

"Yeah, the turkey needed filling!" There was a cherubic smile on McCleland's face.

Haltwhistle harrumphed in irritation. His disgusted expression would hopefully convey his mood, not that Jim would care. He could smell the remnants of perfume on his friend's clothes, and a couple of strands of brown hair clung to the shoulder of Jim's blues where he had held whoever she was close to him.

"Hey man, the stuffing my face was your idea," Jim reminded him. "Do you want to fill me in on what you've found out so far, or what?"

Haltwhistle filled him in on what he had found so far, and who they needed to talk to next.

"Alright. So, we need to shake down this Fliplugs bloke then?" Jim's lopsided smile made Colin want to cringe.

"If you want to put it like that, yes." He began gritting his teeth involuntarily.

"Let's go and bend his ears!"

There was nothing for Colin to do but roll his eyes. Jim was always the same when he had some fun. By the time the lunch break rolled around, he would be more amenable to doing some work, but for now, he knew he was going to have to grin and bear his partner's almost insufferable behavior.

Hoping to make some headway, Haltwhistle said "Maybe you hadn't noticed, but someone died yesterday. In a very suspicious way."

"He was flying a plane he shouldn't have been and got blown up. Seems clear-cut to me. "

"And what about the hows, the whys and the what was he doing?" Haltwhistle knew he was wasting his time trying to get through to his partner.

"Maybe he thought he was Icarus." Jim looked at him. "As The Beatles said: There will be an answer, let it be."

I'm going to kill him, Colin thought.

Sutton Donington's store turned out to be a gigantic warehouse on the edge of the base. It was a converted hangar: the reinforced concrete and corrugated metal roof were dead giveaways.

The drab green side door was typical of the MoD's decor. Jim and Colin were greeted by row after row of ranking shelves reaching up to the ceiling of the hangar. Taking in the gargantuan space, Jim commented on the enormous scale with his usual glibness.

"So where do you want to start, genius?"

"With the sections Woodley and this Fliplugs guy are most associated with, numbnuts," Colin replied. It was obvious Jim was in one of his post-coital glow moods so would not be much use until at least lunchtime.

"They don't just throw someone in here and say go and do it. They have a section allocated to them," Colin went on.

"I know that." Then Jim realized he had been insulted. "Numbnuts? I don't think Sophie would agree with that!"

"I really wanted to know that, mate. And who's Sophie?" Colin suddenly guessed who she must be. "That girl from the crash site?"

"Yep." McCleland wore a cheeky smirk.

Typical. Only Jim could get a date out of a tragic event. Taking another look around at the vast storage space, Colin said, "Alright, let's go and find a shitload of missiles piled up."

"You won't find that in here mate. That's kept in a special bunker away from everything else," Jim pointed out.

"I know that dopey," Colin told him. "What I was looking for was warheads, arming pins, stuff like that."

Colin was about to go on but then realized what he had thought earlier. Jim was the ideal man to say what was air-side and what wasn't. So what were they looking for? Oh yes, the fuses. He took his phone out and enlarged the picture of the dingbat mine's switch. The serial number was of interest. He stopped by a set of brackets that was bagged in clear plastic. The same serial number was printed on the label tag.

Further down the aisle, Colin stopped by a basket of nuts and bolts. Nothing relevant to the investigation, thought Jim, but he kept quiet. Colin again picked up a bag of them and examined the tag. Sure enough, there was the same serial number.

The store itself was an endless maze of aisles and blind corners. Fortunately, everything was numbered by aisle, and a wall chart showed where they should be looking. Heading past rows of detonators and munitions, Colin was genuinely staggered by how much equipment was held in this place. But the real reason for being in here was to talk to Woodley's friend.

He stopped a storekeeper.

"Where can I find a guy called Fliplugs?"

"I think he's taking a coffee break, sir. He's in the staff room," was the helpful reply.

Above the door along the side wall was a sign saying, 'Staff Room.' The room was mostly empty, save for a guy seated who was checking his phone. Vending machines lined the walls offering drinks, snacks and sandwiches and a few tables sat haphazardly around the room.

Getting closer, the man's sleeves were rolled up, revealing his tattoos and he was busily tapping away at the touch screen.

"Excuse me. Would you be Joe Smith, better known as Fliplugs?" Colin walked up to the table.

The man put his phone away and looked up.

"Yes, that's me.' He noticed the ranks on their sleeves and stood to attention. "How can I help, sir?"

"I'm Flt. Lt. Colin Haltwhistle. I'd like to ask you a few questions about Chris Woodley."

Smith offered them both a seat. Colin sat close by while Jim sat further away at the far end of the table.

"He's a good guy. Very thorough," he started. Yes, I know all that from his record, thought Colin impatiently. He kept his tongue in check. "He loves his work, but he doesn't care for his dad very much. He always wanted to be known as his own person, not the boss's son."

"Did he have many friends?"

"Oh yeah. He hung around with me a bit. Johnny in the weapons fitting bay, There was a guy in bomb disposal who he was friendly with. I wouldn't say he was tight with him but got on ok with that guy," Fliplugs explained.

"Would you have his name at all?" Colin asked.

"Erm... that I can't remember. Sorry."

Fliplugs' body language was much more open and straight than Marinell's had been. Haltwhistle could tell he was playing straight cards.

"I could point him out though. Big surly bloke. Goes by the name of Short Fuse," Smith said.

"I hope that's not a reference to his temperament," Jim observed, somewhat wry. Colin gave him a look and sighed. Fliplugs grinned broadly.

"Can I ask what this is all about, sir?"

"Just a few inquiries. We think he may have been in an accident," Colin said slowly.

The corporal looked a bit startled. "I hope nothing bad. He's not been hurt, has he?"

Jim and Colin looked at each other.

"I'm afraid so."

Fliplugs was upset by learning that. He looked down at the tabletop.

"I'm sorry about you friend," said Colin gently.

"Yes. Thank you, sir." The young man was taken aback. "If there's anything I can do..."

Colin rose from the table and smiled. He handed his card to the NCO. "If you think of anything else, call me."

"I will do," Fliplugs also got up and saluted. "I have to get back to work." He excused himself.

Watching him go, Jim sat thoughtfully, rubbing his chin. Colin turned to him.

"What do you think?"

"He seemed straight enough to me," McCleland replied.

"I think he knows more than he's letting on." Colin's take on matters was starker. He drained the dregs from his bottle and threw it in a bin.

"He certainly left quickly and he was pretty cagey about not knowing this bomb disposal guy.

Our next port of call," Jim was catching on to his partner's vibe.

"I might make a detective of you yet," Colin chuckled. His friend was actually beginning to take the task seriously and providing useful input.

"I hope not!" Despite the joke, Jim had indeed picked up on Fliplugs' behavior and body language. While it had started straight and open, at the mention of the gentleman in the bomb disposal section, he had clammed up.

"Don't knock yourself, I think you have a nose for finding answers after all," Colin mused. "It just takes time to develop that instinct."

Then Jim gave Colin the assurance all was well in his part of the world.

"Nah I doubt it. It's much easier to just blast the problem than solve it," he grinned. "People don't complain too much if you drop a thousand pounder on their head."

"Bit bloodthirsty, aren't you?"

Jim looked at him with a serious expression. "Look mate, we do a job where danger is a very real possibility every day. We knew when we signed up that death was a part of the deal. So, you either face it with a cool head, or you get out of it."

"Tell that to Chris Woodley," Colin replied.

But he had to agree with Jim's sentiment. But someone had died in mysterious circumstances and he wanted to know why. The forensics people would by now be crawling over the wreckage and it would be very interesting to find out what they got out of it. That could be some time though.

They would have to go through everything in microscopic detail. And if Woodley had been carrying something that he shouldn't have been, he knew the risks he was taking. One thing that he had neglected to check was Woodley's pilot's license. He made a mental note to look into it.

"I want to know who this bomb disposal guy is. I want to talk to him," Colin said. "I also want to take statements from everyone we've spoken to so far."

"Even Woodley and his family?" Jim asked.

Colin gave his friend a look of stone-faced determination. "Especially the family. Fliplugs there said Chris wasn't close to his father. That is something to follow up on."

"Do you want to talk to them now?" Jim was unsure if they should go back and start asking awkward questions so soon.

"No. Let them stew for a bit. They're more inclined to give something away if we leave it for the moment."

At Jim's questioning look, Colin grinned. "Psychology. Fascinating subject."

Jim shrugged. "I still think dropping a bomb is a lot easier."

Haltwhistle chuckled. "Come on. Let's find some evidence." Colin was most insistent.

They headed out of the staff room and back into the vast confines of the stores warehouse. It was truly mind-boggling just how oversized it seemed. Pretty much everything that the base could need to maintain vehicles, weapons, equipment, hell even the brackets that held the doors on the door frames was here. The wall chart which listed what was where proved fruitful again.

"Twenty-Four G," Haltwhistle kept saying over and over, remembering the section. Eventually they found the right area. A huge row of gun parts spare firing pins, barrels and triggers, along with other odds and ends. Detonators of a different type, spare radio aerials, guidance chips for ordnance, laser guides for bombs and missiles, the parts just went on and on.

"What exactly are you looking for?" Jim asked.

Colin, checking his phone for the pictures he had taken of the blackened Dingbat mine detonator.

"In the wreckage, I found that. And from the serial tag on it, it came from this store. I'm guessing that what destroyed that Cessna was a mine going off."

"That shouldn't be possible," Jim replied. "Unless there was a problem with the detonator or the arming switch on the thing itself or..."

Jim stopped, his voice trailing off.

"Or if the mine was radio-controlled and someone with his finger on the button was close enough to press it," Haltwhistle finished.

"That would mean whoever it was knew where the plane would be, and where it was going, and it had to be flying low enough for it to be in range of the button. He'd have to stay under 300 feet to stay below the radar horizon," Jim said.

"That would explain why he wasn't detected, and why the wreckage wasn't spread over a wide area. It was all in one spot, which means it didn't fall to the ground very far at all from the point of the explosion," Colin finished.

"That definitely pins it on low flying. The guy didn't want to be detected. Wherever he was going, he wanted to get there and get back without anyone finding out about it," McCleland pointed out.

"Alright so we've found what we're looking for here, I think. Let's see this Short Fuse gentleman," said Colin.

The bomb disposal compound was a vast piece of waste ground at the edge of the airfield, littered with burned-out cars and craters where the diffusing of explosives had not gone to plan.

A large concrete bunker surrounded by sandbags which were built up to deflect blasts away and over the angled roof of the building which served as the office block. The entrance was protected by a zig-zag of sandbags which Haltwhistle wound his way around followed by McCleland, who was eyeing up an attractive young WREN who held the door open for them. Colin shook his head. Here they were, investigating a potentially major crime and Jim was still finding time to flirt with the ladies. He walked up to the desk.

"Where can I find the chief of the section?" he asked a bored-looking Aircraftsman.

"In the office at the end of the hall," was the disinterested answer.

Knocking at the door, a sharp reply came from within which instructed them to enter a typical white and drab green office that was heated by an ancient radiator that clattered and banged as it attempted to warm the room. A battered wooden desk sat in the middle of the room and sat seated behind it was the dictionary definition of a senior non-commission officer, in this case a master sergeant.

"My name's Colin Haltwhistle. This is my partner, Jim McCleland," he introduced them.

"What can I do for you gentlemen?" was the businesslike reply.

Colin equally did not beat about the bush.

"You've probably heard about the plane crash by now, the one in Norfolk, and the deceased being one of our own." He waited for a reply but all he got was a raised eyebrow. "We think he was friends with someone in this section. A guy who goes by the name of Short Fuse. Do you know who that might be?"

The master sergeant considered for a bit, tapping his pen on a writing pad.

"Yes. He's one of three corporals who are experts. I don't know too much about his business but feel free to talk to them." He pointed to a blackboard on the far wall, on which a lot of names were written John Chapman, Ron Williams and Kevin Johnson.

Haltwhistle looked at the names thoughtfully.

"John is on the range but should be back any time. Ron is off duty and Kevin-"

"Thank you," Colin interrupted. "We'll start with Corporal Johnson."

A beat and the sergeant said, "Very good sir."

Kevin Johnson was sitting down with his newspaper after finishing his work and taking an afternoon break. A military brat, he had grown up on an army base and moved around a lot with his dead's postings.

When he had shown an interest in aircraft and problem-solving, a career in the RAF seemed a natural choice, although his lack of academic achievement meant ruled him out of being an officer. His dad had been a little miffed that he was not interested in a life in the army, but ultimately supported his son's choice. He had shown an aptitude for preferring high risk situations and reaming cool under pressure. He was placed in the bomb diffusal section, specializing in explosives handling and demolition.

He had done well in trade training and was soon signed off to be the go-to guy for controlled demolitions, hence his nickname Short Fuse.

He enjoyed his work and was a social creature, lapping up the life that the RAF offered. He was not single but was ready to mingle as he put it.

Tucking into a sandwich, he was surprised by the two officers now coming in to speak to him.

The first officer introduced himself.

"Grab yourselves a seat," Johnson said waving his hand at the seats, rickety wooden chairs that had long since seen better days.

"I'd like to talk to you about Chris Woodley," said Haltwhistle.

"Chrissy? What's he got himself into this time?" he asked quickly.

Colin looked at Jim in surprise then back to Johnson. "Does he get in to a lot of trouble?"

"Whenever someone doesn't keep him on the straight and narrow, yes," Kevin joked. "He was a bit easily led. Good lad though. Good for a laugh."

"How long did you know him?" Jim asked.

"I don't know. A couple of years. Since he came from basic. He came into the stores a lot to ask for spares. We got talking and hit it off. You know how it is. We both like the footy so he came around and we watch the match sometimes."

Haltwhistle was feverishly writing in shorthand, making detailed notes. The more detailed, the better case he could build. Clearly, Johnson hadn't picked up on Jim speaking of Woodley in the past tense.

"Is this some sort of interrogation? Why all the questions?" Johnson asked, a little defensively.

"No, nothing like that. Just a friendly chat," Colin assured him. "Please go on. What sort of trouble was he in?"

The corporal shrugged. "He isn't very good with money. I lend him some dough sometimes to help him get by. He is always trying to cadge a tenner from people."

The white cap nodded. "What else can you tell us? Did he have any trouble with anyone?"

"He and his dad argue a lot. Mostly about his position and his spending. He buys stuff all the time."

Kevin shook his head.

"He means well but he's useless with money, he's always broke. I don't know about him hating anyone or anyone hating him or anything like that. He's too nice for that. But he doesn't get on with his sarge." He stopped, considering that. "Then again, no one gets on with him. Can I ask what's happened to Chrissy?"

"What did he usually buy?" Jim interrupted. This investigating business was proving to be quite good fun. He had always liked books about private eyes and maverick cops, Raymond Chandler was a favorite and so was Alistair MacLean. And the films he enjoyed nearly always had an action or cop theme. He had never fancied himself a detective though, a bit too cerebral for his talents.

"DVDs, books, computer games, all sorts of stupid stuff. He just spends and spends. He's a bit obsessed about his car. He has it chipped and remapped and had a body kit added and all of that boy racer stuff. And that doesn't come cheap," Kevin replied.

"What car did he have?" Colin asked.

Johnson took a drink. "Focus ST. It was an older one. He kept going on about the older one being better and faster than the new shape ST." He shook his head. "He's probably right. He's completely car mad."

"What color?"

"Dark blue."

Colin stopped. He read back through his notes. "You said he didn't get on with his sergeant. Who was he?"

Short Fuse gave a rueful look. He tapped his fingers on the tabletop and shook his head. "You'll love him when you meet him. Sergeant Marinell," he said finally.

That fit.

"We've already been exposed to the full force of his charisma," McCleland told him.

It was time to produce the ace in the hole card. Literally in this case. Colin pulled the card from his pocket, but didn't show it to Kevin, not immediately. He kept it cupped in his hand. He wanted to test how truthful this man was.

"Did you meet up with him recently?" he asked.

Kevin scratched his sideburn. "Erm... I saw him two nights ago. We had a beer and then went home. What's happened to him?"

Colin sat back. His notebook and pen could certainly use a break from the frantic scribbling he had been doing.

"He was involved in a plane crash the night before last. He's dead."

Johnson looked positively horrified. "Oh, God. Chrissy!"

"We're very sorry about your friend," Jim said.

Colin nodded, grateful for McCleland's empathy for the situation. "Do you remember what time you saw him that night?"

"I think about 8ish. Like I said, we went to the pub."

Jim leaned forward. "Which pub?"

"The *Dog and Salmon*. In the village just here."

Satisfied for the moment, Colin and Jim stood up. They shook hands.

"Thank you for your help. We'll be in touch. If you remember anything else, drop me a line."

Colin gave Kevin his card. Then he and Jim were heading out of the building. Haltwhistle stopped a little way up the road that led back to the hangars and the main part of the base.

"So, what do you think?" Jim asked, nodding back to the compound.

Colin handed him the card that he had found back in the drawer at the aerodrome. Jim turned it over, reading the details on both sides of it.

"K.J. Same initials as that guy."

"Exactly. I think he's lying about what time he met Woodley. Either that or they spent a long time in that pub. I intend to find out which," said Colin.

"Where did you get that?" Jim passed the card back to him. Colin told him of his search at the airfield and the bag that Woodley had been seen with.

"We need to wait for the forensics report to be sure. But I'll give you 10/1 that he was carrying a ton of explosives on that plane."

"But why? And where was he going?" Jim stuffed his hands in his pockets.

Colin walked with a businesslike air as McCleland had to almost run to keep up.

"That, Watson is what we are here to find out, among other things."

"Alright, Sherlock. Where do you want to go next?"

Colin looked around him and ran his fingers through his hair. He was thinking. Jim knew that he played with his hair when his mind was working. Nervous tic maybe? Or just a funny habit?

Everyone had them. The weather was closing in. Dark clouds were rolling in from the west and the wind was picking up. Rain was on the way.

"I want to check on Woodley's pilot's license I need to make a couple of phone calls, but not here."

"Call from the car, mate. Nice and quiet there."

A quick phone call to the CAA gave the answers that Haltwhistle was looking for. He quickly scribbled the details down in his notebook, which Jim hadn't a hope of reading. Colin's handwriting was akin to a centipede crawling across the paper. He replaced the phone and snapped the book shut.

"The plot definitely thickens," he said.

A rumble of thunder in the distance was accompanied by a flash of lightning. McCleland pulled the collar of his jacket up.

"Something else to add to the pile of paperwork?"

There was a nod from his friend. "Most definitely."

Looking at the incoming weather and his watch, Jim declared his intentions. "I don't know about you mate, but I fancy something to eat. Pub?"

Haltwhistle rolled his eyes. "Do you think of anything other than your middle section?"

The Squadron Leader was about to make a dirty joke. "No, don't answer that!" He had to admit though, that the idea of a hot meal sounded good.

SIX

Sophie read through the report that she had filled out on the crash. She wanted to make sure that she had missed nothing. With this kind of investigation, any details, no matter how big or small could be crucial.

Her hastily scrawled handwritten notes regarding the initial findings had been typed into the official report. Based on the point of impact, it looked as though the Cessna had simply fallen from the sky and landed where it had come to rest, which was unusual. Typically, there was a gouge in the ground where the aircraft had struck and then skated to a stop. Sophie's inquiring mind got some answers from the next piece of information.

The lab report had come back and the traces of explosives found were eye-opening. A little research and she had some answers. If this was an explosive compound, it must surely be used by the military. Why would a civilian aircraft be carrying a military-grade explosive compound?

Reflecting on the previous day and looking at the crash scene, she was still upset about crucial evidence being removed. The dog tag, for instance, was vital to identify the pilot. The type of Cessna, under CAA regulations, didn't require a black box flight recorder to be carried, so there was no data. Fortunately, the photos that they had taken were enough to do some groundwork.

There had been no radar traces logged and neither had there been any flight plan filed for the registered aircraft. Checking on the registry of the Cessna, she quickly discovered who the owner was.

"Group Captain Woodley, RAF," she murmured. No wonder Jim and his colleague had a vested interest in this. And if the pilot was an RAF officer, that meant they were now treading on uncertain ground.

"What was that?" her partner asked.

"The owner of the Cessna. He was an RAF officer. No wonder we had company yesterday."

Phil's eyes narrowed. He was thinking similar thoughts to her own. It had to be called in, of course.

"Did you find out anything about those two? I'll need to file the report."

"I did some checking but nothing came back of any great detail about either of them. The one who took us to dinner is a tanker pilot and I couldn't get anything on the gobby one," she said with a sigh. "Apart from that, I couldn't find anything."

Phil looked over the smattering of information she had put together. He could not remember the guy's name. Jim... McDonald? Callan?

Sophie sifted through the paperwork she had put together. "The whole thing's really strange," she said.

"In what way?" Phil asked.

"It's almost as if the guy at the controls didn't want anyone to know about this flight."

"Would you if you were transporting something you shouldn't be?" Phil looked over her work although he didn't appear to be taking an active interest.

"Well, look at this. If the plane just ended up where it was and there was no impact crater," she warmed to her theme. "That means that it just fell straight down. The thing blew up before it hit the ground."

There was no evidence of a mechanical failure, the aircraft had been well maintained and the pilot had no record of dangerous antics in the air. The way that the fuselage had been disfigured, it was something on board that had exploded. But what?

"I'll get these samples sent off," Phil said. "Whatever caused this, we can get them analyzed." and now it was time to wait. "In the meantime, I'll write up the complaint report about those two but I can't submit it without both of their names. Keep working on it."

Despite getting into a row to begin with, Sophie had very much enjoyed her evening with Jim.

She had legitimately gone to see him to give him a piece of her mind, but truth be told, she did fancy him. And he had made it out of her bad books.

She'd not made any mention of the previous night to her work partner. A conflict of interest was the last thing she wanted.

"Is that the crash scene report?" Phil asked, looking at the piece of paper lying next to her.

"Yeah. Do you want to read it?" She offered the stack of paper to him to check. The thick pile was embossed with the cover of the Air Accidents Investigation Branch.

Phil took the typed document and began flicking through it, comparing it to the handwritten log she kept. Sophie waited for his verdict.

"Hold on. This note about an explosion on board being the cause of the fuselage expanding outwards. How did you come to that?" he asked.

"Easy. Think about it." Sophie said. "The bodywork wouldn't be torn apart like that if it just hit the ground, and there was no engine failure or fire, so it must be something being carried that went off."

The photos of the crash scene were pointed out to support her ideas, and she pointed to the details.

Phil looked unconvinced. "I suppose so, but there wasn't anything visual to confirm that. There was a thunderstorm at the time. Maybe it got hit by lightning."

"A lightning strike wouldn't make an aircraft blow up like that," she pointed out.

He put his hand on his chin which made him look like the statue of The Thinker. "I dunno. Maybe you're right. I'd rather you didn't put it in there until we were sure."

"I am sure. It's not like the crash we looked at the other week. The damage is different," Sophie pointed out. "If you're happy with that, I am and I'll hand this in."

Phil sighed. His coworker was very sure of herself once her mind was made up.

"Yeah, alright." He signed off on the report and it was dropped in to the head of the section's in basket.

Sophie retrieved her bag and headed for the door. "Have a good night." She had a date to keep.

Phil nodded. "You too."

She paused as she reached her car. It wasn't like her colleague to stay late. Looking back at the ugly squat brick building, she could see his office light on. Checking her watch, she had just enough time to reach where Jim had told her to meet him. Something in the back of her mind told her to accidentally deliberately not find out the details he was looking for.

Anna and Sophie arrived at the *Dog and Salmon* separately. It was a typical chain pub with the tacky decor that tried to make it look like a classy olde worlde place when it was nothing of the sort. Anna was thrilled to get an invitation from her husband to spend the evening with him but had hoped for a quiet night for just them. She was less than pleased to find it was a double date with Jim and who she assumed was his latest notch in the bedpost. Her husband meanwhile resisted the urge to deduce his friend's date at his request.

"She doesn't need to hear about how she got into her job through someone else's charity or how you know what color her undies are or some shit like that, ok?"

"I'm guessing you already know what color they are anyway?" was the glib retort. "I dunno why you're bothering, you'll have a new girlfriend by the weekend!"

That got under Jim's skin, especially considering Colin's antics the other morning. "Up yours, man! Anyway, it could be worse." Jim pursed his lips. "She could be sixteen stone with a goatee."

For her part, Sophie was happy to spend some time with her new boyfriend but was a bit put out to see Haltwhistle again. She had not been too impressed with his behavior the other day and intended to tell him what she thought, but here and now wasn't appropriate. The small lady she had seen arriving greeted him with a hug.

"Hello," she said in a neutral tone.

"Hi," Colin greeted her. The height and build matched the girl in the anti-static suit who he had confronted. Unquestionably this was Sophie. He could smell her perfume and recognized it as the same that his friend had been scented with this morning. Her hair was the same color as that which he'd seen on Jim's uniform earlier. No prizes for guessing who he'd entertained last night.

Sophie was surprised by Colin's pleasant greeting to her when he arrived. Because of that she kept an open mind about getting to know Jim's friend. He had been aggressive and pushy at the crash site, and his crime in removing the evidence was far worse than Jim's. But he was clearly intelligent, and he was married, which must count for something.

Taking a circular table in a window alcove, the quartet sat down with Colin taking the spot where he could see the bar and the entrance and who was arriving in the car park.

From Sophie's perspective, Haltwhistle had a slightly standoffish aura which was a bit off putting, but McCleland was something else. While somewhat laddy, she was intrigued by his intelligence and guessed there was a much deeper person behind the macho exterior. She also liked his fun factor. For the second time in two days, she tucked into a salad in a pub.

"How was your day love?" Anna asked Colin.

"Oh, it was alright. A bit trying but alright." Haltwhistle cut his piece of fish with gusto.

"Working with Jim I, can imagine that to be true," she said with a smile, which Jim returned.

"How was putting up with those little monsters?" McCleland asked Anna, testing the waters. It was worth making an effort to get on with her as Colin was his best friend, after all.

"You know, same old same old. Little kids are just… you know… little kids!"

"You're a teacher?" Sophie asked her. Anna nodded. "Wow. You have more patience than me. I couldn't do it. I take my hat off to you."

"It helps that I love my job," Anna said. She looked at the other girl, warming to her. "What do you do?"

Colin had clearly not told his wife about the case that he and Jim were investigating, Sophie guessed. That certainly pointed to an interesting line of work that they both had.

"I'm an air crash investigator," she said simply.

"Is that how you met Don Juan over there?" she pointed her fork at Jim, who set his cutlery down.

"I resent that remark," he replied in mock hurt, then beamed at his date. He was hoping to deflect any awkward questions but Sophie had probably realized what kind of person he was anyway.

"Why be clever when you can be accurate?" Colin chuckled and winked at his wife, who smiled in return.

"Thanks for that, mate," Jim grimaced.

Either oblivious or deliberately diplomatic, Sophie smiled. "And…" She was struggling to remember his name. "Colin here. Yeah."

"Did you have a good day with it?" McCleland asked her, changing the subject before things became uncomfortable.

She looked thoughtful. She was still considering how Phil had been acting. "Yeah, I think so."

"It must be a tough job. That sort of thing can be pretty icky at times," Anna commented.

Sophie half frowned. "It can be. Every job has its ups and downs. Little kids can be a pain."

"Sometimes. Almost as much as putting up with him!" Anna pointed at Colin, who snickered.

Sophie looked between the two of them. It was as if they were mirror images of each other.

"How long have you been married?"

"Four years. Met at another wedding, actually. We got talking and we've been together ever since."

"Yep, we literally bumped into each other," Haltwhistle elaborated. "Then her car broke down and I took her home."

"Dad was really impressed with that. He said you'd be a good guy to be with. He was right!"

Anna was sweet and she had an open, kind nature that cruel people could take advantage of, Sophie guessed. Anna dressed formally but casually, in the manner of all junior school teachers.

The two ladies were getting on well. They shared small talk while Jim watched. He chuckled as he took a sip of whiskey and Colin kept a watching brief on who was coming and going.

"How long have you two worked together?" Sophie finally asked, pointing out McCleland and Haltwhistle.

"About a year, we were just sort of... thrown together. You know how it is." Colin took a drink and set his glass down. "By the way, I'm sorry about yesterday. I acted like a dick."

Sophie laughed it off, glad to have broken the ice. "It's fine. I get you were just trying to do your job, even if you did…" she chose her words carefully for Anna's benefit. "Interpret what was allowed. And we got caught up today, and I was able to smooth things over with the fifth floor, so it's all good." She took a sip of her vodka and tonic. "I assume from yesterday that you're not a pilot, like this one?" She pointed at Jim, who wiggled his eyebrows.

"I wish!" Haltwhistle scoffed. "No, I'm the investigator."

That Colin was the cop was obvious. He had removed the specific items needed to further an investigation and identified what applied to the case very quickly, showing a keen intellect as well as a blatant disregard for the law. With the way he was able to keep up with the conversation and watch what was happening in the pub, his observation skills were clear.

"While he was busy flying his Tonka, I was trying to find who was doing something dodgy," he explained.

She frowned. "Tonka?"

"Tornado," Jim explained. "I'm a... was... a fast jet pilot."

"Is that the one with the swing wings and goes supersonic?"

McCleland nodded. "Yeah. I loved flying it. Just a fantastic aeroplane."

"Did you fly any missions?" Sophie persisted with her line of questioning. She wanted to know as much as possible about her new man and his friends, their line of work, anything she could, as well as anything they knew about the case.

Colin was impressed with Jim's new girlfriend's keen senses. Sophie appeared to be very much on the ball. It could be an asset, but it could be a curse, especially if she started prying into their investigation.

Jim looked at his plate of food for a moment, then at her and Anna and Colin in turn. "If you mean combat missions, yeah. Lots. Lots of bombing raids and low-level attacks and stuff like that. I've taken part in RED FLAG exercises in Nevada. That was fun."

Should he tell her what had happened to him? She would find out anyway one way or another. "I got shot down once."

At that, the other three stared at him. Colin had known this but hadn't asked about it. Cartwright had refused to tell him, reasoning that Jim would reveal all in his own time.

"What happened?" asked Anna. She leaned forward and rested her chin on her hands and her elbows on the table.

He had hoped that he could have kept this quiet but McCleland knew deep down that it would have got out in the end.

"It was a flight over Afghanistan. I was hit and had to bail. Then... well things got tricky." Jim took a large gulp of his drink. "My back-seater, Steve... he was a good bloke. We both went flying without a plane and the Tornado went down. I woke up and I had company... if you know what I mean."

Sophie looked at Anna and despite her misgivings about him, Colin's wife was concerned for McCleland. She had heard about the pilots who had been shot down over Iraq during the first Gulf War and had no wish to see anyone treated in such a manner.

"Did they hurt you?" she asked.

McCleland shook his head. Colin assumed he was being tough but Jim's blue eyes were serious.

"I got out of there before it got too nasty. The first wave of aircraft had already gone in and bombed the air bases and military installations, and now the second wave was mopping up."

He took another sip of his whiskey and looked around the table. The others were staring at him intently.

"It wasn't my first flight in a war zone. My instructor in basic said I had really good aptitude and wasn't afraid of the plane. I was shortlisted for fast jet training, and after it was all done, I was on a Tornado squadron."

Jim had a reputation for being glib and for not taking himself too seriously, but could also drink with the best of them and handle himself in a fight. A tough South London upbringing had helped with that, but serious interest in aircraft and those who flew them made him determined to have a go at piloting, win or lose.

"I wasn't above blagging things to win. It was just finding a good angle. When we played rugby at school, I came up with this thing where we got the other team to go one way, open them up and lob the ball to the other winger. The teacher wasn't convinced until we showed him what we came up with," McCleland explained, holding his audience with interest. "My flight instructor had asked me to perform aerobatics so I went up in the Tucano and I threw it around like a kite in a hurricane, just to prove that it could be done when the guy had insisted it couldn't."

His daring piloting had earned an investigation at which McCleland subsequently argued that the instructions were broad enough to be open to interpretation. He was exonerated of all charges and on XV Squadron had impressed with his 'can do' attitude.

"I didn't mention at the first interview that I'd cheated on my GCSE maths exam!" He had a mischievous smile on his face. Sophie and Anna looked at each other, a little shocked.

"They'd find out surely? We had to do a maths test at the recruitment office?" Colin asked.

McCleland's impish grin said it all. "I got hold of an old paper and wrote all of the answers down on the inside of my fingers, then washed them off afterward. Maths was never my best subject."

Haltwhistle was shocked. If the brass ever found out about that, Jim's career would be over. As resourceful as it was, what he'd done was more than underhanded. Cheating and lying to get in was a huge no-no, despite how clever it was. Anna coughed as she tried to compose herself.

Sophie was just as bemused.

"Anyway, we were hit by a missile, the Tonka started burning and Steve and me ejected. I must have been knocked out because I came around in this room that looked like something out of a *Saw* film and Krasnov of all people was there. He started demanding why we'd bombed him, and he got his bully boys on the case, but I got out of there."

"How?" Sophie asked. She finished her drink, both fascinated and a little on edge by what she was hearing.

Jim paused for a moment. How could he word this? He didn't want to scare her off. "I persuaded them not to bring a knife to a gunfight."

The implication was clear. He reached for an apple in the bowl in the middle of the table and took a bite. "There's no such thing as a no-win situation."

There was an exchange of looks around the table between the others.

"I got some wheels and drove towards home. I got a bit of a hero's welcome back at base which was nice. I was lucky. It could have been much worse," McCleland's cheerful expression faded to a more reflective mood. "Poor old Steve wasn't so lucky. They found his body a few weeks later."

The other three at the table were silent. Sophie nodded and pursed her lips. Colin had known the bare details about this, but now understood why his partner treated life as a game and why Cartwright had recruited him for AID.

Anna considered Colin's friend. No wonder he had such a casual attitude to everything. If he had stared death in the face like that, then it gave him a different perspective. It was a little sad to be honest, but now she knew why McCleland was the way he was, flitting from girl to girl or pub to pub. She was a lot more forgiving of his nature.

"I misjudged you, Jim. I'm sorry," she said softly.

"So that's how you and Krasnov knew each other," Colin murmured.

"Who was this Krasnov guy?" Anna asked, overhearing her husband. She had heard his name mentioned a couple of times.

"Someone you're best off not knowing anything about," Jim told her. "He's also why I transferred to VC10s. I didn't fancy putting myself in a high-risk situation again for a while. It's also how I knew that the only gun I'd ever want at my side is a Ruger."

"And now you're doing high-risk stuff again!" Haltwhistle said, to which McCleland smiled, nodding slowly.

McCleland just smiled a bit. "It's alright. Just keep it between us! It doesn't hurt for the bad guys out there to think they're up against John Rambo."

All four of them laughed.

"Or Inspector Morse!" Anna said, pointing to her husband.

"See? I knew you were a lot deeper than you let on," Sophie touched Jim's elbow. She knew he liked that, but only from her. "What about you, Colin? Why did you join up?" she asked.

"I wanted to travel," he said. "My dad, he served, had said the world was full of wonderful things and I wanted to see them all for myself. It seemed a good way to go about it. Get paid to see the world! I found the discipline a bit hard to get used to. I felt like Patrick McGoohan to start with, but you do these things it goes with the territory."

"What? You're not a number?" Jim teased. "That kind of goes against everything serving in the military is about."

Haltwhistle grinned. "True. I did try the "I will not be pushed, stamped or numbered" thing and got my kit thrown on the floor and told to tidy it up until it was right!"

So, Colin had been as rebellious as he himself was but he either kept it in check or he had mellowed.

Jim considered what it would take to get his friend to come out of his shell a little more.

"If you're given orders which you have to follow, shouldn't you believe in them?" Anna asked.

Jim thought about it for a second, but Colin answered. "I've been in the RAF for nine years. I've had six different COs. If I believed in every order I was given, I'd be both for bombing cities and against it. I'd think nukes were the devil's work and that they were the only thing keeping the peace. I'd be both a hero and a prat, depending on which CO said it. I'd think honor and duty were a curse and a blessing but most of all, I'd be around the twist!"

"What about when you know your orders are wrong?" Sophie asked.

"Almost all orders are wrong, hun," Jim said. "They're just carried out in the best way possible."

"And if I ordered you to..?" she beamed.

"Well..." He met her wicked grin. "There has to be an exception to make a rule true!"

"Why did you want to investigate air crash scenes?" Anna asked her, trying to steer away from the men's banter.

"To make a difference," Sophie said. "To help so bad things wouldn't happen again." She was an idealist. No wonder she appealed to McCleland. "How did you end up as a teacher?"

"Oh, just lucky. It was either that or child care," Anna answered.

"It sounds like you wanted to help people as well," Jim noted. "You are a very… kind of… nurturing person."

Mrs. Haltwhistle smiled. "Why, thank you." She had always made sure to get involved with raising money for charity while at school and supporting the local animal shelter. Seeing animals and children who needed protection was distressing to her sensibilities.

Everyone appeared to be enjoying their meals, with one exception.

"Leave it to Wetherspoons to arse up India's most famous dish. How hard can it be to make curry?" Jim grumbled. His Rogenjosh was unpalatable.

"What's wrong with it?" Colin asked. "And it's not Indian, it's British."

"Don't talk wet, mate. I've been eating curry for longer than I can remember! A piece of cardboard's got more flavor."

McCleland pulled a face, much to Sophie's amusement.

"I'm not. It was invented by British soldiers who were stationed there to cover up the taste of gone-off meat," Haltwhistle insisted.

"What? So are you a food guru on top of everything else?" McCleland pushed the plate away and threw down his napkin in disgust.

"Yeah, I'm a foodie, and I'm telling you, curry isn't Indian," Colin insisted. "If you want an authentic Indian dish, try a Phaal. That'll get your hair standing on end!"

"Which is a type of curry," Jim argued.

Colin sighed. "You just will not be proved wrong, will you?"

"He's right, Jim. The spice trade from India-" Anna began.

"I've heard enough," Jim smiled. He was not in the mood for a lecture.

Sophie was enjoying the banter between the two friends, and at the same time building up a mental picture of their work. Haltwhistle was a fountain of knowledge on almost any subject, it seemed. No wonder he had found a career in detective work. On the other hand, Jim was boisterous and opinionated, but she suspected a keen intelligence in him.

"I never cared for living on base," Jim remarked. "Far too restrictive."

His friend scoffed. "Says the guy who lives in a flash apartment!"

"It was either that or in the mess. The brass don't take kindly to rock music blaring out!"

Colin rolled his eyes. "That's your reasoning, is it? Wow." He considered for a moment. He didn't like to pry, but he had always been intrigued. "How did you get that pad anyway? It must have cost you a bit."

McCleland shrugged. "I cam into some money when I turned 21. I took the money and got a mortgage. I was in the service so they took a punt on me."

"Nice place for a twenty-one year old!" Haltwhistle was impressed with his friend's attitude. Most young guys who had suddenly got rich would have spent it all on frivolities. Despite Jim's outward nonchalance, he had a sense of responsibility, probably drummed into him by his parents.

"I like my freedom," McCleland explained. "Basic was a bloody nightmare. Some supercilious bloke telling you to fold your kit, go to sleep and all of that crap. Give me the bloody aeroplane and let me have at it."

His friend sighed. "It's discipline. It's good for you. I wonder how you even got in sometimes!"

"Try telling that to Keith Moon or Lemmy! And I got in because as much as I hate people getting in my face, it's better than working in an office." He took a breath. "What about your place?"

Colin smiled. "When we moved in together we rented it but we got offered a deal to buy it. We put our money together and there you go."

"Love can you buy you happiness!" McCleland grinned.

"You're a cynical bugger."

"Pragmatic."

The atmosphere had become heavy. Jim's had hoped for a pleasant evening, not darkness.

"Thank you," Sophie said quietly, rubbing Jim's elbow.

"So anyway, let's talk about something happier," her boyfriend said.

"I have to ask. What sort of investigations did you do?" Sophie asked.

Full of curiosity, Jim noticed. It must be the in-depth investigation and putting together the clues that she enjoyed. She was clearly street smart as well as book smart, an attractive quality for him.

"I worked for the Special Intelligence Branch, part of the RAF police. More involved cases, things like that," Haltwhistle told her. "Certainly nothing as challenging as his career in the service." He was indicating to Jim.

"I meant now. You two must see some... interesting things based on what I saw yesterday."

Sophie took a sip of her drink. This would take a bit of cleverness on her part to tempt them into revealing anything that could help her cause with investigating the crash. "We found out the owner of the plane served in the RAF. Not sure if he was the pilot though."

Anna looked at her husband and Jim. This was something that they probably couldn't talk about.

Sophie looked between them, for any clue.

"Yeah. We know," Haltwhistle replied, with a smile. "You probably guessed that something was on board that shouldn't have been too. We're checking it out."

Colin had picked up on how Sophie had noticed that being in their position, they must be involved with extraordinary situations and wanted juicy details. She was intuitive and it was obvious why Jim was so taken with her so quickly. And she was fishing for a hook.

"Do things like this must pop up a lot in your work?"

More probing questions. Jim and Colin shared a look.

"You could say that, but it's not public knowledge, and that's how... other people like it," McCleland answered.

I bet these two had something to do with Vulcan flying over London, she thought.

For her part, Sophie understood the implication. "Did you always want to do that?"

There was a slow nod from Colin. "I wasn't the usual kid at school. I loved murder mysteries on TV and I read detective books and stuff like that. I sneaked in to see *Heat* at the cinema when I was 13 and was blown away by it."

"Ahh." Jim looked whimsical. "I love that film. You sneaked in? I didn't think you'd do things like that. You seem too... straight-laced."

"That's what you think, mate." Colin returned his grin, then moved on before Anna took him to task. "And I loved aircraft. My dad served, so I followed him in. He insisted I played school sports because it would look good later on, so like you, I joined the rugby team."

He excused himself. He intended to get his answers and then finish his food. He was enjoying the evening so far. He had his wife and friend with him and Jim seemed to respect his date, actually listening and paying attention to her.

He was much warmer towards Sophie than he usually was with other ladies. Maybe this was a turning point for him.

The door of the bar opened and in walked the formidable Marinell who he had encountered earlier. He gave a curt acknowledgment to Colin and took a seat at the back of the pub. Aiming to get himself another half an ale, Haltwhistle sidled up to the bar. The barman finished serving another customer and came over. He gave him the empty glass and when the barman returned with a refilled beer, Colin hit him with a question.

"Excuse me. A couple of nights ago a friend of mine came in here. He was with another guy."

He showed the barman a photo on his phone. "Do you remember what time they came in?"

The bartender put a pair of reading glasses on. "Yeah," he said finally. "I remember them. They came in about er..." he was struggling to remember. "I'd say about 8ish I think. They stayed until about 10 or so."

"Do you have any idea what they talked about?"

The barkeep shook his head. "No. It was a busy night. A lot of noise and customers. Sorry."

Colin smiled. "No worries. Thanks."

He went back to the table. He sat down with his fresh drink in time to hear about he and Jim had been in a life-and-death struggle in Afghanistan, complete with the Jim McCleland spin about it being an interesting experience. No, it wasn't an interesting experience. It had been very touch and go, looking back.

Oh God, not that again. He had wanted to banish that adventure to his memory. Sophie was spellbound by the story, little realizing that it was a lot worse than how Jim was describing it and of course, he was not revealing all the details. Anna looked less than impressed and glared at Colin.

Once McCleland had finished, she said pointedly to her husband "You didn't tell me you had nearly been killed, several times over."

Colin shook his head. "I couldn't. It was secret... or it was until now." He looked at Jim with resignation. He took a large gulp of his ale. "Can we talk about something else? Russian spies and assassins do not make for a nice quiet night, which I thought was what we were having."

Jim shrugged. "Hey, Soph just asked me what we actually did. I couldn't exactly turn her down, could I?"

He turned to her. "What did you get up to today?" He thought he might be able to glean some valuable information.

"Oh, it was good," she replied, finishing her leafy salad and taking a swig of her vodka. "Found a few things out. You already knew though so..."

Colin, twigging to what his partner was up to, was interested. "What did you find?"

"I can't talk about it at this stage. I'm sure you understand about that sort of thing," she smiled.

The vodka was having its effect on her.

"Give us a clue," Jim grinned. He'd probably regret it, but they needed to know something.

Anything.

Sophie sighed. "All I'll say is this. It looks like there was something very interesting on that flight. An illegal something. Something that goes bang..."

"That is kind of obvious," Colin smiled, hoping to get a rise out of her. It worked.

"No, you don't understand," she went on. "I mean yeah, something caused it to explode, but then there's this other stuff on board. All sorts. The sort of thing that should be controlled strictly."

She realized she was saying too much and fell silent. Instead of gaining information, Colin had managed to do the reverse, and she was kicking herself.

Colin understood what she was getting at. It was obvious what the main cause of destruction was, but she had let them in on something that filled in a gap before he knew it needed to be filled. There had been munitions on board as well. But where from? An armory would have everything documented down to the last round of ammunition, so that was not an option, but a check of the manifests on the camp wouldn't hurt anything.

Anna however was still seething. She rounded on Jim "You will look after my Colin this time, won't you?"

For his part, Jim finished his whiskey. "I'll do my best," he said seriously.

Anna gave him a look like a teacher staring down an errant pupil in school who had just been caught doing something he shouldn't have done. Not a hard thing to pull off considering her choice of profession.

"You had better, or I'll have your guts for garters!"

"Yes ma'am," was the light response.

"See? I knew there was a hero under that gruff skin of yours!" Colin teased.

"Very funny, man!"

"I thought so!"

But Anna was deadly serious, so much as a scratch on her husband and she would take it out on McCleland. She had not particularly cared for his maverick ways or his cavalier attitude towards women, and despite what she had now learned about him, she'd be damned to see Colin hurt. She told Jim in no uncertain terms.

"He will not come to harm, I assure you," he convinced her.

Jim's girlfriend was intrigued to know what had happened to them and why Anna was so defensive. Maybe she would find out in time.

"And you had better treat Sophie nicely too!" Anna warned Jim. Her new friend grinned at that.

"I'm with you on that one, sister!" They clinked their glasses, then she turned to her date. "See? We're both on your case now, McCleland. So get your arse home and treat me nicely!"

"I thought you'd never ask!" he beamed.

Jim gave them both a cheerful smile and got up, pulling Sophie from the pub after him. Getting into the car, the engine roared.

"Home James," Sophie teased. He looked over and grinned.

"Yes miss."

It left Anna and Colin to spend some precious time together, just as she had hoped for all along.

She looked at her husband, enjoying having him close by. She yawned.

"Long day?" he asked.

"A bit." The teacher nodded to the muscle car that was now leaving. "She's lovely and he's incorrigible." Anna smiled as the Mustang roared off. She was thoughtful.

"Yep," Colin agreed. "But would you have him any other way?"

They got into the Mondeo and drove away, heading for home leaving Anna's Mini at the pub to be picked up later.

"Thank you for a really nice meal," she said.

"Always a pleasure, sweetie."

She settled back into the seat and relaxed.

SEVEN

It was back to the camp at 8 am the following morning. Haltwhistle pulled up to the car park by the front of the main offices and was surprised to find Jim had got there ahead of him. He also looked fresh and ready to go. To say this was a surprise was an understatement. The familiar beat of *Fight the Power* by Public Enemy emanated from his partner's car.

"What are you doing here so early? Did you get dumped already?" he asked Jim, putting his hands in his pockets.

His partner gave him a not-very-impressed look. "No actually. You told me to take this seriously, so I am."

Colin was taken aback by his friend's attitude, but couldn't resist taking a jab at him. "Oh right. I thought you'd been relegated to Pam and her Five Sisters."

Jim grinned. "Nah I had Soph do that!"

"Did she need a microscope and a pair of tweezers?" The white cap pursed his lips. "Well it's nice that you showed up, anyway."

"Jesus there's no pleasing you. I turn up on time and you're still moaning!"

"I just hope you don't finish early either!" Colin smirked.

"What have you been eating, razor blades?" McCleland folded his arms. "You're a real comedian, Haltwhistle. You've got crap hair to match your crap car. And remember who's the higher rank here, Flight Lieutenant."

Colin grinned and took a quick drink of his Mountain Dew. "Kind of ironic that you're pulling rank on me when you're listening to a protest against authority song and you do a job where authority is part and parcel of it!" The song was still blaring noticeably.

"Got to play the game if you want to fly the plane, I say," was Jim's reply as he turned the car off.

Colin chuckled and they went into their allocated office space. The office was a long, draughty cold room with single pane sash windows, a cork pinboard on the far wall and a large table that dominated the center of the room. At either end of the space was a desk which had been hastily moved in, as the trash in the drawers attested to. The layers of paint on the walls gave away the age of the building overall. Jim stamped his feet and rubbed his hands together.

"Bloody cold in here isn't it? Maybe they want us to freeze our bollocks off before we find out what's going on," he remarked.

Haltwhistle, who still had his heavy overcoat on, agreed with the assessment.

"You're probably right!" He looked at McCleland. "I hope you've not let on anything to your missus. Cartwright will be on you like a fly on shit if he finds out, especially if she's a nosy parker."

"Col, I'm not stupid. I've not told her anything that we don't and she doesn't know already."

Haltwhistle unpacked the notes and evidence collected so far. Spreading it out on the table, he looked over what they had learned while Jim tried to coax the heating system into life, mostly by hitting and swearing at it. Once the radiator was in working order, mostly by kicking it a few times, he made his way over to the table.

"I'm thinking that you've got all this on you because you don't trust anyone here, right?" Jim said, looking over their progress so far.

"You catch on quick, Grasshopper."

Like McCleland, Haltwhistle was hesitant to take off his coat. It was April but it was unseasonably cold for the time of year. He looked over the photos of the detonator again and remembered what he had said about his theory of weapons being carried aboard the plane, and what Sophie had told them the previous night at the table, about things going bang. Maybe it wasn't explosives that she was talking about. Maybe it was bullets... and guns? But where would Woodley have got them? There was something about that question that rankled in the back of Colin's mind. Something that could answer that one.

"I'm going to get some statements, then we're going to check out the victim's rooms. Stay here and hold the fort. I don't want any of this left unattended."

"Have you ever heard of a lock?" Jim asked.

"Would you trust it based on what we've learned so far? Sod that." He had a good point there.

"Alright, no worries," The Squadron Leader agreed.

Colin took his leave, while Jim looked over the photos and evidence bags they had accumulated so far. Suspected weapons and explosives, a meeting that took place, an aeroplane that wasn't registered flying under radar. It all looked like pieces of a jigsaw puzzle that they didn't know what the final picture would look like. McCleland wondered how these detectives that handled murder investigations put up with the stress and the horror of the case and lived with it over and over again for several years. He had read accounts of some cases taking six or seven years to solve and trials, re-trials and appeals that caused the thing to drag on even longer.

That must cause a lot of distress for all concerned. Frankly, that would bore him rigid, but Colin lived for that stuff. Oh well, to each his own.

McCleland had a drink of his coffee that a helpful WREN presented to him at the door. He was tempted to give her a quick look over but remembered Sophie's interest in him and let it go.

Taking a quick sip of his hot drink, Jim sat down at his desk. The sunlight poured through the windows of this crisp spring morning and he placed his feet on the desktop as he stared out onto the grounds, deep in thought. Being involved in something like this certainly gave you a different perspective to someone on the outside.

Damn, Colin was rubbing off on him. He now wanted to solve this mystery. His mind wandered to the day he arrived at the camp. That truck that had nearly wiped him out when he drove on to the base.

It was as if a light bulb went on in his head. Sometimes the mind was funny. It could guide you to an answer that was there in completely unexpected ways. The guy had said that new weapons were being delivered and old stuff being taken away. What if what had been on board was some of that old gear?

Convinced he had something, Jim quickly scribbled down his theory as he had seen Colin do and added it to their stash of information that now littered the tabletop.

Happy that he had made a breakthrough of some sort, Jim finished his coffee and plopped himself back down at his desk. Again, he put his feet on the desktop like some sort of 1920s gangster in old Chicago.

Then another thought struck him. It was all very well discovering what had been on the aeroplane, but the questions of who took them, for what reason, and to be delivered to who and why remained. But it was a start at least.

"We'll find this bastard," said Jim before he caught himself talking to no one but himself. He chuckled and fell silent. It'd be interesting to find out what else Colin could get out of these people now that a bit of time had gone by since their first meeting with the main players in this mess.

Something that someone said may give them away. Or, McCleland thought grimly, it could open a can of worms far bigger than the one they had opened now.

EIGHT

"I'm sorry sir. I don't mean to offend but I need to ask you why there was friction between you and your son," Haltwhistle had tracked Woodley down to his office, where he was trying to bury himself in work rather than sit at home moping. It had been fairly successful, going over orders for AVTUR and requests for transfers until Colin Haltwhistle had arrived at his door with more questions.

Woodley set his fountain pen down and steepled his fingers.

"I don't see why I should answer such a personal question, Flight Lieutenant." He emphasized Colin's rank, as if to make himself seem more important. "Are you insinuating I had something to do with this? That I killed my own son?"

If the pulling rank was meant to be intimidating, the white cap was undeterred. In matters such as these, his authority was absolute, especially with his department's influence. He tapped his pen on his notebook. "Sir, with all due respect, I'd like an answer. It could very well help."

The base commander was not pleased. "I find this question crass and insulting. My son is not yet buried and you are raking old coals over. I find it disgraceful that you come in here and begin this line of questioning."

Colin sucked his tongue for a moment. It helped concentration. Woodley wouldn't like this at all, but it was a good way of bringing about a little order. He opened his notebook.

"I did a little check with the CAA regarding Chris's PPL. It turns out that his single-engine rating had expired and he hadn't renewed it. And he never took a night rating. In effect, he was doing the equivalent of driving a car without a license I'm sure you know how serious that is."

Haltwhistle looked at the Group Captain. "I want to know why he'd take such a risk. He was flying in dangerous conditions without paperwork and with a deadly cargo.

Any lead I can get is going to be useful, and I want to know right now, sir."

Woodley was livid, partly hat his son's stupidity and partly at the white cap's dogged insistence.

"You are dismissed, Haltwhistle," he barked.

Unmoved, Colin lowered his cap. "Sir, it's an offense to obstruct a police officer in the execution of his duty, irrespective of rank. I mean no disrespect, but I want an answer. Right now." He was insistent.

Woodley was steaming at the ears and could have tried to order him out, but he knew that as the investigator, Haltwhistle had authority in this situation. Any strong-arm tactics would just make things a hell of a lot worse for him. Colin's last statement had got him thinking, and he softened a little.

"You're right." He stood up, came around the desk and leaned himself up against the window sill, blocking out a lot of natural light. This also made his face pretty much unreadable because of the surrounding glare, Colin noted. "Alright. He was very much into doing his own thing. He didn't want to listen to reason, always wanted his own way."

He looked at the floor and wiped his nose. "He didn't want to go to university, which would have made things a lot easier for himself, but he didn't want that." Woodley emoted and went on to explain his frustrations at how he had not been present much because of his work.

How he had missed out on a lot of his children's growing-up time. "I hope I can be a better father to Cassie," he finished sadly.

"How much did you know about his work here on the base?" Colin wanted to build up a picture of the man and his job, how he went about it and who he was associated with regularly beyond those he had already spoken to.

"I know he was very hard working. He was very proud of being in the service. I was pleased to hear he was getting on well with his work. I didn't talk much with him, but I know he was close to a guy with a funny nickname."

"It wouldn't be Fliplugs, would it?"

Woodley frowned. "No, I don't think that was it. Erm... something to do with explosives I think."

"Do you know what department this guy worked in?" Colin stopped writing and looked at the base commander.

The Group Captain looked at some paperwork in a file. He had taken it from a filing cabinet of which several lined his office.

"Bomb disposal," he said finally.

That made sense. Haltwhistle knew who Woodley was talking about and wrote the man's name down on his pad.

"I just want to say thank you, Mr. Haltwhistle. Thank you," Woodley said. "From me and my family. Please find out what happened. We loved Chris, but we just want to know what happened."

He handed over a copy of his son's phone bill. "You may find this useful."

Colin looked it over. One number was recorded repeatedly.

"It could very well, sir. I'm waiting for a listing, but this helps a lot."

"Just find my son's killer, Mr. Haltwhistle," Woodley insisted.

Colin nodded. The family was grieving and just wanted peace of mind. It was understandable.

The base commander was a good man, a bit too devoted to his career than to his family and now he had realized that. But it had taken a loved one to die to come to terms with that, and that was sad.

Woodley resolved to devote as much time as possible to his daughter and not to be so negligent.

Maybe if he paid more attention to Chris, he wouldn't now be missing his son.

"I'll do my best, sir. I've got a lot of information to put together so thank you. If you could provide me with a written, signed statement that would be very helpful, sir," Haltwhistle was determined to be as thorough as possible.

"Of course. I read your file. A good investigator. Mr. McCleland, however, is a bit of a loose cannon, I feel."

That's putting it mildly, Colin thought. "He has his moments, but he's a good guy. I'm trying to teach him to be a detective. It's hard work, but we'll get there. Not his natural set of skills, if you like." He turned off his dictation machine and slipped it into his pocket.

"Call me if you need anything else." Woodley stuck his hand out and Colin headed out of the office. Aiming to get back to his and McCleland's new digs, he went over what he had been told in his mind. Taking a shortcut, he recognized he was close to the weapons fitting area. And accompanying the usual sounds of work and dirty jokes that was part and parcel of station life was the sound of raised voices and arguing.

He was about to put it down to the usual scuttlebutt until the words Chris Woodley being said loudly got his attention.

Colin moved closer to get a better level of things. Rounding the corner he saw the familiar features of Marinell and Fliplugs standing shouting at each other and pointing fingers while other people looked on in bewilderment.

"Did you do it? Did you kill him?" Fliplugs demanded.

"I would advise you not to shout, and be careful of who you"re talking to," Marinell told him with an edge. "You are a corporal and in case you hadn't noticed, I am a sergeant. Remember that mister!"

"Oh yeah, pull rank on me. If I find out it was you, I'll nail you!" Fliplugs glared at the superior, absolutely determined not to be intimidated.

"If you have a problem, you go through your sarge. Get out of my sight!"

"Oh no. I want an answer, or I'll get an answer!" Fliplugs was unmoved.

"Are you threatening me?" Marinell tutted. "That will definitely get you thrown out. Do you really want to go there?" Marinell was condescending and used to getting how own way. Clearly that was something that had to be stamped on. What worried Colin was that no one watching was saying anything, until he reasoned this guy ruled by fear and no-one dared to buck him.

Colin was disgusted by that. He had been bullied as a kid and had an almost pathological dislike for anything behavior of the sort.

"Gentlemen is there a problem?" he inquired, putting his hands on his hips.

Marinell simply saluted him. "No sir, no problem. I think this man is just trying to feel his oats, that's all."

Fliplugs was fuming. "No I don't think so -!"

Colin cut him off. "It's inappropriate to talk back to a superior, so I'm forced to agree with Sergeant Marinell on that." Fliplugs looked crestfallen. Marinell looked beyond smug and began to say something. 'shut it, Marinell. I haven't even begun with you."

He got between them. "I want to see you both in my office in thirty minutes. No excuses. Is that clear enough for you, sergeant?" He was going to enjoy putting the squeeze on this arsehole, that's for sure.

"As crystal sir," was the slightly smug reply. Hmm. Maybe ten minutes with Jim would straighten this guy out? Not exactly within the regulations, but it would get the message across.

Colin intended to let his partner loose on this joker.

"Thirty minutes." Then he had second thoughts. He turned to Fliplugs and pointed a finger.

"You. Come with me now."

Sitting Fliplugs down in the office, Haltwhistle offered him a drink.

"No thank you, sir. I'm fine," he took Colin's offer of a seat, however. He pulled the chair up to the desk, which Jim was perched on.

"So, tell us. What was that argument all about?"

Fliplugs looked like a little boy who had just been caught by his parents with his hand in the cookie jar. "I went to deliver some parts, they needed some pieces for warheads. I dropped them off. Marinell -" he paused at Colin's raised eyebrow. "Sorry, Sergeant Marinell was joking about Chris passing away and said he had it coming. So I told him that's not fair to him or his friends or family and we got into it."

"I see." Colin thought for a moment. "It's not your place to take a superior officer to task, is it? I believe the proper procedure is to log a complaint with your superior."

Fliplugs took a breath. "You know that there is a code of honor sir. We watch each other's backs. We have to. So for someone to come along and disrespect someone who is gone is not the done thing."

Colin smiled and Jim nodded. "You're right there. But next time, do it properly and go through your boss. It protects everyone."

Haltwhistle, as he had with Woodley, asked Fliplugs for a signed, written statement. Ten minutes later it was done and in the file.

"Thank you. You can go," Colin said. As Fliplugs went to leave, Colin spoke again. "If you have any more problems with Sergeant Marinell, come and see us. It'll be off the record. You're among friends here."

Fliplugs saluted and thanked them both, then he strode out. Haltwhistle looked at his clock. It was five minutes before Marinell was going to show.

A notification popped up on Colin's inbox.

"Great. We've got the phone records."

Unfolding the phone bill, he quickly matched up the repeated number. A good two dozen calls and texts between Woodley and whoever it was. Curious, Haltwhistle dialled it. Only a dead tone came back.

"That's no good," Jim grumbled. "We're no further forward than we were!"

"I'd have been more surprised if it was still working. I'll get it checked."

"I thought I knew this guy and when I saw his name, I became certain of it," Colin said looking at a file on his desk.

"Where did you know him from?" Jim asked.

"It was back when I had just passed out. It was around the time of the wedding when I met Anna. The wedding was a real drag. I'd been invited to this thing and had to be arm twisted by my CO to represent the section." Colin smiled at the memory. "I don't like weddings. Too much emotional baggage and clingy people who you would never see again afterward. I was investigating a case of harassment at the time, and he was the suspect but the person who was being harassed wouldn't talk. The case was dropped. Lack of evidence."

"Then, this is your chance to nail him?" McCleland looked at his friend and pursed his lips.

"No. You never make it personal. that's not professional."

A loud tap on the door heralded their visitor's arrival. The two friends looked at each other.

"Talk of the devil!"

NINE

Jim cracked the door a touch. He heard the irritating sergeant outside being snide to Fliplugs.

Something about being the pet in the pocket. Colin nodded to Jim to deal with it. He of course was all for it.

Marinell was in mid-sentence and poking Fliplugs in the chest when Jim stuck his head around the door frame.

"Oi, Fuckface. Get your worthless bullying arse in here, now."

Fliplugs just grinned at Jim and was gone. The errant Sergeant Marinell trudged his way in, standing to attention and saluted.

"Sit down, Sergeant," Colin said.

"I'd prefer to stand sir." There was a bit of a sneer in his speech. Jim simply grabbed him by the shoulders from behind and pulled him down into the chair, which swayed under the sudden impact.

"He said sit down," he growled in his ear.

"Assault of an officer is a court martial offense! I'll have you!" Marinell jabbed a finger angrily at McCleland.

Jim simply looked down and stood over the Sergeant with his arms folded. He wore a ghoulish smile on his face.

"Who's looking son?" Jim raised an eyebrow. "No witnesses."

Marinell shook his head and chuckled. "Oh, I'll have you both. Mark my words," he jeered.

Jim leaned down by his ear and put his arm around Marinell's shoulder. "I'd watch what I say if I was you. So shut the fuck up you prick, you're on our territory now."

Suitably uncomfortable, Marinell piped down while McCleland loitered behind him.

"I know you, don't I sir? We've met before," Marinell said to Colin. For his part, Colin placed his clasped hands on the desktop.

"You do. We met a few years ago. It was a bullying case then, too."

Marinell shrugged and said nothing. Jim, unmoving continued to glower down at the despicable man.

"What is this? Good cop bad cop? I didn't read that in the Queen's Regulations," Marinell complained, looking up at McCleland, who was letting his demeanor and behavior be as unpleasant as possible.

Essentially he was giving Marinell a taste of his own medicine and was thoroughly enjoying himself. Looking on, Colin was also secretly loving every second of the odious man's misfortune.

"We're both bad cops, pal. And strictly speaking, we're not RAF. My friend here is going to ask you some questions. Your answers are required to those questions. You get where I'm coming from?"

Marinell smiled thinly. "And if I say no comment?"

Colin, gleeful, leaned forward and cracked his knuckles. "Then Sergeant Marinell. My colleague here is going to make sure you answer."

To emphasize the point, Jim clapped his hand on the sergeant's shoulder. He spun him around in the chair as Colin joined his partner in looming over their suspect.

"I have the right to legal counsel," Marinell said coldly.

Jim mocked him openly. "Legal counsel he said. Did you hear that Col? He wants legal counsel!"

Colin played along. "You'll want a dentist by the time we're done!"

For the first time, Marinell looked genuinely alarmed.

"You can't do this to people! There are regulations!"

"For someone with a history of bullying, I'd say regulations don't matter to you," Haltwhistle said, absently thumbing through Marinell's personnel record. It was full of personal warnings and better conduct required recommendations. How the hell this guy was still seen as fit to serve was anyone's guess.

"It's up to you to prove me wrong," Colin told him, sitting back down and folding his arms.

For his part, Marinell looked deeply troubled. "So you're above the law? This AID department doesn't answer to anyone?"

McCleland spun him around in the chair to face him and leaned over him menacingly.

"We are the law as far as you're concerned," he told him. "So play nice or you get cut out. All the way out." He put his face in the sergeant's again to get the point across. "Know what I mean?"

Marinell looked down at the floor and then back at Colin, who rose from behind the desk.

"Your demeanor is a front, sergeant. The body language says insecurity, as does your behavior in trying to coerce people who you see as weaker than yourself. You recently lost your lady friend, which you are still upset about. And you got the job you're in only by fortune, which goes some way to explaining the chip on your shoulder."

Surprised, Marinell looked at the white cap. "And how did you work all that out?"

"A confident person would not be constantly adjusting his posture to make himself look bigger than he was. You flex your shoulders three times a minute." Haltwhistle pointed at the sergeant's hand. "You're wearing a bangle on your right wrist, one of a pair, but it hasn't been cleaned recently, hence you're hoping the person who gave it to you will come back but you don't hold out hope. A female someone because the scroll work on the bangle is a women's his and hers design."

Jim grinned. "And what about Mr. Lover Lover Man here's way of getting his job?"

Colin looked at his friend. "His predecessor was killed on active duty. I read the file. He was next in line, so got the job. It annoys him to know he didn't get the job on merit."

Suitably humbled, Marinell nodded. "Ask your questions."

Colin tried his best imitation of one of Jim's evil smiles. He didn't know how effective it was.

"Good boy. Where were you on the night of Chris Woodley's death?"

"I was in the pub. You can check if you like."

"Oh we will," Jim assured him. "Which pub?"

Marinell glared up at Jim. "Do I have to have this untrained gorilla breathe on me? Tell your lackey to back off or-" Jim pushed the back of Marinell's head down fast, slamming his face into the desk top. He yelped in pain as a thin trail of blood oozed from his nose.

"That's for speaking out of line to a superior officer," Jim said as he backed away and leaned against the big table behind them.

Marinell nursed his nose and tried to stop the bleeding.

"He asked you which pub," Colin persisted.

"The one you saw me in last night. Who were the women you were with? Did you pay them-"

Marinell was getting cocky and trying to get back on level terms with the two of them. He had his manners minded by McCleland lifting him up by the lapels and landing his fist a good blow on Marinell's jaw which sent him onto the cold concrete floor.

"We keep telling you to behave. I'd take that advice if I were you."

Marinell got back on his feet and nursed his injured jaw. "Can't you take a joke? It's like trying to explain to my ex why I enjoy using my green fingers in the garden!"

"Yeah, it was very exciting. Tomorrow I'll take you to a theme park!" Jim shot back.

"Not the kind of banter we enjoy," Colin said briskly. "So. How well did you know Mr. Woodley?"

Still nursing his jaw, Marinell got back in the chair.

"Not well. I only met him a couple of times. He was a bit meek," Marinell said. "He needed toughening up." He gave a sly smile.

"Did you bully him too?" Haltwhistle was grim and didn't disguise his dislike for the man sitting opposite.

Marinell fixed him with a superior look but had got the message to keep his tongue in check around McCleland.

"I don't bully. I make people stronger by being tough with them. If people don't like that, then get out of the service." He was smug. "He probably deserved what he got."

Jim shook his head in disgust. "People like you make me sick. A man has died. Probably a far better man than you."

Marinell was equally dismissive. "If you think I had something to do with his croaking, you're wrong. I couldn't care less about him. I was miles away from him. I don't know how he died, and I don't care. Are you happy now?"

He looked from Jim to Colin and back again. For his part, Colin turned the Dictaphone off and put a piece of paper in front of the sergeant.

"Sign it and date it."

Marinell did so. "Can I go now?" he demanded.

"Get the fuck out of my sight," McCleland growled, thumbing the door.

Colin sat back in his chair and dismissed him with a disdainful wave of his hand. "Sqn. Ldr. McCleland here will show you the door."

Marinell got up, and Jim showed him the door alright.

"Well, I hope you find whoever did it. But don't try too hard as they did us all a favor Woodley was a useless piece of-" The unpleasant sergeant was cut off with a kick to the ribs which sent him flying out of the room. He crashed into the wall opposite and dropped to the floor. He groaned as he sat up.

"We'll let you know if we need anything else," Jim told him as he closed the door on the surly man's face.

Coming back to the table, Jim leaned against it and looked at his partner. "What do you think? Think he's the guy?"

Colin scratched his chin thoughtfully. Finally, he shook his head. "No, he's not smart enough. His motive is pretty shallow as well."

"I wouldn't go for a circumcision if I was him." McCleland sighed. "The doctor would never find the end of the prick!"

There was a giggle from Haltwhistle. "There is that! No, he didn't do it. He was telling the truth when he said no." To ward off his friend's question, Colin went on. "His eyes didn't dart around and he didn't start sweating."

Jim considered that with his arms folded.

"People have killed for a lot less mate. Money, love, hell people have died over a disagreement."

Colin was impressed. Jim had been paying attention and understood a lot more about this line of work than he was letting on. It was a little frustrating that he hid his intelligence.

"I get the point mate, but he's far too dumb. He could dead eye me at point blank range with a Kalashnikov and still miss," Haltwhistle said firmly.

Jim chuckled. "Bloody hell mate. You sound like me!" They both laughed but then Jim got serious.

"We'd better check and see if anyone's listening at the door." A quick look revealed there were no unwanted eavesdroppers and the door was closed again. "We're good, so what's the next move?"

Colin finished scribbling on his writing pad where he was ticking off the list of today's jobs. He produced two bottles of Mountain Dew and began drinking.

"Christ mate! How much of that stuff can you put away before you blow apart?"

"It's a double bubble problem, mate," Haltwhistle replied. "It's my only vice!" He thought for a moment while sipping on the first of the drinks.

"We need to talk to that Short Fuse guy again," he said, looking at the business card with the scribbled handwriting on it again and turned it over. "And I want to check out Woodley's apartment and car."

"You think he had something to do with it?" McCleland pointed at the card.

"At this point, i think everyone has something to do with this in some way," was the response. "But I want to check everything out. Remember what Sherlock Holmes said?"

Jim frowned. "What? 'The game's afoot' ?"

"No, the other thing. I dunno, it's a long while since I read one of those stories." Haltwhistle looked at his friend, surprised. "You read those books?"

"No, I just watched the Jeremy Brett episodes. Mum loved them." There was the briefest whimsical expression on Jim's face.

Colin guessed his friend had something on his mind and wanted to tell him what he had not wanted anyone else, especially Marinell to hear. He showed Haltwhistle the notes he had written.

"Remember when I told you about the truck that ran me off the road?"

Colin screwed his forehead up. "Yeah, I think so. Why?"

Jim sat on the desk next to Colin. "What I'm going to lay on you may sound crazy, but here's what I think." He folded his arms again. "What if the weapons he carried on the plane came from this camp. We know the detonator did, so why not everything? We know there was a lot of surplus stuff going out, guns, equipment and all that jazz. Who'd miss them? Sophie said there was something on the plane that shouldn't have been besides explosives. Why not that?"

Colin's eyes went wide. He could see what Jim was driving at, despite how ridiculous it sounded. Military-grade weapons, retired or not would make a lot of money on the black market.

And if a great deal of equipment suddenly became available, who knew whose hands it would fall into? What Jim was suggesting was terrifying but yet it made perfect sense. It put the security of the Ministry of Defence and the services into jeopardy but it had to be checked out.

Once you disregard what's impossible, whatever is left, no matter how unlikely must be right, Haltwhistle thought, remembering the infamous line. "Sadly we need evidence, all we've got is a theory which just happens to hold up. We need to get over to the stores and check it out."

Quickly stuffing the work into his knapsack, Colin headed out of the office with Jim in tow. He kept hold of the bag religiously. He wanted nothing falling into the wrong hands or compromising their investigation through the loss of evidence or information. He locked the bag in the Mondeo's boot and they made their way over to the store.

Once there, they collared the duty officer.

"I'd like Corporal Smith to report to us in the quartermaster's office," Jim told the man. He saluted and disappeared into the immense interior of the warehouse. He and Colin took a seat in the office, surrounded by piles of paperwork and box files. It was chaos, but somehow there seemed to be an order in it. Well, as long as they could find what they had come for. A few minutes went by before Fliplugs appeared. He stood to attention.

"At ease, Fliplugs. We need your help again," said Colin.

"Anything sir." Fliplugs had so far been unfailingly helpful and enthusiastic in all their meetings with him.

"We need all the manifests and records for the store and the transfers of the weapons and equipment that was exchanged in the last round of changeover," Haltwhistle told him.

"All of it?" Fliplugs' jaw dropped.

"Yes, Corporal. All of it," Jim confirmed.

Slightly shocked, Fliplugs stepped out of the office. Jim and Colin burst out laughing.

"Perks of being an officer. Leave the grunt work to the working man," McCleland smirked.

Fliplugs reappeared a few minutes later loaded down with ring binders and several rolled up papers in his arms.

"Here it is." He dumped the stuff on the desk. All three looked at the rather large pile of paperwork that was now piled up.

"Don't you keep records on a computer?" McCleland asked, a bit put out and dreading having to plow through the vast pile of papers that now filled the desktop.

"We had a computer problem a few weeks ago, sir. We had to do everything the old-fashioned way," Fliplugs explained glumly.

"Do you have discs or USB sticks? You don't keep a backup? That's standard procedure."

Haltwhistle was equally unenthused to dig through this lot. The corporal's expression told the story.

"What the hell, man?" Jim groaned. He looked despairingly at his colleagues. "They must be around somewhere!"

"They were wiped at the same time. It was one afternoon about six weeks ago. Everything just went down. They said the server was overloaded," Fliplugs explained.

"How convenient," McCleland said petulantly.

"Well, the sooner we start, the sooner we finish," sighed Colin. "So much for being an officer, eh Jim?"

McCleland rolled his eyes and took a reluctant seat, grabbed a binder and set to work.

Fortunately, they were in date order, so each person took a file for the last month, Colin on inventory, Jim on stock in and Fliplugs on stock out. Matching up the lists took a bit of juggling as whoever had written up the orders and slapped them in the folders in any order. Once that was straightened out they were able to call out the items listed in the correct order. Until the details in the stock out logs abruptly stopped.

"There's nothing. No details past the 15th of March," said Fliplugs.

"Are you sure? Check back again," Colin told him.

Fliplugs did so, but he had been right. There was nothing past the 15th of the month prior. A thorough check of the other files turned up nothing as well. Haltwhistle slammed the file down in frustration and looked at the stuff put away on the shelves. They were all dated for months and years gone by. A good auditor would be able to sort through it, but they just did not have the time for that.

"Someone has either lost the paperwork, or they didn't file it, or..." Jim started.

"Or someone took it and destroyed it," Colin finished.

With no records of what went out of the base in the last three weeks, it meant someone could have taken the surplus with impunity, but the lack of records means there was indeed something shady going on that someone didn't want them to find out about. And down the line, the

MoD would have written the stock off as 'lost presumed destroyed.' It was a perfect crime.

Perhaps it had gone missing while people were on active duty, or damaged on maneuvers or some such. In any case, deadly weapons could potentially be with people who had no business having them.

"Do you realize how much could be missing?" Jim thought aloud, horrified.

"I'm trying not to." Haltwhistle cringed at the thought of all the weapons and explosives that could be in people who shouldn't have them's possession.

"And there are no records anywhere else?" Jim asked Fliplugs.

The young man shook his head. "I'm sorry sir. Nothing."

"Shit," Colin murmured. "Alright Fliplugs. Thanks for your help."

Outside, Haltwhistle stood with his hands on his hips and thought things over.

"This is all a bit too convenient," he said. The fact the very records they needed were nowhere to be found was more than just a coincidence, and it backed up his partner's idea about surplus weapons going missing. With no records and no way of checking what was missing, it gave whoever was behind this a free hand to take whatever he or she wanted.

Jim looked his friend over. "Reckon we should check the crime records? See if there's anything there?"

"Yeah. Good idea." Colin exhaled noisily.

The pair trudged over to the WWII-era administration block, its brown bricks and old-fashioned sash windows giving away its vintage. Inside the foyer, an old wooden counter greeted them with a straight-backed female officer on duty attending it.

"Sirs," she said stiffly.

"At ease," Colin assured her. "Who's the senior officer here?"

"Flight Lieutenant Irwin, sir."

"I need to see him or her now."

Knowing that Haltwhistle's demeanor brooked no delays, she disappeared into the office beyond the counter. A few moments later a tall immaculately turned-out officer appeared. His hair, his countenance, his entire being was austere.

"Good afternoon, gentlemen. How can I help you?"

Colin produced his warrant card. "I need to see the criminal reports for the last three months."

Inspecting his identification, Irwin nodded. "Please follow me."

McCleland and Haltwhistle exchanged a glance. Everyone in this department looked as if they were on tenterhooks. There was no humor, no jokes, no camaraderie in this entire building.

"We have both computerized and paper files, which would you like to see?" Irwin asked.

"Both."

Jim groaned inwardly. All this paper pushing was getting on his nerves.

"I can feel the vibes, mate," Haltwhistle murmured to him. "It's in everyone's interests to check everything."

The Flt. Lt. showed them into a side office lined with shelf after shelf of box files. At one end of the room under the window, a pair of computers sat. Checking the dates listed on the folders, he pulled down three of them and placed them on the desk beside the two computer terminals.

"Here they are. Is there anything else you need?"

"Has anything unusual been happening around here in the last few months?" Jim asked.

"Nothing that would warrant the presence of the police, sir," Irwin said. "I was only posted here last month but nothing was reported."

"Really?" Colin produced the dingbat mine fuse. "This came from here."

Irwin frowned looking at it. "Where did you get this?"

"It was pulled out of Chris Woodley's Cessna. You might have heard it crashed?" Haltwhistle looked at his opposite number.

That brought Irwin up short. "I heard about the crash, but not about this!"

"Which is why we need to read through all of this. So far we've found out all of the store goods out records are gone. I'm wondering what else hasn't been reported so far." Colin folded his arms.

"Of course." Irwin seemed genuinely concerned and pulled up a chair. He opened up the first of the boxes and showed them the reports had been hand-written and submitted which Colin cross referenced on the computer.

Everything matched up.

"And no reports of anything missing, nothing turned in?" Jim wondered, knowing the answer.

It didn't make Irwin, as the head of the base's police department, feel comfortable. Especially as he did not know what Colin and Jim had dug up in the last twenty-four hours.

"Who was the officer in charge before you took over?"

"Flight Lieutenant Glover." Irwin was thoughtful. "I didn't need to look into anything like this. Nothing was ever brought up and no one reported anything untoward."

"Then I suggest you and your team to look at everything, and I mean everything that's going on around here. You want to wear the white cap, prove you've got what it takes to do that."

Colin looked at Irwin squarely.

TEN

Chris Woodley had lived in the barracks near the main hangar. While Jim went to look for the Focus ST, Colin concentrated on the rooms allocated to him. They were quite extensive:

Woodley must have used his father's reputation to get a nicer place. A bad relationship did not equate to a bad place to live in this case. Stepping around the front room, Haltwhistle took in the small DVD collection and the personal effects. An iPod, laptop, the usual gadgets for a young man in his early 20's.

Pictures of himself in uniform and with his family adorned the walls. Interestingly, none of the images included his father. Colin was careful not to touch anything. The base's crime team had gone over the place but found nothing. They didn't have an allocated investigator, just a police dog handler and a handful of white caps whose duties were limited to finding people drinking on duty. No evidence had been collected either. Conversely, there was a forensics lab, but it wasn't generally manned.

A look at the kitchen and its drawers turned up nothing but cutlery and bills. Lots of bills. Over on the credit card, behind on a loan and he owed a lot to the utility companies. A quick calculation showed he owed about £15,000.

Ouch. No wonder you were transporting weapons. If you owed this, maybe you were offered a way out to pay it off, he thought.

Outside, McCleland had not found a trace of the Focus and several phone calls to the different section officers turned up nothing.

Apparently, the car had simply disappeared into thin air. Colin came outside after checking the place over and found his partner with a glum look on his face.

"This doesn't look good," he said.

"No mate it's not. No trace of that car at all on the camp."

Colin stood back. "You're joking. It was his car, the guy's dead. A car that has no driver can't just disappear!" He was not happy.

Every time they seemed to make some progress, another blind corner came up to send things off the rails.

"Unless someone else has got the keys," Jim pointed out.

They trudged back to the Mondeo. Haltwhistle pulled the receiver out of the center console and put in a call to Black Jack.

"Rapier 2 to Wren's Nest. Come in."

"Wrens Nest." Jim smiled to himself. He was convinced Cartwright sat at his desk 24/7 just in case anything happened.

"Request General APB for a blue Ford Focus ST." He gave the license plate number.

Deciding to follow up with Kevin Johnson, Colin and Jim went over to the bomb disposal unit, only to find Short Fuse had checked out for the day and gone home. The home was a small house in the mess quarters that they now approached. Typically whitewashed, the house was as ordered as anything else. A dark-haired woman with a Brummie accent answered the door.

"Yes?"

"Hi is Kevin in please?" Colin asked.

"Yeah. He's having his supper. Kev?" she called out.

After a moment, Johnson's broad-chested physique framed the doorway. "Sirs. What can I help you with?"

"Can we come in for a few minutes?" Jim asked. He was fully aware of the fact he and Colin could march into the quarters at any time unannounced, but he decided politeness was the order of business.

"Erm.. sure."

They went inside the typically spartan house with whitewashed walls and ceilings. MoD quarters were never the friendliest places. Johnson invited them to sit down.

"This is my missus, Gemma," he said, gesturing to the woman who had answered the door.

"What can I do you both for?"

"Nothing too major. We just need a signed statement from you about everything you know about what has happened."

Colin put a piece of paper in front of him and Johnson leaned forward across the table from his chair and signed the slip off.

"I just want to ask you a few more questions as well."

Colin pulled the Dictaphone from his pocket and set it down.

"Did you know Tim Marinell?" Jim asked.

Kevin adjusted himself in the seat. "I've met him once or twice, but I've not had much to do with him. Bit of a prick, pardon my language, sirs." The smiles from Jim and Colin told him he was on safe ground. He continued. "Likes to bully people. That's not the sort of person I want anything to do with. Like I said before, Chrissy had some trouble with him."

Both officers could see the merits of the statement.

"How about the guy in the stores, Fliplugs? Do you have much to do with him?" Colin was scribbling as well as recording him.

"Oh everyone knows Fliplugs. He's a good lad, I don't know him personally but he's okay."

"He and Marinell got into it earlier, Fliplugs was accusing Marinell of killing Woodley," Jim said.

Kevin looked down. "I wouldn't put it past him to do that."

Colin and Jim looked at each other with a frown.

"What do you mean?"

"Marinell is a bully. A thoroughly unpleasant man." He looked at Gemma who was standing in the doorway.

"And how do you know that if you don't know him well?" Colin wanted some real answers.

Johnson took a sip of coffee from his mug. "Word gets around on a camp. You know that, sirs."

Colin sighed. It was clear Short Fuse would not give much away at this stage. He tapped Jim's arm and they both got up to leave.

"Well, thanks. Have a good night."

The two stepped back out into the cool spring evening which was rapidly closing in. After the door closed, Jim said in a low voice "He definitely knows more than he's letting on. Did you see how he looked at the girl when you asked him how he knew our friend?"

Colin nodded. "You are getting into this detective stuff aren't you, clever clogs? Yeah." He headed back for his car with Jim. "I'm going home. I'll see you in the morning mate."

Fliplugs arrived home late after pulling a cover shift for a friend. Setting down his kit, he just wanted something to eat and to get his head down and have some sleep. He had the early shift tomorrow. His tiny quarters were functional but comfortable, consisting of not much more than a bedroom/sitting room, bathroom and kitchen. He put the kettle on and grabbed a can of baked beans. A couple of slices of toast would make a tasty and quick snack. Switching on the TV, he flicked around the channels. Not much on, just current affairs shows and the news. Not much on Forces TV either.

He went back to the kitchen and got a plate ready for his supper. The beans were bubbling away nicely. Then his eyes fell on something on the wall flickering. It was a shimmering red dot. For a second he thought it was a laser pointer but that was silly as no one he knew had one. Then it disappeared. He thought about it for a second then put it down to a trick of the light. He was tired, after all.

The toast popped up at the same instant a cracking noise came from behind him. Fliplugs was vaguely aware of himself losing consciousness and blood spraying across the white tiles. And then everything went dark.

The beans on toast would never be eaten.

Among a clump of trees half a mile away, the sniper looked through his night scope and watched the unfortunate store worker fall against his oven, a smear of red liquid bathed the tiled wall of the kitchen above the countertop. Satisfied his job was done, he disassembled the rifle and put it away in its carry case. More than aware that even a suppressed gunshot could still be heard, he quickly withdrew from his vantage point and took the path which skirted the base. It was doubtful he would encounter anyone at this time of the evening. Quietly, he slipped away into the night.

ELEVEN

The phone rang urgently on Colin's bedside table. Next to him, Anna stirred and rolled over. She realized it was a call from his superior, the mysterious Mr. Cartwright. She shook her husband awake as he was always a fairly deep sleeper.

Groggy and still half drowsy, he answered the call.

"Get over to Sutton Donington, now! I'll meet you there," Cartwright's voice said urgently.

Colin slammed the phone down and looked at the clock. Two Thirty A.M. He groaned and pulled the bedclothes back.

"What is it?" Anna asked sleepily.

"I don't know. But I'm needed," he said. He kissed her gently and went downstairs. From the bed, Anna heard the engine start and he drove off in a screech of tyres. That wasn't like him: he usually drove carefully. It must be important. His work was making him come home at weird hours, but he was enjoying the change, even if it kept him away sometimes. She laid back on the pillow and went back to sleep.

McCleland had also been called out of bed, much to his annoyance as he'd only had two hours' sleep. Sophie required a lot of attention, he had learned. Not that he was complaining much.

The Mustang flew down the road towards the base and as he approached the turning for the gate, he performed a perfect handbrake turn which half spun the Mustang into the entrance. Jim locked up the brakes and screeched to a stop, only to be confronted with three guards holding rifles and standing to attention. He had only seen a lockdown once before when 9/11 happened.

The base was on high alert and was sealed up tight. Armed sentries now manned the gate while others were walking the fences. He produced his pass and they admitted him. Rather irritated, Jim saw Colin was waiting for him as the first strains of dawn raked the horizon to the east.

Added to that, Cartwright and Woodley and a pair of white caps were also standing close by.

"On your toes, McCleland. I thought we said hurry," Black Jack chided him.

"Sorry sir. I had a bit of a way to come."

"Well, I hope she was worth it because now we really have got work to do." Cartwright led them into Woodley's office, where the base commander was standing ready to greet the AVM. Black Jack simply strode past him and sat behind the desk.

"Report." he demanded briskly.

"The base is on top priority alert, sir." Flt. Lt. Irwin presented his findings. "We have a Level One search underway and guards have been posted at every entrance to the camp. All aircraft movements have been canceled and every arrival and departure by road has been restricted."

"Very good." Cartwright looked at the people present in the office. "I'm assuming temporary command of this station as of 06:35 hours this date. Enter it in the station log."

Woodley looked very unhappy at that development.

"Sir, I thought you were in command of the investigation, not the whole base?"

Black Jack took his horn-rimmed spectacles off and set them on the table.

"This is now a murder investigation. Your son was killed and now a man has been shot dead within the grounds of your command posting. That doesn't look very good on you, does it?" He looked at Woodley with something which verged on pity.

"This station has been the pride of the service, sir," the base commander countered.

"Murder? On at an RAF base?" Cartwright wasn't looking for an answer. "It's unthinkable, it's shocking! And yet here we are. Until this is cleared up, I am in command." The firm tone in his voice told the Group Captain everything he needed to know.

Woodley looked like he had dropped a tenner and picked up a quid in its place.

"Sir, I must protest. This station has a very high efficiency-rating under my command!"

"Well, now it has a very high crime rating as well. This is not open for debate." Cartwright looked up at him. "Dismissed Woodley."

Jim opened the door for him.

"You lot have just waltzed in here, taken over and all without so much as a by your leave! I hope you know what you're doing," he grumbled as the door was closed on him. It hadn't escaped Colin's notice that Irwin was keeping watch at the door frame. Satisfied that Woodley was out of earshot, Cartwright looked at his two men who were standing to attention.

"Apparently more than he does," Black Jack snorted. "Don't stand there looking like a couple of scarecrows. How far has your investigation got you?"

He waved them to the seats. Colin produced his knapsack.

"We're pretty satisfied it was an internal explosion that caused the Cessna to be destroyed. I'm certain it was a mine. We checked the stores, the weapons loading section and the bomb disposal areas, all the places Woodley fraternized and spoke to his friends and colleagues. One of those was the dead man last night," Colin explained.

"Anything missing from the stores?" Cartwright's instincts were sharp.

"The dingbat mine fuse I found definitely came from this base, sir. As you know those are currently being decommissioned," Haltwhistle explained. "They're at the tail end of getting new equipment, weapons and all that sort of thing so the place is a mess. We've checked the paperwork. Everything is in order until you get to the 15th of last month and then the stock-out forms are just not there."

"Hmm. Beware the Ides of March," Cartwright sighed as he drummed his fingers on the tabletop. "What about electronic records? Databases?"

Jim pulled a face. "All of that has been conveniently wiped. Apparently, their server went down or had a power surge or some such."

Cartwright raised an eyebrow. "That's no accident." He had half expected it, though. "What about the station's police unit? What have they found?"

Haltwhistle gritted his teeth. "The regular white cap was reassigned a month ago. The new guy is good but he's getting up to speed. There's nothing listed in any of their files of anything dodgy."

"Why was this fella reassigned?" Cartwright demanded.

"I was about to pull his file today and check, sir. I was told it was a regular posting."

"It seems convenient to offload the guy before all this started coming out of the woodwork." Cartwright tapped his pen on the desktop. "Any theories who the guilty party is?"

Jim and Colin seemed quiet.

"I'm waiting gentlemen, don't keep me in suspense. We're not playing bloody Cluedo here."

Colin sighed. "I saw an argument between the deceased and a guy whose file shows a history of bullying. I don't think he's our man." He twiddled his thumbs a little.

"What makes you think he's not the prime suspect, based on that?"

"He's not clever enough to pull something like this off, sir. I think it's someone else. Who, I don't know yet."

"It seems to me this guy arguing is your prime suspect. You'd best check him out again," Black Jack replied. "Just to be sure."

Colin and Jim got up and headed for the door. "Try to be subtle, eh?" Cartwright said before they left.

Jim turned in the doorway. "Us sir? Would we be anything else?" he asked cheekily. He was relishing another showdown with Marinell.

"Sir?" Haltwhistle asked from the doorway.

Cartwright looked up from his paperwork. "Yes, Colin?"

"I'd like your permission to find the shooter's location. See if there are any traces before we shake the suspect down."

Black Jack nodded. "Very good, carry on."

Walking out of the building, Colin asked to be taken to the crime scene with Irwin hot on his heels. As the lead investigator, he and Jim were driven over to the barracks which housed the NCOs on camp. A red brick building of 1970s vintage looked oppressive. It reminded him of the quarters in basic. He headed up the concrete steps and down the hallway to the unfortunate Fliplugs' room with Jim on his heels. At the far end of the hall, he was shown into the right-hand living space. It was as tidy and ordered as you'd expect.

"My people have gone over the rooms with a fine toothcomb," Irwin explained. "No traces, no fingerprints, there was nothing but Fliplugs... sorry Corporal Smith's fingerprints."

The window above the settee had a telltale hole splintered and shattered through it with shards of glass littering the settee and the floor in front of it. Using the line of glass as a starting point, Colin worked out the trajectory of the bullet to a point by the oven, which had a very burned pan of baked beans and two stone-cold pieces of toast still popped up in the toaster. An empty plate sat to one side.

"The last supper," Jim murmured.

Looking over the place, Colin suddenly felt guilty. Fliplugs had been a nice lad with a good career ahead of him and now he was dead. He had been helping them, and if whoever killed him had done it to hinder the investigation, that made Colin responsible. It was a thought which weighed heavily on him.

The taped outline on the floor and the dried blood gave away where Fliplugs had fallen. He turned to the guard at the door.

"I want this room photographed and everything documented," he ordered. "I want this apartment sealed. No one allowed in or out without AID clearance. Absolutely nothing is to be touched."

"Already taken care of," Irwin replied evenly. "I have sentries posted outside as you saw. I really hope this doesn't turn out like Jack the Ripper."

"Last time I heard, prozzies didn't work for the RAF," Jim replied and tried to get rid of the wicked grin on his face as the others glared at him.

"Any idea of the time of death?" Colin asked.

The station's coroner was stood by the doorway with a clipboard of information. Glancing at the paperwork, he gave him the estimate. "Between 7:30 and 9:30 pm last night."

Colin went to the window and looked out. The roofs of the buildings were dotted about directly in the line of sight. No, the trajectory would be wrong if the shooter was on a rooftop. Looking down to the ground he noticed all of the roads and thoroughfares would make the idea all but impossible as whoever it was would have been seen as he came down from his vantage point.

His eyes were drawn to an embankment on the other side of the camp with a line of trees on it's ridge.

Doing a rough line-of-sight, Colin worked out that a good marksman could make the shot, depending on the weapon and ammunition used.

Deciding he wanted to check it out, Haltwhistle waved to Irwin and pointed to the ridge.

"Take me over there," he said.

They went down to the Focus police car and the corporal drove Colin and Jim over to where he had indicated. It was a fair distance from the buildings, so it would have made a nice hiding place.

Scrambling up the bank, Colin was surprised by how steep it was. It was almost a sheer if short climb. Behind him, Irwin was curious to see what Haltwhistle could make out of this grubby patch of land. His people had already scoured the area.

Getting to the top of the bank, he looked around, ducking to avoid being hit in the head by the low-hanging branches of the evergreen trees. He crouched down and checked the ground, searching for anything that would give away the shooter's position. Looking for the window of the barrack block, Colin made his way along the line of trees until the window he knew was there came into view. He noticed the grass here had been pushed down flat and the exposed tree roots had been scuffed. He knew from this he had found the spot.

"Anything up there?" Jim called.

"I'll let you know in a minute," Colin told him.

Getting down on his knees, he knew he had to get himself in the shooter's position to properly see how whoever had done the deed, had.

"What are you looking for?" Irwin asked.

"The shooter's line of sight. I want you to take notes. Aren't you familiar with this place?"

"I told you, I was only given this posting last month," he protested. "The guy I took over from was reassigned."

Adjusting his bearings, Haltwhistle could see the window between the side of the building which housed the canteen to its left and the ops room on the right.

Yes, this was the shooter's position all right. If this was the place and it was a night shot, then using a torch to find the shell casing would have given the killer away. The spent shell may still be around here somewhere.

Colin stood up again and checked around. It was an overcast day, so sunlight glare would not have given away a brass cartridge on the ground. He scouted about himself, looking for anything unusual. The twigs, sticks and pine cones fallen from the trees were making things very difficult.

Fascinated by Colin's working methods, Irwin was watching his every move.

"Look around for a bullet casing. You're probably looking for a rifle cartridge," Colin told him.

They searched the mucky ground for a few more minutes. Then Irwin spotted something away among the stubby twigs.

"Over here," he shouted. Colin sprinted over to where the eager young man was standing, pointing at the ground. A dull bronze-colored cartridge lay there, just to the right of where the shooter had been. The base's chief of police bent down and reached for it, his hands gloved.

"Don't touch it," Colin warned him.

"I'm wearing gloves!" Irwin protested.

"I can see that, but still." Haltwhistle produced a pen from his pocket and slipped it in to the casing. He dropped it in a clear evidence bag and put it away. Haltwhistle was about to head back to the car when something on the ground caught his eye. Moving closer, he saw it was a footprint. Not the pattern of the MoD boots, and not the wedge or look of training shoes.

These were deep blocky treads, more like hiking boots. Colin took several pictures of it.

"I'd like to be kept in the loop with your investigation," Irwin said. "As head of the base's police unit, I feel I should know what's going on."

"All information is given on a need-to-know basis," Haltwhistle replied. "This investigation falls under the remit of our department, so for the time being I'm not at liberty to inform you of anything. Maybe that'll change." He pointed to the treaded pattern pushed into the ground. "Stay here and I'll have someone over. I want a cast taken of that footprint."

Irwin nodded in acknowledgment. "You must see some... exciting action."

"Sometimes. It's certainly interesting."

Jim and Colin drove back over to the weapons fitting area.

"What do you reckon to our friend back there?" Jim asked.

"We'll find out. If the footprint comes back okay then he's trustworthy. If not, then he's under the microscope as well."

"You left him there deliberately?"

Colin gave his friend a grin.

Knowing better than to ask more, Jim asked "How do you want to go about this?"

"Not like last time, mate. We can't beat a confession out of him, as much as you'd like to."

"Awww!" McCleland complained in mock annoyance.

Climbing out of the police car, Colin put his white cap on and went into the administration building.

"Where is Sergeant Marinell?" he asked the desk clerk.

Looking at the roster, he gave them an answer. "He's working on warhead fitting, over in hangar one."

The two men strode across the pan towards the imposing hangar. Eurofighter Typhoons, looking sleek and impressive sat in neat rows on either side of the hangar with mechanics and technicians swarming around them. The familiar shape of Marinell, his face still marked after his last encounter with Jim was hunched over a missile in the process of being prepped to be fitted to a wing pylon. He saw them approach and seeing Jim, stood to attention. Clearly, he was intimidated by McCleland, which worked to their advantage.

"Yes sirs?" he stood stiffly to attention.

Colin looked at him with a steely glint in his eye. "Where were you last night between 7 pm and 10 pm?"

Marinell's reply was immediate. "I was here, working. Then the base was locked down about 10:30 and we all confined ourselves to our quarters."

A corporal popped his head up from the loading trolley. "I can confirm that, sir. I was here with him."

Haltwhistle clenched his jaw. Of course, he would check it out, but this alibi was a thorn in the side. Beside him, Jim was on the balls of his feet ready to spring into action if it happened.

"Alright Sergeant. Thank you." They turned on their heels and headed away from air-side.

Colin walked back to the main block. He could do with the fresh air and the time it took to cross the distance to think.

"We're going to look at the body," Haltwhistle said. "Maybe we'll get something there."

"Yeah, we'll get to look at a corpse!"

The station's morgue was behind the medical center. The small space was freezing cold.

Presenting his ID, Haltwhistle made his presence known.

"I'd like to see Fliplugs' body."

The refrigeration unit was opened and the prone form of the young man was pulled out on a cart. Putting on a pair of latex gloves, Haltwhistle began his examination of the corpse.

Jim grimaced at the sight. He could stomach a lot of things, but not seeing an actual dead body being checked over. Somehow, it seemed wrong to Fliplugs. His head was a bloody mess. Conversely, Colin seemed able to put the gruesome sight out of his mind.

"Single tap entry wound at the back of the head. No powder burns, which ties in with the bullet casing found at the shooting location," Colin said into his Dictaphone. "The victim was shot once in the back of the head. The bullet exited the skull on the same trajectory."

"So he had his brains blown out? I could have told you that," McCleland snorted. "A hole is a hole is a hole, as the saying goes."

Colin shot him a dangerous look and Jim went quiet.

"Has the body been dusted for prints, fibers, anything of that sort?" Haltwhistle asked.

"Yes, sir. There was nothing found. The body was not interfered with in any way," the coroner replied.

"Alright. I've seen enough, you can put Fliplugs back."

"I hope I don't go out like a box of fish fingers," Jim said as the body was closed up again.

"You're sick, do you know that?" Haltwhistle told him. "And a hole isn't just a hole! Different bullet calibers? Different grain, ballistics, barrel rifling, need I go on?"

With the base still under a lockdown, everyone was being held to the confines of the camp apart from the AID men, of course. Cartwright had been allocated some smart rooms on camp and it was there he,

Haltwhistle and McCleland met to debrief. The cast had been made of the footprint, so Colin was enthused about an idea he had.

"All we have to do is match up the footprint to the boot. Do that and we find our killer," he enthused. He was quite taken and Jim could swear he thought Colin would personally search every single person on the base to do so.

"What if more than one person on the base has got the same boots?" Jim asked.

"Shoe size, scuff marks, mud in the treads," Haltwhistle said.

"It seems logical," Cartwright agreed. "But that could take a couple of days. There are three thousand people in this camp. It takes time. And who is to say the person in question hasn't thrown them away?"

"Have forensics found anything on the bullet we found?" Haltwhistle asked.

Black Jack shook his head. "No. Same problem as your shoe theory Colin. It takes time."

The autopsy would also be up against a ticking clock, so Jim told Colin to relax. Haltwhistle however was restless. They had come so far with this but it was frustrating to come up against a brick wall when it felt like they were so close to an answer.

"Instead of getting impatient, have something to drink and then get out of here 'til morning. There's nothing more to do tonight," said Cartwright. "We've had a good day and learned a lot, so let's have a good night's rest and come back fresh tomorrow."

"Sir, I'd like to continue with this –"

Black Jack interrupted. "Tomorrow Haltwhistle. I don't want my best men burning themselves out."

The lead investigator looked irritable. "I need to pay my respects to the deceased's family," he said. "I owe Fliplugs that much."

"Of course." The head of AID replied. "Now. Dismissed, both of you."

"Yes sir," said Jim. Colin was about to say something but his partner grabbed him and pulled him out of the room, virtually dragging him to his car.

"We could do this now!" Haltwhistle insisted. "We could pull the goods in sheets from the surplus stores where the stuff was dropped off and see what was missing!"

"You need to learn to switch your brain off and just chill out, mate. You heard what the old man said. Now let's get out of here."

"Jim, you don't understand. If he died because of us, that makes us responsible until we get the bastard who did this!" When Colin called McCleland by his first name, Jim knew things were serious.

McCleland turned to face his friend. "Even if we find out who did it, it won't bring him back. The state of play will be exactly the same tomorrow as it is now. So go home and spend some time with Anna." Jim looked at him. "Do I have to order you?"

Colin thought about that. Jim was right but it didn't justify Fliplug's needless death.

"No," was his simple reply. Colin turned and headed for his car, his mind still racing with ideas.

TWELVE

The throaty growl of the V8 engine filled the late afternoon air. With Motorhead's *Ace of Spades* blaring from the stereo, Jim was heading out of the main gate when a familiar blue Ford Focus passed by.

Jim noticed it was identical to the one that they were looking for. A quick look at the license plate revealed it was indeed Chris Woodley's car.

The very car that they had been looking for.

Flooring the throttle, Jim set off in pursuit. Who would have access to his car? The answer may well be the answer to everything. Apparently, the driver saw Jim coming as his speed increased noticeably as well.

Reaching for the intercom, Jim urgently called Cartwright.

"Rapier 1 to Wren's Nest. Come in," Jim barked.

"Wren's Nest. You've not even left the base, have you? What is it?"

Jim was trying to keep up with the Focus which had a good turn of speed thanks to its turbo, and speak into the radio at the same time.

"Scramble a chopper fast. I've got the Focus we're after in front of me. Confirm!"

"Rapier 1, are you sure of this?"

Jim rolled his eyes. The old man could be so obtuse at times.

"Yes. Confirmed. I am sure of the car. Get a chopper up now!"

"McCleland. There are no choppers at Sutton Donington. Keep up with them and report."

Well, that was a total waste of time, Jim thought. Cartwright signed off.

How had the car left the base if it was locked down? There was no side gate, so it must be somewhere off camp. Jim had no more time to think about what was going on as the driver of the Focus was trying to stay clear of the big red American muscle car in his mirrors with lights ablaze. He was now taking the corners he was coming into at speed and sliding around, trying to shake off his pursuer.

The smaller Eurobox possessed superior handling and had a punchier throttle response, it's exhaust note rasping in the cool air.

On the straight sections, the Mustang was much faster. Jim had had the engine and suspension tweaked to give the car better handling and more power so the car handled reasonably well but it looked like the driver of the other car was a pretty handy pedaler, as he was able to make the Focus dance around.

McCleland could hear the change in the exhaust note as he double-declutched. They came up to a tight bend which the Focus bounced around, skipping on its suspension as the tyres squealed.

The Mustang drifted sideways as Jim skidded broadside, trying not to scrape off too much speed but the sheer weight of the car dragged it to the outside of the corner in a cloud of blue-gray rubber smoke. The barriers on the outside of the corner approaching rapidly caused Jim to throw his car across the road in a huge skid, and the car stopped, facing backward. Ramming the gear stick into reverse, he backed the car up then touched the brakes and hauled the wheel hard over, flipping the Mustang around in a nice J-turn. A roar from the engine and a bark from the exhaust and Jim was off again.

A long straight downhill section lined with trees on both sides of the road followed where Jim gained ground, but the peppy ST still had some legs. Cars coming in the opposite direction gave the speeding vehicles a wide berth as each driver breezed along in excess of 100 miles per hour.

Dodging in and out of the traffic that appeared in front of them, the Focus swerved around the offending drivers just trying to get home for the night. Furious horn blasts filled the air. Jim meanwhile used his outright straight-line speed to outrun them and begin to gain ground.

In the gathering gloom, the Focus' headlights went on. A village came up in front of them. The pretty stone cottages reverberated to the sound of engines screaming at flat chat. The Focus flew through a red traffic light. Forced to jam on his brakes as the traffic started to move across in front of him, Jim cursed and floored it the instant the coast was clear, red light or not. Twirling the steering wheel to avoid a crash, the car fishtailed.

Screeching brakes, horn blasts and yells which turned the air blue fell on deaf ears as Jim got up to speed again. In the rear-view mirror, Jim could see several cars piling into each other in a multiple collision, the mass of tangled bodywork and smashed glass littering the roadway.

Two more cars joined the mess, which sent one car skyward, crashing down on its nose and rolling over in an explosion of debris.

Hoping no one was too badly hurt, Jim hunched at the wheel, determined to get back on terms with his pursuit. The big Mustang's engine roared as McCleland put his foot to the floor and the speedometer needle pointed towards 140.

About a mile ahead, he could see the Focus turn off to the left.

Knowing he had to keep a discreet distance, Jim took the same turning but slowed dramatically.

He kept well back and avoided being seen. The spires and building of a big town came into view, so McCleland kept a few cars between himself and the Focus.

Eventually, the target stopped in a car park surrounded by trees. Jim pulled over on the opposite side of the road and pulled up at a petrol station. Taking a pair of camera binoculars from the glovebox, Jim rounded the corner of the garage and peered across the road. The hooded, dark figure walked from the car over to a restaurant carrying a large duffel bag. He met another man of a dark complexion and long wavy black hair, standing next to a silver Mercedes. The bag seemed to be quite heavy as the man was having trouble lifting it into the boot of the car. Once the lid was slammed shut, they went into the restaurant. The two cars were both parked far enough away for the registration numbers to not show up on CCTV. Smart move.

The Focus driver frustratingly had his back to the window so Jim could not see his face. But the other man was in plain view. He was a swarthy Latin gentleman with stubble and piercing brown eyes.

Jim vaguely recognized him. He watched as they shared a drink and the dark-haired man pushed something across the table to the other gentleman.

"Hey, what are you doing?" a voice called. Jim turned around to see an elderly man with a walking stick glaring at him.

"Bird watching," was the lame reply. *And not the ornithology I enjoy,* he thought.

"At this time of the evening? You're a peeping tom! I have a good mind to call the police!" he chided.

Jim had no time for this. "Get lost, Grandad."

The old gentleman was visibly angry at being disrespected in such a way.

"How dare you? I shall report you to your superior for speaking to me like that!"

Jim rolled his eyes, trying to get on with watching the two men again. They were in a very animated discussion about something, that's for sure. There was a lot of finger-pointing and banging on the table they were seated at. But again, the old man interrupted him.

"I want your name, young man. You are extremely rude and ignorant. I fought for this country and-"

Jim turned and faced his septuagenarian critic. "Your country would owe you a great deal more if you just shut up and let me do my job," he interrupted, impatient. He turned to see the man heading back to the Focus while the Mercedes was already leaving the car park.

"Shit!" he cursed.

"Now I definitely want your name, sir," the craggy face of the elderly gentleman was very stern and disgusted with the younger man's attitude.

"Oh, I dunno. Carroll Shelby and Performance is my Business." Jim shot back as he jumped in his car.

The engine started at once and the squeal of tyres left the intoxicating aroma of burned rubber in the old man's face.

So much for the state of play being the same tomorrow.

***

"I take it you lost him?' Cartwright tapped the desk irritably at Jim's report.

McCleland shuffled from foot to foot. Failure did not sit well with him and if not for the interfering old coffin dodger he could very well have the bad guy here with them.

"Yes sir. Sorry sir. This old codger got in the way and wouldn't take a hint," was the conciliatory reply.

"And whoever was driving the Focus got out of a locked-down military base with full sentries on duty."

"It must be someone on the base who knew where to look and when, sir," Haltwhistle offered.

"The security in this place is a joke," McCleland agreed.

"I'm not interested in excuses, gentlemen!" Cartwright looked at them both, seething.

Jim stood to attention in front of the desk as he did when he thought a bollocking was in the offing. It came, alright.

"Not only did you not get to know who our man is, you also did your usual party piece and destroyed a lot of property!" Cartwright flicked the television which sat at the side of the room on and changed channels. "Do you realize how much damage you did with the move at the crossroads? Four cars were written off with two people hospitalized," said Cartwright, showing him the TV news report which showed smashed up cars in various states of disrepair and a police presence with the area cordoned off.

"You did tell me to keep up with them and report, sir," McCleland said trying to keep a straight face. Colin, who had been halfway home when he was recalled, had to bite the inside of his mouth to keep from laughing. Black Jack appeared to turn a fetching shade of red.

"I never said to cause a major traffic accident which took three hours to clean up! Fortunately, you were going so fast that no one got your details, so there will be no comeback for you, or AID. Not that you seem to care about those things."

Jim looked puzzled. "Then with respect, sir. How did you know it was me who caused the crash?"

Cartwright threw his pen down in frustration and fixed the former fast jet pilot with one of his patented dead eyed glares.

"You don't have to be a genius to know who was involved with a high-speed incident in this area. I don't think there are too many people around these parts who think they're Nigel Mansell, Rapier 1!"

At Colin's amused look and attempt to hide his glee by biting his lip, Black Jack turned on him.

"This is not a laughing matter, Rapier 2!" he barked. Unable to help himself, Colin erupted in guffaws. Likewise, Jim snickered and was shaking with mirth.

"You will not be laughing so much when I put you both on a fizzer for a week!" Cartwright softened a bit and stifled a smile.

The light-hearted interlude had relieved some of the stress built up over the last few days.

Haltwhistle's phone pinged. Checking it, his good humor disappeared.

"There's no record of that phone number. It was an unregistered mobile. Bollocks!" he cursed.

"At least you got details in this." Black Jack waved the binoculars in front of McCleland's face.

"Let's load it up and see what's on there," said Colin eagerly.

A quick USB lead connection into the laptop allowed the pictures to be uploaded, and in a minute they were looking at the features of the Latino gentleman.

"I'll get a match," Colin said, transferring the images to the facial recognition database.

Cartwright was still considering what Jim had reported back.

"And the driver of Woodley's car never turned around, you say?" he asked.

Jim shook his head. "No sir." He was clearly disappointed.

"And you're absolutely sure it was Woodley's car?"

There was no question in Jim's mind about it. "Positive sir. The license plate matched and so did the make and color."

Cartwright folded his arms and pursed his lips. "We've had an APB out on that blasted car and it seems to have been close by all the time." He cursed himself. "I want that car found. Tear the base apart if you have to. I want all of the base personnel and private quarters searched, whether on camp or not."

"That'll take time, sir," Colin commented, quoting his boss's earlier comment.

"Do you have anything better to do?" Cartwright looked at him over his spectacles. "Get everyone on it. I don't care what it takes!"

Haltwhistle's computer chirped, the database search was finished. The three men clamored around the screen. The picture of the man Jim had seen was displayed along with his information: Hector Montalban.

"I want to know who this man associates with, his history, everything." Black Jack pointed to the screen.

Colin went back to his laptop and checked the database. A bit of cross-referencing took only a few moments to send a file to the boss's computer. Opening it up, Cartwright brought up the PDF files. The first name and picture got their attention.

Inigo Montalban, Hector's brother.

"I think I know that guy," Jim moved to look closely. Haltwhistle printed off the details, which came to quite a stack of paper. He started reading.

"Jesus, this guy is raw," he said.

"I don't suppose you'd care to share the information with us, would you?" Cartwright asked dryly.

Colin, knowing Cartwright didn't like being kept in the dark at the best of times, read aloud.

"Inigo Montalban. Born Madrid in 1968, emigrated to Britain in 1982. No criminal record but suspected of smuggling activities. Has links to organized gambling, European crime syndicates-."

The mention of smuggling and criminal gangs was enough to pique interest, especially on the strength of what had been discovered so far.

"Stop. Smuggling. Is there anything on that?" Cartwright pressed.

Colin read through his pages, searching for clues. "No, not really. Vague allusions to jewelry, money, weapons..." He stopped.

You could have heard a pin drop in the office. Cartwright knew they had an answer.

"Alright. What is there on his hobbies, interests and that stuff?"

Haltwhistle leafed through his block of paperwork. Now that they were on a tangent that lead somewhere, he was scouring the print. "Okay. This man enjoys gambling and cars, he plays pool well. He lives a luxurious lifestyle. He's a member of the London and Area Pool League. Has a good record with them. He goes to a club under their banner most evenings."

"Any known associates?"

"Nothing solid. Rumors of ties to street gangs in London, some other less than reputable people," Colin finished.

Cartwright thought for a moment. Then he and Colin looked at Jim, who was smiling. He knew what Black Jack had in mind, and was relishing it.

"You're a handy pool player." The boss of AID sat back, regarding Rapier 1. "I want you to go to this club. Meet this Montalban character. Get close to him and find out what the fuck is going on. Report progress."

Black Jack sat back, considering the gravity of his next order. This was crossing a line from which there as no coming back, but it seemed the only appropriate course of action in the circumstances. He drew two pieces of paper from his briefcase and put them in front of of his men.

"Under the terms of Section 7 of the Intelligence Services Act 1994, I am granting you both the right to terminate with extreme prejudice. Under British law, you are both granted immunity from prosecution for acts carried out in the execution of your duty which take place on British soil."

"What about overseas action?" Colin asked.

"You'll have to rely on your wits to get out of the country," Cartwright said. "This get out of jail free card ends at the limit of Britain's territorial waters."

"I dunno about you, but I don't fancy finding out if the prisoners elsewhere have seen *Deliverance*," McCleland grimaced.

Colin looked horrified at the implication and shook his head.

"We need to talk about your inappropriate sense of humor, Rapier 1!" The AVM looked Jim over and sighed. "This is purely discretionary, it does not give you the right to become The Terminator. Is that clear?"

"Very, sir," the Squadron Leader nodded.

He would never admit as much, but inwardly Jim was thrilled. There were some people who simply could not be dealt with in any other way than with brute force. And now he had the means to meet those people on equal terms.

Conversely, Colin gulped. Despite his actions in Afghanistan, he hated the idea of taking a life, despite the nature of the service.

Although he was going to enjoy the hell out of this, Jim had a couple of things on his mind.

"They will have seen my car. And if this guy is flashy, I'll also need to appear as such, sir."

Colin pretty much face-palmed and McCleland nearly let out a belly laugh. Cartwright, knowing what was going through both of his subordinates' minds felt like a father chastising his two naughty sons and failing dismally. Cartwright wondered why he bothered, sometimes.

"You'll have an expenses account. And I can get you a set of wheels that'll catch the eye, for sure," Black Jack assured him. "This could be dangerous for you, McCleland, so watch yourself. You'd best take a young lady with you, which for you shouldn't be difficult to sort out, given your interest in air hostesses and nurses."

Jim needed no second urging. He turned and headed for the door, beaming.

"Rapier 1?" Cartwright wagged a finger at him in warning. "Try not to over-indulge. Don't shoot Montalban, don't Karate Kwon-do him, don't damage him unless he starts first. Clear?"

"Kung fu, sir," Jim said.

"It's all much of a muchness. Just don't kick him in or fill him full of holes," Cartwright insisted.

"You have my word, sir," he replied with a smile.

"McCleland? This does not give you the go-ahead to turn a situation into a shooting gallery."

Jim left the office, leaving Cartwright and Haltwhistle to deal with the rest of the evidence gathering. Colin shook his head.

"Permission to speak freely sir," Haltwhistle stood at attention. Black Jack knew what he had to say, but let him vent anyway.

"'Don't overindulge'? I'm sorry, sir but you've just given a license to have fun to Jim McCleland!" Colin couldn't believe how brazen this move was. It could be a disaster. It most certainly would put a dent in the department's operational budget.

"It'll look good for Montalban though, won't it?" Cartwright grinned.

Haltwhistle took his leave. He shook his head and went back to work, resisting the urge to question his commanding officer's judgment.

THIRTEEN

McCleland reported to the garage on the north side of London near Enfield Cartwright had instructed him to visit. It belonged to an old friend of Black Jack's, who answered the door. A steel-gray haired man with a big robust build, he looked like a lock in a rugby team. Hawk-like eyes regarded Jim with somewhat amused enjoyment. Apparently, Jim didn't know what he was about to be given.

"Ah yes. Black Jack's friend. Come in." The gentleman, Lt. Colonel Robbins led him into the dark confines of the garage and switched on the light.

"Good God!" Jim exclaimed. Under anti-dust sheets, the shape and form of sports cars and supercars sat patiently waiting for someone to come along and drive them, as they were meant to be. This was a very rare and expensive collection indeed.

"Feel free to have a look around," Robbins told him.

Jim counted 20 cars in this place. He walked up and down them, admiring their looks. Peeling back the covers of the nearest one revealed a Porsche 911 Turbo S. Very nice. The bright yellow color would certainly grab attention but it was a bit too flashy for him, and he didn't like the reputation of the car's drivers. Next to it, a Ferrari 458. Hmm. He preferred the older models like the 355 or the 550. The newer ones just didn't have the same wow factor as the older ones. A poster of an F40 had adorned his wall as a youngster, after all. Further along the row, an Aston Martin DB9 sat purposefully. Definitely a thing of beauty, but not quite what he was looking for.

He flat-out dismissed the Pagani Zonda in the far corner. There was being flash and then there was stupid.

"How did you come by all this?" Jim breathed, a bit disbelieving.

"I love cars, what can I say?" Robbins said.

"Yeah, but… this lot must have cost a fortune!"

He was about to decide on the DB9 when a shape at the back of the lock-up caught his eye.

There was no mistaking a muscle car.

While he loved the Ferraris and Lambos, he always loved a good muscle car. Weaving through the other vehicles, Jim looked at the bulging machine under the sheet.

Pulling the cover off completely revealed what was underneath. Jim's jaw dropped. There was no mistaking what this beast was. It could run rings around the car he currently had.

It just oozed aggression and coolness. It sat on huge snowflake-effect wheels. A low stance made it look like it was hugging the road.

Just like its legendary inspiration it had quad headlamps and removable glass panels in the roof that made up the T-Tops. It was a glossy black color with gold pinstripes and a stylized fire- breathing eagle emblazoned across the bonnet. McCleland could feel his inner 12 year old taking hold. The film was on his shelf at home and it had meant an awful lot to him as a kid.

"I think I'll have this," Jim said, clearly unable to contain his excitement.

Robbins nodded knowingly. "Jack said you'd go for this one," he said.

He pushed open the garage door and Jim started the engine which he knew had over 800 horsepower on tap. While the Mustang growled, this baby flat-out roared. He pointed the very limited edition Pontiac Trans Am onto the dark street. The 455 Super Duty engine rumbled, power burbling noticeably.

He had an insatiable need to floor it but the huge power and torque would tear the tyres to shreds in moments if he did so. So, he took a sedate drive to pick up Sophie from her work.

***

It had been a trying day. Even a news report which could only be about her boyfriend's antics doing couldn't lighten the mood. The report she had finished had mysteriously gone missing when she arrived that morning. After half an hour of searching her desk, there was no sign of it.

Sheepishly, she knocked at Phil's door and poked her head inside.

"That report we were working on? It's gone," Sophie admitted.

"What do you mean, it's gone?" Phil asked.

"I handed it to you before I left. Are you sure you don't have it?" Sophie asked. "You left after I did."

"I countersigned it and put it back on your desk. Check again," her co-worker replied.

There was no sign of the offending folder anywhere in either office. Fortunately, Sophie had a habit of making two copies of everything and produced a fresh version of the report in short order. To her surprise, Phil wasn't pleased at seeing it in front of him.

"All you have to do is sign it," Sophie told him. "Then I can hand it in."

"No, I'll hand it in. I like to make sure these things are done," he said testily.

She bit her tongue with what she actually wanted to say. "Of course."

He scribbled his signature on the dotted line and she did likewise, and Phil got up, approaching the chief investigative officer, Fernest's office with Sophie in tow. A rap on the door and the command to come in was given.

"What have we got here?" Fernest asked, a forthright man in his late 30s.

"The initial report on the Cessna crash," Sophie explained quickly.

"Very good." He flicked through the pile of papers and photos. "Good work, although it appears there's evidence missing. Are those the details you told me about?"

"We had a problem at the scene with a couple of guys, the ones we reported. We think one of them removed the items," Phil said. "Whoever they were they've got probably half of what we need to solve this."

Fernest nodded. "I read your report about that. I put a few feelers out. There was nothing found, there's no record of an RAF-based investigative team on file. Whoever you met, there's no report on them."

"He had a flash car, an American one I think. There's got to be something there," Sophie played along.

"Without a registration number, you've got no chance. We'll just have to go on this and hope for the best."

"Wait," Phil interrupted. "He gave you his card. Do you still have it?"

Sophie frowned. "Somewhere, yeah."

"Hand it over when you've got it," Fernest told her. "With what they have, they've only got the answers to half the puzzle as well. Any idea what you think caused this?"

Sophie pointed to the report. "On page 3, you'll see we found traces of Tetryl, but it was of an older type compound. It's a highly unstable explosive, especially when it's aged. We think that was the cause."

The folder was placed in his briefcase which was snapped shut.

"Alright. It's a good start and we'll go from there."

They left the office. Phil, not saying a word. He quickly retreated to his hovel and closed the door.

Sophie wondered why he was behaving so oddly. She looked at the clock. Nearly 5:30. Jim would be here any minute.

There was a throaty growl from the street below. Sophie looked out of her office window to see a black and gold sports car pulling up on the street opposite. She grinned when she saw who was driving, grabbed her bag and locked her office door.

"What the hell is that?" she exclaimed, pointing at the Trans Am as she saw what he had arrived in.

"New car," he beamed. He opened the passenger door for her and she slipped into the black and gold leather interior. A quick kiss and she looked around the retro-style interior.

"It's certainly very you," she grinned. "Does it come with an ejector seat and machine guns?"

"Sadly not!"

She held on as he shot off in the direction of her house.

"How was your day, apart from causing a massive pile-up?" she giggled.

"Oh, don't you start as well!" Jim grimaced. "I was on a job."

"It was you though, wasn't it? Let's face it, it couldn't have been anyone else!" Sophie put her work bag on the cramped back seat of the car and put her hand on his knee.

"If this is meant to be for undercover work, you're doing it wrong," she said, picking up on why he actually had this ridiculous machine on hand.

"There's method to the madness. It has to be flashy to get attention. I just hope it's enough," Jim explained, accelerating the powerful car and getting used to its speed and handling.

"You don't need to worry, it'll do that alright!" His girlfriend was teasing him which Jim liked.

Most girls he couldn't joke around with, but Sophie had a sense of humor as subversive as his own.

A small two-bedroomed brick house with her little MG Rover on the inclined driveway beckoned as he pulled up outside where she lived. The two cars certainly made strange bedfellows.

Bounding up the path to the front door, Jim followed Sophie into the cozy, welcoming home.

Her coats and various pairs of footwear were arranged by the door as they went in. His jaw dropped when he saw the collection of shoes and boots.

"Why do you need so many shoes? What is it with girls and shoes?"

"They're so pretty! And I have to match my outfits. Think of it like you have so many action movies, I have these," she countered.

"I make do with four pairs." McCleland scratched his head.

Sophie kissed him again. "Shut up. What's going on tonight?"

"Date night," he explained. "I'm taking you somewhere special. Get your best out."

He plopped down on her settee and waited while Sophie disappeared upstairs to get changed as he had requested. He heard her showering and saw she had brought a file home with her.

Noticing the title referred to the air crash he had a quick peek, but it was nothing more than photos and measurements Colin already had. *Wow, these crash investigators dragged their heels,* he thought.

He made himself at home on her two-seater settee and waited. The home was warm, and he could tell she was house-proud. The place was spotless and ordered especially the kitchen. He guessed she spent most of her time in that room. Eventually, she reappeared wearing a very fetching sparkly gold ball gown. It clung to her in all the right places and was definitely flattering.

"What do you think?" Sophie twirled in front of her boyfriend.

"You look fantastic. It'll do nicely," he smiled, genuinely impressed with the view. *Lovely eye candy,* he thought.

"You don't think it's a bit in your face?" she fussed. She felt self-conscious in a backless dress.

Sophie had never considered herself to be beautiful or shapely, and such a garment may be a little too much.

She had once worn one to a party and her dad had not been impressed, telling her to get changed at once. Jim being Jim however, was rather less conservative.

"No. Not at all. You look fabulous," he assured her. She realized he had more to tell her.

"What is it?"

"There is something I need to tell you. It's a date night but there's something else," Jim admitted.

He told her as much as he dared, and the reason for going to the club in as roundabout way as he could. Fortunately, she smiled.

"I knew something was up." Sophie looked up at him. "Well, don't worry McCleland, you'll pull it off."

It was her turn to look serious. She turned to face him.

"The other night in the pub, you and Colin tried to get me to reveal sensitive information about the Cessna crash," she folded her arms and gave Jim a similar look to the one she had fixed him with the first night she had come to his place. "Don't do that again. If my boss finds out, I'll lose my job, and I can't afford to run this house without a wage. Alright?"

Her expression showed how serious she was.

"Alright," he agreed.

He looked down at his clothes. Leather jacket, black shirt and dark jeans, the standard casual dress for AID personnel when not on official air force or undercover business.

"I need to get into my best as well," he said. Sophie moved very close to him again and hugged him.

"I've seen that over the last few nights!" she grinned. She could not stay mad at him for more than a couple of minutes.

FOURTEEN

Pool Hall was not the right expression to describe the truly palatial building they were now pulling up to.

The establishment, called The Flying Flamingo was lit up like a Christmas tree. It was much more than a pool hall. It was a restaurant, casino and place to come and have fun. The car park was full of very expensive vehicles, just like the one Jim now slowed to a stop in front of the doors.

"Good evening, sir, madam. Welcome to The Flying Flamingo. May I take your car?" the valet said.

"Sure."

Jim climbed out of the Trans Am. He straightened his tuxedo and dress shirt. He pulled his cuffs down then went around the car and helped Sophie out of the passenger side. Elegantly, she stepped out of the ground hugging muscle car. They certainly made a very attractive couple.

They went up the steps into the building. It was so plush inside, the walls were painted in deep reds and purple with gold scrollwork and detailing. The restaurant was set back behind the gambling tables of which there were a lot. Baccarat, Texas Hold-Em, Blackjack, Roulette, pretty much anything you could want in that regard. Rows of gambling machines, one-armed bandits and a bingo hall stretched to the back of the building. The array of pool and snooker tables were positioned to their left with big TVs showing the football and motor racing which was currently being televised fitted overhead.

A quick look at the restaurant showed a menu to salivate over. Gourmet food alongside fish, steaks vegetables and world cuisine from Italian to Chinese was offered. All very tempting, all expensive.

"Would you like something to eat first?" Jim asked his date.

Sophie smiled and sat down. A waiter came over and took their order. It appeared promptly and was nicely cooked, looked great and smelled intoxicating.

Jim had no taste for gourmet food. A bad experience with caviar had put him off the stuff for life.

Instead, he treated himself to a nice piece of baked fish with vegetables while Sophie had a leafy salad. Looking around, he spotted the two Montalban brothers sitting by the pool tables.

Both were dressed in immaculate white suits with matching highly polished slip-on shoes. The pool tables were, of course, their next port of call after they had finished dinner. The food was very good, had a nice flavor and was filling. The drink, a nicely aged whiskey was exceptional.

Jim guessed it was an aged cask, probably Glenfiddich. Sophie was impressed with her vodka and tonic as well.

"This is classy. I like it," she enthused.

"Don't get used to it. Ill-gotten gains are funding this place. I need to know how ill-gotten and how many gains this guy has got."

She looked crestfallen, then remembered what her boyfriend had told her earlier. It was sketchy, but probably forced on him.

"We got the forensics back on that crash," she said in a low voice. "There were traces of gunpowder, ball bearing, chemicals. It looks as if it was a chain reaction explosion, but it would have been instantaneous."

"I thought you said you couldn't discuss anything?" Jim murmured. "I was expecting a hollowed out volcano."

"I can tell you that, as it's in the public domain, but I can't go into lots of detail," Sophie explained.

Jim nodded. This was not the place or time to discuss it. Who knew who was listening?

"You should tell Colin that. He'd be interested. It may answer some questions he has about the whole thing."

Sophie set her fork down as she finished her meal.

"They're checking on the explosive itself. We identified it but it's being investigated." She couldn't help it. Jim should know as much as she did and he smiled. He was still looking over at Montalban.

"Okay, what do we do now?" she asked.

Jim was considering how to approach this man. He was a large, muscular gentleman with aquiline features and an air of superiority hung over him. His hair was swept back in a duck hairstyle which complimented his tanned skin. He was all ego and appearance. His immaculate way of dress, his perfectly presented shoes and hair and his presentation of the club just screamed egomaniac.

"Now... we play pool. Keep close by me and try not to say too much." It wasn't meant to be an insult but it came out a little harsh.

Jim immediately felt guilty at the hurt look on Sophie's face. "Sorry. It wasn't meant to sound nasty."

They got up and left the table, heading for the section set aside for pool and snooker games.

Taking a seat at a table close to the action, Jim watched as a table racked for 8-ball pool and Montalban and his opponent went at it. One was skilled, being able to play long pots and cushion shots to sink his set of reds.

The other player struggled with anything over half a table to make a successful play.

Sophie ordered another vodka and tonic as Jim continued to watch the game. If he played, he would have to be in good form, but not so good it looked as if he was showing off. Too much alcohol would dull his edge too, so he ordered water.

In the corner, Montalban eyed the newcomers with detached interest. He too was focused on the table and the game that he was playing.

Jim eyed the positioning of the balls, but that wasn't the only thing holding his attention.

Montalban's shots were played with firm aggressiveness, but the balls he sank were potted with finesse. More than that, they traveled straight and true into their pockets. His opponent, clearly a skillful player managed to pot only a couple of his shots, despite being clearly on target.

Almost as if the game was rigged so that an opponent couldn't win.

The table had metal detailing running around the entire edge of it. Montalban never strayed more than a foot from the side of the construction. It was enough to arouse suspicion.

Leaning towards his date, Jim whispered softly. "Do you have a nail file? A metal one?"

"Sure." Sophie was confused. "Why are you whispering?"

"I'll explain later. Hand it to me but don't make it obvious."

The small sliver of metal was passed to her boyfriend under a handkerchief, who proceeded to slip it into the inside breast pocket of his tuxedo.

The game ended with a predictable comfortable victory for the owner of the establishment.

"Who wants to play the winner?" asked the victor.

Montalban and McCleland looked at each other. "I'm game," was Jim's offer.

The Spaniard gestured to the table.

"After you," said Jim politely. Montalban bowed slightly and made his way to the table. He picked up a cue. It looked like it was putty in his hands. The man had charisma, an almost magnetic presence.

"Thank you." A deep Spanish accent to go with the charisma. He allowed the other man to rack up the balls. He made the break, and two reds and a yellow went down. He cleaned up the balls with ease, with his opponent only able to sink a single yellow. Jim took a sip of water as he continued to watch. He had made a smart choice by borrowing Sophie's grooming tool.

"Would you care to break or rack up?" Montalban asked, holding out a cue to McCleland, who stood up.

"I'm easy either way." Jim took the cue. The wood was beautifully made, smooth and it was perfectly straight. Brand new. He chalked it up and drew a coin from his pocket.

"Heads or tails?" he asked Montalban.

"Heads," came the confident reply. Jim flipped. Tails.

"I will set up, Mr...?"

"Neal. Jim Neal," he offered his hand. Montalban took it.

"Inigo Montalban. This is my brother, Hector. Welcome to The Flying Flamingo." Hector nodded but said nothing. "And who is your lady friend?"

Out of anyone else's mouth, the question would have sounded creepy but Montalban was a perfect gentleman.

"Sophie. Sophie Hawkesworth," she said.

"A pleasure." Smooth, very smooth Jim thought. "In your own time, Mr. Neal."

Montalban took away the triangle and Jim made the break, leaning down over the cue and almost laying chest down on the table. A perfect scatter of the pack led to a potted yellow which McCleland's opponent watched with the faintest of frowns. Clearly, that was not in the game plan.

Sophie breathed a sigh of relief. She watched as Jim lined up his next shot, again hunkering low over the cue. A medium long into the bottom left pocket. Jim took the shot and the yellow sunk.

Measuring up his next play, he had to get a rebound off of the cushion for the shot after to be playable, between the middle and top left pockets. The third yellow went down but the cue ball didn't have enough pace.

Despite seeming a little disgruntled, Montalban, back in the game, quickly sunk two reds and lined up a third. The angle was narrow but the red went in. He didn't have a good angle on his next ball, but took the shot anyway, expecting his shot to be potted anyway. The red hit the cushion of the pocket and rebounded. From his crouched position at the other end of the table, McCleland was amused to see his opponent irritated as he conceded a turn to him.

Jim realized Montalban did not like holding play or tactical safety, preferring long, spectacular shots and fast gameplay. All aided by how the table had been specifically set up to assist him. He knew for sure he had something to work with now.

His yellow went in, but he didn't have open play on another ball. So Jim played for a safety shot behind a yellow and red which he got.

"Would you like to up the stakes?" Montalban said with a broad smile. He seemed certain of the outcome of the game.

"It depends. What have you got in mind?" Jim replied.

The white-suited man spread his hands expansively. "How does £50,000 to the winner sound?"

Sophie looked aghast. Her brown eyes widened noticeably and she shook her head at Jim. But Montalban was offering a handshake. Jim looked at the table, then at Sophie, and finally at the positioning of the balls. He turned.

"You have a deal." He shook on that.

Oh my God, she thought. *What the hell is he thinking? His apartment, his car that he loves so much...*

Montalban tried to go for a shot on a clear red but didn't have a good angle. The red just missed the pocket, helped by McCleland maintaining a watching brief near it as was his right, which let Jim sink a further yellow. Again, McCleland didn't have a follow-up play, so he went for another safety. The cue ball however swerved slightly and didn't go completely safe.

Montalban, confident, took a chance and found his red a home in the top corner pocket. Another two reds went down and he was on the black. Fifty thousand pounds were now at stake.

Oh shit, Sophie's mind screamed.

Before Montalban could line up his shot, Jim spoke.

"How about a counter-offer. Your 50 plus another 50?" He offered his hand. Montalban looked at it and then at Jim.

"Can you afford such a wager, sir?" He looked at the table and then back to his opponent. "The odds and the balls are not on your side." He sounded a little on the arrogant side.

Jim looked at Sophie again who was simply frozen in sheer disbelief. How had she got herself in to this?

"I can afford it, Mr. Montalban," he said.

Hector merely smirked and covered his mouth, stifling a laugh. He could not believe how this guy was behaving. He was either incredibly stupid or incredibly brave. Probably a bit of both.

Inigo shrugged. "Very well."

He went for the shot, but the black rebounded off the corner cushion beside the pocket where McCleland was observing from.

"*Mierda!*" he cursed.

Jim looked up from the pot over to Montalban and smiled to himself. Sophie saw she was sweating profusely and her heart was racing, but her date did not appear to be at all ruffled.

McCleland sank his remaining yellows in quick succession and lined up a long pot on the black.

If this did not go down he would be in a heap of trouble with Cartwright.

Drawing the queue back, the white hit the black with pace and the 8 ball sailed towards the pocket, deviating on its course just enough to make Jim's mouth fall open in horror. The black brushed the cushion along the side of the table.

And mercifully, the ball dropped into the pocket.

Sophie let out a slow breath.

Laying down the cue, Jim offered his hand.

"A good game sir," he smiled. As well he might. He was £100,000 richer, probably to his opponent's extreme irritation, not that he was showing it.

Montalban looked at him with a slightly ghoulish expression, then his face softened and he smiled.

"A good game, Mr. Neal." He produced a chequebook and wrote Jim a slip for his winnings.

Handing it over, he said: "As agreed."

"Would you care to have a drink with Sophie and me?" Jim asked. For her part, Sophie was horrified at her boyfriend rubbing this dangerous guy's nose in it.

But Montalban continued to be a most gracious host. "I would enjoy that very much," he replied.

He looked McCleland over. "Are you as graceful in defeat as you are in victory?"

Jim's gaze didn't waver. "I couldn't tell you. I don't set out to lose."

The dark eyes narrowed a little. "I will hold you to a drink. But at my place."

FIFTEEN

He led them up a thickly carpeted staircase that was similarly painted in the deep purple and red that the rest of the club was.

Turning right at the top, he led them into a spacious room, tastefully decorated and upholstered with leather furniture and artifacts collected from his travels around the world. A huge wooden desk with a wing-backed leather chair sat in front of a curved window beyond which the inky black of night showed. In the center of the room, a long conference table sat. This was a nice office, indeed thought Jim.

Sophie had half expected to be in a torture chamber and have her throat cut open, so it was with relief she took the glass which was offered to her.

Montalban poured Jim and Sophie a drink and invited them to sit. His brother stood to one side of the room, by the door. Their host got right down to it.

"Mr. Neal, I can't decide if you are courageous or irresponsible. You come to my club, you gamble and win big despite you never having come here before. I admire your fortitude but your rationale for being here mystifies me."

The uncompromising Latin sat down behind his palatial desk. "Perhaps you would care to enlighten me why you're really here."

Jim took a breath. "We heard it made for a pleasant evening and I wanted to treat my good lady to a night out. It's been a long week."

Montalban smiled and pressed his hands together, touching his fingertips to his lips. "Please don't think of me as a fool, Mr. Neal. I can assure you I am not. I also value honesty above all else so I would advise you to be truthful." He nodded toward Sophie. "Perhaps your lady friend will be more forthcoming."

He tapped his right index finger on the desk top in a manner suggesing any answer which he considered wrong would be met with something unpleasant. Hector remained utterly impassive, Jim noticed, as if this was par for the course.

"Well, it's true I enjoy a game of pool and a good night out. And good company of course!"

Jim smiled.

"That does not answer my question, Mr. Neal," was the icy comeback. The dark brown eyes narrowed suspiciously and burned into Jim.

He'd better come up with something, Sophie thought. *I rather like him with his knees in one piece.*

She could easily imagine this man having a couple of thugs take Jim into a back alley and do unspeakable things to him.

Montalban rose from his thickly padded seat and paced around his desk to stand in front of them.

"This establishment is run on trust. All of my business interests are carefully monitored to make sure my trust is not misplaced. My people are happy and work well in a team. There is no place for ego or self-promotion here. I believe people are happy and fulfilled when they work for me.

"The same goes for my customers. Without them, I would not have a business to provide my services to. I ask in return that they respect all and behave courteously."

Jim sat taking all this in and watching Montalban's behavior. So many hidden agendas and mixed metaphors from this bloke.

Hector was still looking on, silent and impenetrable. He was taking all of this in. Yeah. He was the ideas man. Jim took some comfort in the Ruger he was packing and fortunately had not been patted down, considering the fact that weapons were virtually illegal in Britain.

If Sophie knew he was carrying, although she probably had guessed that he did, she might freak out.

"I established this business based on hard work. My family gave me strong values: honesty, honor and hard work. My people answer my demands. I now ask you for the same treatment towards me. So, I ask you again, Mr. Neal. Why are you really here?"

Hector finally made a move, putting his hands in his pockets, probably more eager to hear this than his brother.

Jim looked sad for a moment, or as sad as he could muster. "I wanted a night out because I'm out of a job at the moment. It's been a hard few months."

Montalban's eyebrows went up. "And you gambled a hundred thousand pounds when you are without an income? You are quite crazy. And what of that interesting car of yours? Such a vehicle is not cheap."

"Not really. I have my payout to fall back on," Jim explained. He went quiet, expecting a follow up. He expected correctly.

"And what, pray to tell, did you do to earn such a large fortune to potentially squander on a whim?"

Montalban was full of curiosity for his guest and was impressively verbose. He also wasn't averse to using his vocabulary. Sophie guessed he enjoyed showing off how smart he was.

Making up for something, maybe?

For his part, Jim simply found him to be a flash git with too much mouth.

"I used to be a pilot," was Jim's quiet summation of the facts. "An RAF pilot."

That piece of information most certainly got the Roman's attention. Montalban looked from Jim to Sophie, trying to detect any kind of falseness.

His brother's expression remained unreadable but his eyes... The eyes gave away a multitude of things.

Because of the open expressions on their guest's faces it was clear this was legitimate.

"How did you come to leave the service?"

Jim sighed. "It was the end of the engagement. In other words, it was time to go."

Inigo Montalban's face was unreadable. He simply looked at Jim squarely. Sophie knew there was some sort of psychological chess game going on., with each of them trying to outstare the other. Jim remembered what Colin had told him: 'Psychology, fascinating subject.' He could see now that it was.

Finally, Montalban smiled. "I see." He stopped in front of Sophie, watching her like an eagle looks at its prey.

"And what occupation takes up your time, may I ask?" He asked of her, his full concentration boring into hers.

The girl smiled. She had the perfect answer. "Putting up with him!" she laughed, pointing at Jim.

Montalban smiled but his eyes didn't. "It must be a full-time position?"

"Oh, you could say that! Jim certainly keeps me on my toes."

Jim had to hand it to her. She was doing brilliantly. Sophie has never been asked to be put in this position and thinking about it, it had been selfish and crazy to drag her into this. If Montalban found out she was investigating the air crash he was probably involved in, who knew what he would do to either of them?

He knew it was irresponsible. Jim would be sure to make it up to her, providing they got themselves out of this mess.

Montalban retook his seat. He did not need Sophie as she presented no threat and so no use to him. Or so he thought. Jim however could prove useful...

"I am pleased to make your acquaintances. I would very much enjoy calling on your unique services at some point, Mr. Neal. Let us exchange our details. In the meantime, please enjoy my hospitality."

Jim gave him his details and took Montalban's slipping the piece of paper into his pocket. The owner of The Flying Flamingo led them back downstairs and into the club again.

"If you wish, we have a regular pool league to which you can add your name to. There is someone on the list who I feel would make a good opponent for you," said Montalban.

"Really? I thought you were a most worthy foe," Jim told him seriously. Montalban stopped, turned and regarded his guest.

"Generous in victory, Mr. Neal. A most pleasant quality I also appreciate. You are both welcome here anytime you wish."

He snapped his fingers and Hector appeared by his side. "Brother. You are to extend every courtesy to my guests." He gestured to Jim and Sophie. "Anything they wish is on the house."

McCleland smiled to himself. He was in. Yes, he had the skills Montalban wanted to exploit, but that had to be an advantage.

However, Sophie was his number one priority. He promised himself she would not come to harm.

Holding his hand tightly, she just hoped that Jim was not on this man's hit list.

***

Sophie's place was closer to London than Jim's was, positioned near the end of the Jubilee Line, and with him doing this ridiculous undertaking, he rolled the big Trans Am into her driveway and parked behind her car and the Mustang. Sophie got out, and unlocked the door, leading him inside. A comfortable little house, her living room wasn't as expansive as Jim's and her front room was decorated in a far less in-your-face way. Her kitchen was divided from the living room by a bar divider. The room was painted in a warm pale mauve color and a couple of small sofas sat ready to be used. On the left-hand wall, the staircase stretched upstairs to the upper parts of the house.

Despite having visited before, Jim looked around. "It's nice. It's comfy."

"I'm glad you think so. Your place is a bit too... how can I say it? Lad pad for me," Sophie smiled.

She went upstairs to get changed while McCleland made his call to Cartwright.

"Rapier 1 to Wren's Nest. Come in." He had taken the portable intercom from his car into the house. After a few moments, Cartwright's voice came back.

"Wren's Nest. Go ahead."

"Contact made with target. Proceeding with assignment. Bait laid. Over."

"Very good, Rapier 1. Report progress."

Before Cartwright could sign off, Jim jumped in. "Tell your friend thanks for the car. I'll be buying it."

The old man's voice was seriously unimpressed. "This line is for work purposes only. It is not for you to conduct your personal business on. That can wait for your own time. Over."

"It is work business sir!" Jim protested innocently.

Cartwright tutted. "If you say so, Rapier 1. I will pass on the message. Continue to report. Out."

The line went dead as Sophie came back downstairs dressed in her lounging clothes of a baggy t-shirt and jogging bottoms. "Who was that?" she asked.

"My boss. I was just checking in," he said.

She went to her DVD shelf, which Jim had taken a brief look at. Aside from the obligatory chick flicks, Sophie had the complete *Harry Potter* series and the *Lord of the Rings* films, none of which he was interested in. His girlfriend was a top-to-bottom science fiction and fantasy fan.

"I can see why you got into your chosen profession," he said gently.

"Why's that?"

"You're a nerd!" His smile was genuine.

Sophie took down a box set. Popping the disc in to the machine, the girl loaded the show up.

"What is it?" Jim asked.

She looked at her boyfriend and sat down with him. "Well, it's not blood, explosions and car chases but I think you'll like it."

"Hey, I like blood, explosions and car chases!" he protested. She punched him on the arm good naturedly.

The programme started and Jim quickly came to the conclusion it was *Buffy*.

Oh great, he thought. *She's a Trekkie and likes this as well?*

Sophie gave him a look. Apparently, his expression had given away what he was thinking.

"Hey. Do you really want to get the girl? Give a little back and share something she likes," she insisted.

"I always made sure I was busy doing other things when this was on," he admitted. "*Demolition Man* and *The Running Man* are about as far as I go with stuff like this."

Jim was never much of a science fiction fan. He liked *Predator* and its ilk, and thoroughly enjoyed *The Terminator* but a straight-up action thriller was his purple patch. It was funny how the two movies he had spoken of seemed to sum up the current state of society, he thought.

"*Demolition Man* isn't a feminine movie! It's stuff blowing up!" Sophie protested.

"You're forgetting the bit where Sandra Bullock falls for Sly. I'd say that was pretty feminine. And she was hot in that movie." He grinned in a ghoulish manner. "I totally agree with Sly about the sex machine though!" He pointed at the TV. "This is a teenage girl's show."

"Then you missed out! It's a good show, and you need to give it a chance." Sophie fixed him with a look similar to when his mum looked at him when telling young Jim to eat his vegetables.

Hmm. She had a point there. He had been a little selfish with her as well as reckless enough to get her involved in all of this. Something in the back of Jim's mind told him he should have thrown her out that first night, just to save her from the trouble that must surely be coming but what was done was done.

And anyway, the fact he cared about her meant he had feelings for her. It was a new experience for him.

"It's not really my thing," Jim said. "But, I'll give it a try."

"That's all I ask. How do you know you won't enjoy it unless you try it?"

Again, she had made a fair point. Sophie just became sweeter and more appealing the more he hung out with her. He did not need of food or drink after sampling the delights of Montalban's restaurant cuisine.

Jim remembered he had never asked Sophie her last name. "Is your surname really Hawkesworth?"

"Yes. Why?"

Dammit. She had given her real name. That meant people could come to get her right now!

Apparently, Sophie was also a mind reader.

"What's the plan for tomorrow? Are we going back to that club?"

Jim thought. If they simply turn up at the club again, it could arouse suspicion. On the flipside, Montalban's office might be loaded with evidence. What to do?

"Maybe." He didn't commit to one action or the other.

"You took a horrible risk, playing him for all that money," she said, apparently forgetting her show.

McCleland nodded slowly. "It was calculated. I knew I could beat him. The second I raised the stakes, it went to his head. That's what gave me the edge."

"Still, a hundred grand?" Sophie was not convinced. "That's more money than I could earn in three years! Why did you ask me for the nail file?"

At the mention of it, he opened his tuxedo and handed it back to her.

"He was cheating. The table was rigged with magnets on each pocket. He had magnets in each of the yellow balls. The metal in that..." he pointed to the file.

"Disrupted the magnets," she finished. "You out-cheated him at his own game!"

"Right. If you noticed, I was hanging around each of the pockets and making the balls go off course."

"What if this magnet trick hadn't worked? You'd be a hundred grand in the hole!" she protested. "What if he'd searched you? He could have skewered you!"

"If he'd done that, he'd have been admitting his guilt in front of all those people, babe." Jim wasn't about to tell her about the perks of being an AID agent on assignment, but he had to concede she raised good points. Then a thought occurred to him. He went upstairs and keeping back from the windows, he peeped out onto the street. Looking up and down he sighed with relief that they had not been followed. He went back downstairs.

"Can you just relax and not think about work?" It sounded like a question, but it wasn't. Sophie batted her eyelashes at him.

"I'm sorry. I just had to be sure we were safe." He sat back down with her. She cuddled up to him.

"You're sweet when you're being protective," she pecked him on the cheek. Despite himself he blushed.

Sophie beamed. "That's adorable."

"Give over," Jim fussed, embarrassed.

Sophie sighed. "My ex... He didn't care. Nothing was ever good enough for him. I'd cook a meal and he'd say things like 'I'm not eating this.' He'd take the piss out of everything I liked." She looked at him, who was clearly listening. "I felt really unappreciated. I felt like a spare part for him most of the time."

He grimaced. "That's horrible. I'm sorry. If someone was good enough to cook me a nice meal after a long day, I'd be dead chuffed!"

She took his hands in hers and faced him, touched.

"Seriously, you're a lot deeper than I thought. You care, even though you like to pretend you don't. You believe in something and don't tell me you don't, otherwise you wouldn't have chosen to serve."

She stopped the DVD and waited for him to respond. He looked around the room. She had cornered him.

"Well... I believe water's wet and the sky is blue." It was a very broad answer and Sophie wasn't having any of it.

"Don't avoid the question. I want to know what goes on in your head." Jim opened his mouth to reply but she interrupted. "And don't try to be evasive. Don't be cheeky or try to wriggle your way out of this. I want to know the real you."

McCleland looked sheepish. He didn't enjoy put on the spot and any other time he would have got up and left, making an excuse.

But Sophie was different. "Alright. Ask away. I don't enjoy being under the spotlight."

She scoffed. "You are in the middle of an investigation and are out to take down some crime boss, you fly fighter jets and don't want to be under the spotlight? Try again, Jim. I've been very open with you, so you owe me that."

Jim thought about it for a moment. How could he word this? He wasn't very creative, but he'd have a go.

"It's different. That's my job. You have to think on your feet to get the result but mostly you take your orders and follow them. There are no gray areas. When you're up there," he said pointing at the ceiling. "You're free. It's wonderful. It's like..." he hesitated, looking at her.

"Being with a really lovely girl and knowing she really likes you too."

Sophie was taken aback. She had not expected to hear something so simple yet so profound. But it told her everything she needed to know about this man. She snuggled up to Jim again and resumed the show.

"That's just about the most romantic thing I've heard you say!"

"Piss off," Jim grumbled.

SIXTEEN

Anna Haltwhistle was waiting for Colin to come home. She had supper ready for them both and he had called to let her know he was on his way. She had finished marking the children's homework for Monday morning and was sitting back, watching the news.

The phone rang and she went to answer it.

"Hello love, are you on your way?" she asked, thinking it was Colin.

"Is this Anna Haltwhistle?" said a distorted voice.

"Yes. Who's this?"

The voice sounded like it had been filtered and she couldn't pick up an accent, as her husband had told her to do if she got something like this. "Listen carefully. Your husband and his partner had best back off, they'd better destroy all the evidence they have and leave the base with that prick Cartwright, or you will find the angels welcoming you to the afterlife, Mrs. Haltwhistle."

"Who is this?" Anna spat angrily. "I hope you know who -"

'shut up. They stop their work, or your time is up."

The line went dead.

Shaking, Anna immediately dialed Colin's mobile phone. He answered shortly.

"I'll be there in a few minutes sweetie. Hope you"re ready for some snuggle time tonight," he said.

"Colin, come and get me. I just got a phone call," she sounded panicky and the words were just pouring out of her. To Colin on the other end, she sounded very upset.

"What phone call? What's going on?"

For the only time in their relationship, she shouted at her husband. "Just get here!!" Anna hung up.

Two minutes later, the Mondeo locked up it's brakes outside and a screech of tyres heralded Colin's arrival. He ran inside. Anna was in a mood somewhere between abject panic and murderous fury. He sat down and asked what had happened, taker her hands in his.

"This call came. He said for you and Jim to stop chasing him, whoever he is, or I'd be dead. He threatened to kill me, Colin!"

"Did you get an accent, a name or anything like that?" Haltwhistle tried to be as gentle as possible.

"No! His voice was distorted. He just said I'd be dead!" She looked at him tearfully. "What the hell have you and Jim got yourselves in to? What's going on here?" Anna was inconsolable.

Colin shook his head. He was livid. "I can't tell you too much, sweetie. I'm sorry. But we"re going to sort this out," he promised. "Get some things together, we're going somewhere safe -"

"Really? Where? Where's safe? After what I just got told, where is safe exactly?" Colin had to admit, she had a point. He wished he knew a genuine answer.

The Mondeo stopped by the main gate barrier at Sutton Donington. Colin lowered the window and flashed his pass at the guard.

"Who is the lady? I'm sorry sir, but no access to civilians at this time," the duty corporal said.

"I haven't got time to argue. Open the gate. That is a direct order," Colin told him.

But the guard stood fast. "I'm sorry sir, no -"

"Open the fucking gate, now!" Colin barked angrily. He was not in the mood to play nice. Anna was startled by how much venom he had in his voice. He never swore, well not in front of her anyway. Colin called Cartwright, who came down to the gate a few minutes later accompanied by a very disgruntled Group Captain Woodley and Flt. Lt. Irwin.

"Let them pass," said Cartwright to the poor corporal. The gate opened and the Mondeo passed in to the grounds of the base. It had been a long day.

Sitting Anna down in Cartwright's office, Black Jack himself offered the scared young woman a cup of her go-to comfort, hot chocolate while Colin sat down with her and held her hand in his.

She was a little calmer now her husband and his intimidating boss were close by. Anna had only met him once, briefly at the passing out ceremony when he had congratulated then Flying Officer Haltwhistle and shaken them both by the hand. She gulped down the drink quickly, despite it being piping hot.

"Mrs. Haltwhistle, I'm very sorry you had to be put through that." Cartwright's voice was soothing.

"Thank you," she said timidly. Colin squeezed her fingers.

"It's very important you remember everything you can. Tell me what happened."

She reiterated the events of the previous hour and became upset again.

"He called me, this voice.. it sounded distorted told me to tell you and Jim to back off." Anna looked down. She looked ashamed, even though she had no reason to be.

"Easy. It's ok," Colin rubbed her shoulder.

"What else did he say, miss?" Irwin asked. At Colin's agreement he continued. "I'm the base's lead police officer, Mrs. Haltwhistle."

"Well, you'd better get on it sharpish and find this man!" she snapped. Then Anna frowned. "He did say one thing, now I think about it. He said 'You and your partner'." She looked up at Colin.

"He said destroy all the evidence."

Cartwright leaned across the desk. "Are you sure? Are you absolutely sure he said that?" He looked to Colin as well.

"Yes... I think so. Shit! Why is it so hard to remember?" She cursed herself and bit her lip, realizing Cartwright thought that women swearing was not very lady like. "Sorry. I swore in front of you, Mr. Cartwright. I mean sir. I mean..." she stumbled over her words.

"It's perfectly understandable," Black Jack assured her.

"If this bastard said 'You and your partner', then he knows about our investigation. That means we're close to an answer," said Colin. He was fuming, almost shaking with fury.

"I should think the entire base knows that you're doing an investigation, so I wouldn't go jumping to conclusions yet." Black Jack pointed out.

Colin had an answer. "Stop me if I'm wrong, sir, but who would know about evidence gathering apart from those we'd spoken to?"

"Any investigation collects evidence," said Anna, her voice barely a whisper.

Her husband knelt down beside her again and gave her a reassuring hug. "It's alright. We can do this another way."

Cartwright smiled a little.

"I'd like to and get some rest," said Anna.

"Of course," Cartwright agreed. He nodded to a sergeant waiting at the door. "Find this young lady some rooms in the mess. you'll be perfectly safe there."

Considering the events of the last few days, the words 'perfectly safe' in association with this camp did not sit well.

She got up and left with the sergeant, making her way out of the office somewhat shakily.

Watching her go, Haltwhistle turned to his boss.

"I want an armed guard on her," he demanded. Cartwright began to protest but Colin placed his hands on the desk and ranted. "No one upsets my wife. No one! You understand, sir?" He was almost bending over the desk towards his commanding officer.

Black Jack rose from his desk and looked at Colin over the brow of his spectacles. "I do not appreciate that, Haltwhistle." He pushed his chair under the desk. "I believe that you're emotionally involved, and after what's happened this evening, I'm going to relieve you of this investigation and assign Flt. Lt. Irwin to carry on."

Mollified, Colin clasped his hands behind his back. He was close to an answer and he'd be damned to see it given to someone else. He had to toe the line of course.

"I'm very sorry sir. It won't happen again." He looked at his CO squarely. "I will continue in the spirit you suggest but I request to remain as part of this until it's finished. I want to crack this son of a bitch!"

For his part Cartwright took his spectacles off and placed them on to the papers in front of him, rose and came around the desk.

"That's enough." He looked over his officer and finally nodded. "I for one, would not want all of that pent up aggression let out on me. I think the guard can be arranged."

Black Jack called out Irwin, who was standing beside the desk saying nothing. "See to it."

"I want your permission to have the phone records pulled for my phone line at home, sir." Colin was going to leave no stone unturned on this one. He was even more determined to get this man... whoever he was.

"Of course. Do you need me to write something up?" Cartwright asked. Haltwhistle nodded.

"Yes. The request has to come from higher up."

Both Colin and Cartwright had noticed Woodley was keeping himself to himself. He had said nothing for the entire meeting and had not reacted at all during Anna or Colin's outbursts.

"You're not saying very much, Woodley. What do you make of all of this?" Black Jack demanded.

"Well, I'm glad someone is asking me something around here!" was the sarcastic response.

Cartwright rounded on him. He was fast running out of patience with this rather officious man.

"Have you organized your men to search their quarters for anything and everything? Have you set up a search for this bloody Ford Focus which magically reappeared?" Cartwright asked.

Woodley was defensive. "Yes I have. It's all in place. And if you don't mind, myself and my family are still grieving, so get off my back!" he fired back.

Cartwright gave him a cold glare and clasped his hands behind his back. Colin knew what that meant. Woodley was in for a major ticking off.

"Unfortunately for you, the stakes are now a lot higher than a tragic accident, which I don't think was one. A man has been murdered on your base, we have weapons, munitions missing, we have a case of stolen property."

The base commander looked unhappy at being put on the spot, but Black Jack was not letting up.

"Added to that, we apparently have someone who got out of a supposedly locked down military base with ease. The last I checked, no one around here went by the name of Harry Houdini!"

What the hell were your men doing, because they sure weren't looking for anything!"

Now he was on a roll, Cartwright nodded to Haltwhistle. 'We also have the small matter of one of my men's wives having death threats made against her. And all on this supposedly highly efficiently run base. From where I'm sitting, you couldn't manage a piss up in a brewery, Woodley!"

Colin could not help but jump in and fully expected to be knocked back by his CO, but sod it, he wanted to vent. "If I find someone on this base was the one who threatened my wife, I'll have your balls on a barb wire plate... sir!"

"You can't speak to me like that!' Woodley retorted. "I'm a group captain, so how would you like to spend the night in a cell, Haltwhistle?" Woodley flared. He was on his feet and jabbing his finger in Colin's face.

"Shut the fuck up, Woodley!" Black Jack bellowed. "Colin is right."

"Why did the police unit get shaken up?" Haltwhistle demanded. "Was the head of the section about to find out something dodgy and you wanted him gone before he opened his mouth?"

"How dare you insinuate that?" The Group Captain looked drawn. "He accepted a new posting as a matter of course!"

"I'll be checking that!"

The mood in the room was getting ugly and Cartwright was certain fists were going to fly at any moment. If it came to that, even he could not stop the proper channels from having a field day with Colin.

The tension was high, tempers were short and emotions were at boiling point.

Colin and Woodley stood glowering at each other, almost daring the other to make the first move. Cartwright broke the tension.

"Let's all turn in and get some sleep, shall we? Come back fresh in the morning." He was trying to be as controlled as he could be, but he too was now simmering with anger.

"Yes sir." Colin saluted and walked out, slamming the door behind him. The same sergeant who had led Anna away walked with him over to the rooms she had been placed in. They were large and well furnished. Obviously set up for a high ranking officer who wasn't on camp. Anna was seated on the settee when Colin came in, she rushed to him and he held her tight as she let it all flow out.

"It's alright," he assured her as best as he could.

"Is it?" she asked, her cheeks wet.

Haltwhistle nodded. "Yes. It'll be alright. I'll make it so. And if I don't, Jim and Cartwright will."

Anna smiled a little at that and Colin grinned at his inadvertent reference. "Make it so?" she asked him. He chuckled, despite it all. She touched his cheeks and he wiped her eyes and face.

"I love you," she said gently.

He hugged her tightly again and whispered in her ear.

"Can I get you anything?" he asked.

She looked up at him. "Yes. You can get us as far away from here as possible!" she snapped.

He knew exactly where she was coming from. She had had a horrible fright and had become involved in what was turning out to be a very messy and unpleasant business which she should not have to. Colin held her again.

"We will. As soon as I crack this case, we'll be away from here and down the road again."

Anna looked up at him. "How long will it take, do you think?"

"That I don't know. It's all... it's all very complicated and it's getting deeper the more we check it out," he admitted. "There's a lot of bad things going on here."

Mrs. Haltwhistle pondered for a moment. "Yes. Judging from what happened tonight, I agree."

Colin dried Anna's face with his fingers. "I'll get him. I promise you."

She laid her head on his chest.

"Let's get some rest," Anna finally said. She headed for bed with Colin in tow.

But he did not sleep well at all, with the case running through his head and now this. Anna fell asleep late and stirred any time her husband took his hands away from her.

The following morning, Haltwhistle was up early, shaved, dressed and ready to go at 6.30am.

Overnight, Cartwright had arranged the phone trace procedure but the result was negative, so from that Colin deduced whoever had made the call had used a jammer or scrambler. If they had called from a mobile, an app would have done the same thing.

The entire base was deep in to the business of turning their rooms inside out, searching for anything which could be a clue. Haltwhistle and Cartwright walked through the stores, the vehicle sheds and the hangars, watching the men searching high and low for clues.

The stores especially were meticulously searched, with each section fully emptied, contents checked and then replaced methodically. It was time consuming, but it was the only way to make sure nothing was missed.

Under Irwin's direction, teams of NCOs were scouring the grounds of the camp for the Focus which had proved to elusive, except of course when Jim had tried to chase it down.

However, a thorough search had turned up nothing at all. The hard work seemed to have been for nothing. The vehicle sheds, hangars, even looking in the Typhoons housed in them and the stores were clear of anything that shouldn't be there. The barracks, mess and outbuildings beyond the runways had turned up nothing at all.

Picking up a phone receiver in the office, Haltwhistle was about to make a call.

"What are you doing?" Cartwright asked.

"Call it a hunch sir. I'm gonna call DGM and ask them for their inventory for the surplus left here the other day. I wanted to do it last night but you ordered us to head home."

"Do what you need to get done. The idea of our guns and explosives falling in to the wrong hands doesn't bear thinking about," Black Jack agreed.

A few minutes later, an email arrived with an attachment listing all that had been advised for delivery compared with what had been for the last three months from Sutton Donington. The extensive print out was lengthy to say the least and Haltwhistle, magnifying glass in hand was intently reading the small print. Glad to be seeing the details he had wanted at last, Colin was hard at work.

Despite the urgency, Cartwright was amused at his agent's antics. No wonder he had been given such a literary nickname.

Looking up from the listings, the younger man rubbed his eyes and offered the magnifying glass to his CO.

"Give me the short version," was his reply.

Cracking his trademark bottle of his favorite tipple, Colin began. "Everything matches up apart from the number of certain items, specifically rifles, handguns and grenades, mines and such. They're getting the stock, just not as much as they should. A clarification request was sent, but no reply received yet."

Haltwhistle showed the spreadsheet to Cartwright, and was pointing to what he had found. Black Jack nodded and smiled wanly.

"It's a bit small for me to read. I believe you." He stood up. "The response to the clarification would have to come from Woodley himself as base commander. If he's been slack..."

"Either a clerical error or failure to do his duty, sir," Haltwhistle replied.

Cartwright was grim. "This proves beyond a shadow of doubt someone has been light fingered."

He went to retrieve his top coat from the hook. "Come along, Haltwhistle."

Deciding to pay a personal visit to Tim Marinell's rooms, just to keep him on his toes, Colin and Cartwright entered the smart quarters and looked around as Marinell looked under his settee. He stood to attention, although somewhat reluctantly.

"Sirs," was the stiff comment.

"How is the search coming, sergeant?" Cartwright asked looking around at the soft furnishings.

Little ornaments and magnets collected from around the world were placed on a metal tablet leaning against the wall. Clearly, it was a memento of his travels. An unusual quirk of the personality of a man who had so far shown very little signs of being an approachable person.

"Nothing unusual so far, sirs," Marinell continued to be on the rigid side.

"You've not found guns under your bed then?" Colin said coldly. He didn't expect an answer either way.

He went in to Marinell's bedroom, just to see if there was anything there, but a look through the wardrobes and drawers revealed nothing beyond perfectly folded fatigues and dress blues.

A look around the rest of the quarters did indeed reveal nothing out of the ordinary, so the two AID men took their leave. Colin had been sure Marinell was not who they were after, and this just cemented in his mind that they needed to think of something else.

Stomping back into the office, Haltwhistle slumped down into the chair. Cartwright looked at his agent.

"I take it we didn't find anything anywhere else, then?"

Colin gave him a look of forlorn annoyance. "No sir. Sorry sir."

Black Jack spun in his chair from side to side. "Well let's hope McCleland isn't enjoying himself too much he can't turn up something, anything."

SEVENTEEN

In another part of the country, Jim awoke to sunlight coming through the bedroom window.

Sophie had already got up and he could hear her downstairs, rattling around in the kitchen making breakfast. The smell of eggs and toast wafted through the house. He got up and got dressed quickly. Heading downstairs he found her making coffee.

"Morning," he mumbled, trying to straighten his bed hair. He never had been much of a morning person, despite military insistence on being up and out by 6am.

"Good morning, gorgeous," she greeted him. He gave her a kiss.

"Did you sleep well?" he rubbed the sleep from his eyes.

"Very well, thanks. I had a big teddy bear to cuddle me all night!"

Then, Jim's mobile rang.

Answering it, Jim held it up to his ear.

"Good morning, Mr. Neal," came Montalban's voice. "I hope you had a pleasant night."

"Yeah, it was fine," Jim said absently.

"I would be delighted if you and Miss Hawkesworth drank with me at my house," Montalban was not messing about. That brought Jim up short. He reiterated to Sophie what the man on the other end of the line had said. At Sophie's expression to him and Jim's reticence Montalban tried to persuade them.

"Come. Stay. I would enjoy your company."

McCleland and his lady friend were looking at each other, and both were not too keen on this idea. It was a sudden move, but realizing this was his way in, Jim smiled.

"We'd be delighted."

If Jim was nervous he certainly didn't show it. Sophie however had an inkling of the danger at hand and just wanted to stay at home, but she played along.

"That'd be lovely," she said in a small voice.

"Excellent. I will meet you at the club, and you can follow me." Montalban hung up.

"Looks like our day has been decided for us," Sophie grimaced.

"Yeah," Jim was equally unhappy. But it was part of his job so he did not want to pass this up.

An hour later, they were ready to go. Jim made a call from the portable transmitter to Cartwright to inform him of the situation.

"Rapier 1 to Wren's Nest. Come in."

Cartwright's voice sounded tired and drawn. "Come in McCleland." He skipped the Rapier 1 part, Jim noticed.

"We are going to attend a meeting with the target tonight at his club. We're going to his residence now. Over."

"Explain what you mean by we, Rapier 1?" By his tone of voice, Cartwright was suspicious.

"Sophie and I have been invited. You said take some company."

Cartwright was furious. And rightly so.

"Yes I did, McCleland, but civilians aware of the situation are not under any circumstances to be involved with our operations or to be endangered! Your lady friend was supposed to be part of your cover, not the mission!"

Jim gritted his teeth. "Yes sir. Sorry sir."

"This is a serious breach of protocol, McCleland," Black Jack went on. He sighed. Black Jack knew McCleland flaunting the regulations was nothing new. "Very well, what's done is done. Keep us posted on your progress. Out."

Sophie had not heard the conversation, but she was seeing the aftermath. Jim looked something like a child who had been shouted at by his father. Sophie thought he looked rather cute.

He put his jacket on and she saw the holstered gun inside the coat.

"Is that what I think it is?" she asked. He produced the big revolver and let her see it. She was perturbed.

"I have to carry when on duty," Jim explained. "Which in my department is 24/7."

"I get that, but I don't feel comfortable with guns in my house, Jim. I don't like guns," she said.

Once they arrived on the street where the club was, Jim parked up and waited for Inigo Montalban to arrive. He drummed his fingers on the steering wheel. He looked around. A doorman was watching for anyone who may make any untoward moves, but clearly hadn't noticed them.

"Wait here. I want to check something," McCleland said.

"Where are you going?" Sophie asked, a little surprised. She suspected what he had in mind and didn't want him to be caught.

"It'll only be a minute. Text me if you see our dear friend, okay?"

Sophie frowned, clearly irritated with his impetuousness. "Fine."

Jim clambered out of the car and headed across the street, making sure the man in front of the Flying Flamingo didn't see him. Trying to look as casual as possible, McCleland headed between the club and the medical clinic next door to it.

The alley was narrow and there was no entrance to the building. There were no cameras keeping their watchful eye on him, thankfully. Jim made his way to the back of the club where a door was unlocked. Carefully twisting the handle, he went inside.

The room was very well organized, as befitting a professionally owned and run business.

Beyond the cases of alcohol and sundries, including crates of fresh vegetables which gave the space a distinctive earthy aroma, a room with a temperature gauge to his left was the cold storage unit. He didn't have long to inspect everything, and the crates was stacked against the walls, four high. If there was anything hidden, it would be underneath what was visible.

A quick look showed nothing out of the ordinary. He moved a couple of boxes full of sweet treats to the floor and took a glance at the plastic crates below. Without opening them up and examining the contents, which there wasn't time for, the goods seemed normal.

Jim crossed to the room and headed for the cold storage. He pulled the heavy door open. The chill in the air was immediate. The frost clung to the packets of poultry and fish. Reaching in to the refrigeration units, McCleland pushed aside the frozen foods, but there was nothing beneath the various trays of chicken to attract his attention. The unit was full of similar fridges, the largest one was next to his first port of call. Jim opened it up. Whole fish were presented packed in ice.

Wiggling his fingers, Jim plunged his hand in to the frigid display. The cold was excruciating, but determined, he pushed further in. If he started pulling ice out of the freezer, it would be obvious someone had tampered with the unit. Feeling around, all that he felt were more stingily glacial crystals. If there was anything in there, he couldn't be sure.

He withdrew his increasingly frostbitten hand and stuffed it deeply into his coat. If Montalban had any weapons in his possession, it would take a team of guys with a warrant to find.

He left discreetly and headed back up the alley way. Taking a furtive look both ways, there was no one around that should not be. He headed back to the car.

"Anything?" Sophie asked.

"Nope. Not that I could see anyway."

She looked at him as he rubbed his frigid hands and blew on his fingers. His skin had begun to turn red.

"What if you'd gotten yourself caught?"

"The risk you run when you're doing something like this." The same Mercedes Jim had seen earlier meeting whoever had been in the Focus appeared at the end of the street and parked up.

"Hold on, we're on ceremony," he said. He drove the car in to the frontage of the club and stopped.

"That's a lovely car," Inigo said, admiring it's lines. He had seen it before on CCTV of course, but not in person.

"Thanks," Jim replied. Inigo admired the squared off stance and screaming chicken emblem emblazoned across the bonnet. Jim let Sophie in to the passenger's seat.

"Follow me," Montalban said as he drove off. Jim followed him for a few miles before the Mercedes pulled in to a large gated driveway.

The gate swung open and the driveway stretched ahead for about half a mile, with both sides lined with small trees. At the end of the drive was a grand house, illuminated against the night sky by spotlights.

"Nice pad," Jim murmured.

"I wonder how many people he shafted to get this." Sophie was as unimpressed as Jim had been at the start of the night.

"You're not wrong there."

"How did you know you'd win that game?" she asked. "He was on the black and lined up perfectly. And don't tell me it was just because he used magnets in the balls."

Jim grinned. "He let his ego get in the way. Also I distracted him at the right time. People like him want money and they want to win at all costs. That's his weakness," he explained. Colin is rubbing off on me too, he thought.

"Talking of ego, yours got stroked last night," she said, Jim gave her a raised eyebrow. "No place for ego when you're a pilot. You've got to take yourself out of the equation completely. It's simply a job to be done."

"I hope it will get us through." Sophie sucked her tongue and looked at him.

He squeezed her hand a little. "We'll be fine. Just stick close by me."

Jim stopped and they got out, heading into the impressive house Montalban was holding the door open for them to enter.

The house was decorated in the same way the Flying Flamingo was. Deep red and purple shades adorned the walls with gold trim and it gave the rooms a very warm feel.

Montalban loved antiques and knickknacks and the drawing room and dining space was almost akin to a museum, with glass cases lining the walls full of things collected for their historic or artistic merit.

In the basement, a full gym was fitted which Jim was envious of, and under the cover of a glass roofed and walled conservatory was a 20 foot long indoor swimming pool.

Jim was served with a fruity cocktail and he sat beside the pool sipping this large drink. He had to get some answers quickly. On the sunlounger next to him, Sophie seemed similarly relaxed.

She had just gotten out of the pool and was drying off. Jim allowed himself a quick peek of her attributes. She didn't have any tattoos fortunately, but she had a couple of piercings which he didn't mind. Predictably his attention was a bit too obvious and she caught him. Sophie winked.

"Enjoying the view?" she asked.

"Oh yes. I love a bit of ornithology!" he quipped. Sophie lay down on the lounger and spent a bit of time taking in Jim's muscly physique. He wasn't absolutely ripped to shreds but he was in shape, which in turn she liked.

Montalban appeared with a man who appeared to have a permanent scowl on his face. He was stocky with short cropped hair. He was tall but thin, almost wiry.

"Ah. Wilsoncroft. How are you."

The other man was not friendly.

"Who are these two?" he demanded, skipping pleasantries entirely.

"These are my friends, James and Sophie. They are to be treated well," Montalban insisted.

He looked at them both and fixed his sights on Jim. "You get in my way, or cause me shit and I'll fuck you up!" he said gruffly and walked off.

"Charming fellow." Jim shrugged it off. "Where do you keep him caged up?"

Montalban shook his head disgustedly. "You must forgive my friend and his lack of manners," he apologized He knelt down near them. "Are you enjoying yourselves? Is everything good for you?"

"Just fine, thank you," Sophie said, a little blandly.

"I would like for both of you to join me for dinner at the club tonight. I would hope to introduce you to some of my friends."

"Yeah alright. Sounds good," Jim agreed. Fortunately Sophie was wearing sunglasses which hid her expression.

"I hope you will enjoy the evening." Montalban headed back in to the house.

Once he was out of earshot, Sophie leaned towards him. "How long are we going to play this game? The guy is a gangster. Probably a killer and he's dodgy as hell. We've got to get out of here and tell Colin and Phil what's going on."

"Phil couldn't find his own arse with two hands if he used a compass and a map!"

Sophie giggled. "Don't hold back!" She was about to mention the odd behavior she had seen in her colleague, but Jim continued.

"It'll look suspicious if I'm on the phone. And if we say a family emergency came up, it'll raise too many questions." He was trying to work out furiously what to do. "I'll come up with something."

He was looking at the door which led in to the house and from Sophie's perspective, appeared to be considering something.

"What now?" She was becoming irritated by McCleland's cagey mood.

"I need to check something out."

"Be quick about it, alright?"

Letting her be, Jim ventured into the house and took a look around. It was indeed a very grand establishment, built over three stories. It appeared to be a Georgian style building. The Upper floors were made up of bedrooms, while the first floor came with a gym and a massage room, and a huge ballroom was set aside for dancing and entertaining large numbers of people.

There was nothing in any of the rooms which gave away anything untoward.

The ground floor featured the kitchen, dining room and Montalban's office which he seemed to spend most of his time in, and in which he was presently ensconced with his brother. No chance to check it out at this point. The drawing room was huge with high white painted ceilings and walls, giving it a very airy feel. Large full length doors ran from floor to ceiling giving access to a wide stone patio with steps leading to lovely gardens.

A mysterious black painted door sat just off the entrance hall. It turned out to be locked. No matter, a credit card to the lock would soon take care of that, but Jim knew he would have to be quick to avoid suspicion.

Deftly, he had the lock undone and was down a set of stone steps which led to a wine cellar.

Many, many bottles of rare red and white wines sat in wooden racks. Clarets, Chardonnay, Bougelais. Montalban had expensive and classy taste.

But there was something sinister about being down here. There was nothing that shouldn't be in a cellar like this, no stashes of guns yet, but the unmistakable smell of gun oil was quite pungent.

Looking around, Jim crept behind the racks of wine bottles where the oily odor was more noticeable. He knelt down and in the dim light, made out a brown piece of paper, which had a waxy feel when he touched it.

He smelled it and the smell of the oil coated the paper, which he recognized as ammunition wrapping.

So there had been weapons here at some point recently.

McCleland folded up the stiff paper and put it in his pocket. He went to the stairs when above him, the door opened, the lights illuminated the cellar and he heard footsteps coming down the stone stairs. He headed back to his hiding place behind the long rack and waited.

A slick gentleman with heavily gelled hair went to the rack at the far end of the room and picked out a bottle of wine. He appeared to be heading for the stairs, but then turned. He came towards the rack McCleland was concealed by. The rack was made up of a cross hatch of wooden slats which was open at both ends. It would be easy for apparent sommelier to spot Jim, who crouched down and remained in the shadows.

The man had apparently not seen the person in hiding and went about his business, collecting more bottles of wine. Satisfied with his haul, he turned and headed back up the stairs, taking care not to drop any of his collection.

One of the bottles he had been considering was now perched precariously in its slot, and as Jim stood up, he carelessly used the rack as a handhold. The errant bottle shook loose and headed for it's encounter with the floor. McCleland watched in horror as the bottle of Mouton Rothschild shattered just as the door above closed.

He waited for a few moments, but the door did not re-open and no-one came to investigate what had happened. Apparently, the accident had not been heard. Jim made his way back up to the entrance hall and headed back through the house to the pool. Sophie was still there, looking relaxed.

"Did you find anything?" she asked in a soft voice.

"I'll tell you later. Has anyone been back here?"

"No. It's been quiet."

McCleland retook his place next to her and tried to relax, but his mind was abuzz with thought.

In his grand study, Montalban had his wine served and he took a sip. Instantly, he pulled a face.

"This is corked!"

"I'm very sorry, sir. I will attend to it." The sommelier went to one of the other bottles of wine and unwrapped the cork.

"I want Mouton Rothschild," the formidable Hispanic said softly.

"Yes, sir."

"See that you do," Hector told him.

The man went down in to the wine cellar once again, to be confronted by the smashed bottle of wine on the floor. He was sure he had not dropped it. He made an effort to clean up the mess and retrieved another large magnum of claret.

Returning to the study, he presented the bottle and uncorked it.

"I can smell wine on your person," Montalban commented. "How so?"

"There was a smashed bottle on the floor, sir. I cleared it up."

"You smashed one of my bottles of wine? Which one?" The voice was soft and dangerous.

"I didn't break it sir, it was already broken." The sommelier falling over his words.

Montalban bared down on him.

"I do not tolerate incompetence, especially with my property." Hector was at his brother's side in an instant and both were staring down the unfortunate server.

"Is that oil on your fingers? How did you come by that in my cellar?" The sommelier looked at his hands.

How had it got on to his hands, indeed?

Montalban grasped the smaller man by the lapels. 'Did you go snooping in to business which was not yours?"

From the poolside, Jim and Sophie could hear the man's screams as his punishment was mercilessly wrought on him and exchanged a look.

"I want to go home, right now," she insisted.

McCleland was having second thoughts about the whole thing. How had he gotten himself in to this?

EIGHTEEN

The forensics on the shell casing had finally come back, and Haltwhistle's hope for a breakthrough came up short. Whoever had fired it had loaded it into the gun wearing gloves, so no fingerprints to go on. The only glimmer of hope being the confirmation the weapon used was an AWL96A1. The groove and twist was obvious.

"We have turned this base upside down and inside out and turned up the exact square root of fuck all. All we have is incidental evidence and a few theories which tie it together. How do you propose to break out of this legal friend zone?" Cartwright summed up matters in his uniquely succinct manner.

"Well we do know based on that, the shooter may be a skilled marksman, so if we go back to the personnel files and tie down who has shooting experience in that way, it could narrow down the field of fire, so to speak," said Colin.

"If you think it will help, but it'll be like looking for a needle in a haystack," Cartwright replied.

"Bear in mind every man is graded on his ability to shoot well."

Haltwhistle was resolute. "I think we could still go on the basis of being good with a rifle, sir."

"Alright. It's worth a try. But we've got to think outside the box to solve this one," was the offhand comment. Colin's eyes widened in realization.

"Think outside the box…" he muttered. "Sir, we've been going about this all wrong. We've been looking in the wrong place!"

Cartwright sat back in the seat. Woodley was not sure where this was going and after being eaten for breakfast the previous night, he was quiet but keen to understand what Colin had in mind.

"Go on," the base commander said.

"What if… whoever we are after has property outside of the base's ground? It'd be no wonder we can't find anything because it's being kept there. It's worth a shot."

"I wish you wouldn't keep saying 'worth a shot.' It's kind of unsettling considering recent events," Woodley complained.

"Grow a fucking backbone," Cartwright told him.

Colin went back to his notes and evidence bag. He pulled a copy of the personnel files he had photocopied. Quickly scanning through the details on Chris revealed nothing, now was there for Marinell but something that he had said about green fingers and enjoying gardening, despite there being nowhere on the base for someone to enjoy a horticultural pastime, niggled at the back of his mind. Suppose…

Something Marinell said while being interrogated was now in his mind.

"Are there any gardens or allotments around these parts?" Haltwhistle asked. Being surrounded by countryside surely meant something like that around here. Woodley looked blank.

Gardening was not something he or his family went in for. Lofty, the base's groundskeeper handled that sort of thing. He would more than likely know, so Cartwright ordered him to report.

Ten minutes later, an older man shuffled in to the office. He was a small, ratty looking gentleman.

"Can I help you sir?" he asked meekly.

Cartwright pointed him to a seat.

"This is important, sir. Are there any allotments or gardens people can rent, here roundabouts?"

Black Jack could not believe they were going down this road which results were probably not going to be forthcoming from, but anyway.

"Yes," said Lofty. "There's a big allotment in the village. A few of the lads on camp have a plot there."

Haltwhistle, knowing he had hit on the answer, seized the moment. He put a picture of Marinell in front of the grizzled man at the desk. "Would this man have a plot there, do you know?"

Lofty squinted at the picture, screwing up his face as he did.

"Yes. Yes he has one of the largest lots. He grows all kinds of vegetables and things."

Colin grabbed his coat and was heading out of the door before the sentence was finished.

Cartwright rolled his eyes, knowing without a warrant, any evidence would be inadmissible at a potential legal hearing. McCleland's get up and go attitude had indeed rubbed off on his partner in good and bad ways.

"Haltwhistle!" Cartwright's bark stopped Colin in his tracks. "Best wait for the warrant to arrive before you go kicking doors in."

The paperwork was retrieved in short order and countersigned by the AVM. Guided by the groundskeeper, Colin drove through the village that gave the airbase its name. A typical small English village, it was not much more than a church with a tower, the pub that he, Anna, Jim and Sophie had enjoyed the other night, a post office and some pretty stone built cottages that lined the main road through it on the way from the bigger towns in the area.

Just past the village green, Colin was told to turn left which took him down a lane which quickly turned into a dirt track.

The allotments were off to the right, behind a playing field which doubled as a football pitch.

Cartwright, in his MG Rover ZT260 gave the mucky, muddy entrance ot the allotment a miss as he stopped and followed on foot. A couple of white caps brought up the rear.

"Which one is Marinell's allotment?" Colin asked. The groundskeeper pointed to a large type building surrounded by canes which bore beans of various types. Neat rows of dug up earth gave away where the vegetables were grown... or were they? He instructed the white caps to start digging up the vegetables.

After a few moments, the shovels gave a heavy metallic thumping noise. Quickly sweeping the dirt away, a large metal trunk was unearthed, padlocked and earth stained. Cartwright nodded and the lock was quickly broken.

"Sir," Irwin said. "This is breaking and entering."

"Think of it as like Robin Hood, my friend," Colin told him.

Opening the trunk revealed pots, pans, jewelry and money. All of the ornaments were gold, platinum and other precious metals.

But there were no weapons.

"Bag all this up. I want it checked out," Colin ordered. Irwin and his team went to work, cataloging and wrapping up the finds. As he suspected, there was no trace of any produce. The beans were there as a diversion, and he instructed his men to dig up the other vegetable patch while he and Cartwright looked at the garage itself.

Breaking the lock, inside was a slightly dusty and rain spattered Ford Focus ST in metallic blue.

The registration number matched the missing car belonging to Chris Woodley.

"Here's the car, sir," Haltwhistle observed.

"Yes. I can see that," Cartwright replied from behind him.

They stepped around the car, checking it out. The Focus was unlocked, but there were no keys to be found. Cartwright put his gloves on, as did Colin, and the driver's door was opened. It was the older style ST as opposed to the global Focus and featured the 2.5 V6 turbo engine. If Jim was here he'd probably be saying how superior this one was over the newer shape, being faster, more powerful, lighter and far more hardcore or something along those lines.

The glovebox had nothing but the logbook and owner's manual in it and the center console had a couple of CDs for contents. The boot was more interesting. A piece of waxy paper with the distinctive smell of gun oil on it.

"You'll want to see this, sir," Haltwhistle said.

Cartwright came around to the back of the car where Colin was pointing at the ammunition wrapping.

"There's your proof of what Woodley was carrying, I'd say," Black Jack said.

Forensics would go over the car; there was little doubt what they would find but they still needed the positive ID.

Behind the Focus sat a big plastic sheet which stretched backwards and up to the back of the garage. Pulling the sheet back, Irwin's jaw dropped.

"Colin, sir. Come and take a look."

Rows of dingbat mines, guns of various types including rifles, automatic pistols and machine guns sat. Grenades and boxes of ammunition was neatly stacked, all stamped with the base's identity codes.

"Oh my God," Colin exclaimed.

And a telephone jamming and signal deflector. Colin was tempted to smash it, safe in the knowledge it had more than likely been used to frighten Anna. But then his duty took over and he knew it had to be bagged up along with the rest of this haul.

A small, round box sat on the floor which Cartwright picked up and unclipped to get at the contents.

"I wouldn't do that, sir," Colin warned.

"Why not, Haltwhistle?" Black Jack asked, looking at his subordinate and back to the box.

"That could be anything, an IED or something like that."

Understanding that his agent had a good point, Cartwright put the box down.

"You're quite persuasive when you want to be!"

He looked around at the rest of the stash. The collection was enough to supply a small army. Jim had been right. All of the equipment was labeled as surplus, and was marked for sale or destruction depending on condition. What was worse to think about was how much of this equipment had been taken and gotten to wherever it had ended up. It was a truly horrifying thing to consider.

"I want all of this equipment impounded and logged," Colin told the white caps who had appeared at the doorway, looking hot and sweaty after some hard manual labor.

"I'll handle it, sir," Irwin assured him, disappearing through the door.

"There's nothing else in those vegetable patches except... well... vegetables," said the first snow drop.

Colin was too gentlemanly to make them all put it back. They had done their job and done it well. To recover this stash and the car was the break they had been looking for.

"We're going to need a truck for this lot," Cartwright said, taking a hard look at the pile of munitions. He looked at the Focus. "I want that impounded too. And have the boffins give it a good once over. See what else is in there."

Colin sat down outside the garage looking at the gray sky. The whole sorry affair was making sense now.

All they had to do now was prove once and for all who was behind all of this. Cartwright patted his shoulder.

"Well done, Haltwhistle. Between you and McCleland your instincts have proved right on," he said proudly.

But Colin was a little more pragmatic. "Let's not get ahead of ourselves, sir. We have to prove who did all of this, and find out what Jim has got." He stood up. "Jim. I wonder how he's getting on? I should head down to that club and find -"

Cartwright stopped him. "He radioed in this morning, he is investigating his end and thinks he's gotten close to this Montalban character. Until we hear anything, let's let him do his thing."

Colin gave a small sigh of relief. "I hope he's alright. That Montalban guy is not to be taken lightly."

Cartwright smiled. "Jim McCleland can take care of himself. He's just mad enough to become his right-hand man if he wanted to be."

A bottle of Mountain Dew was opened and Haltwhistle took a deep drink from it. "Yeah, he does like to think of himself as a bit of a reprobate." He paused, thoughtful. "I'm praying he hasn't brought Sophie into this mess. I think she means a bit more to him than the girls he usually dates."

"How much of that vile stuff do you get through?" Cartwright pointed to the bottle and looked sour. "He did indeed take the young lady with him." Colin started but Black Jack cut him off.

"That one is on me, I told him to, and he chose her. That's on him. I have no doubt he will take care of her."

Haltwhistle looked at the ground then back to his CO. "I think he has feelings for her, sir."

The head of AID stuffed his hands into the pockets of his thick topcoat and stifled a laugh. "The idea of Jim McCleland actually taking the time to get to know a woman instead of just bedding her is difficult to fathom."

Colin smiled. "From what I've seen, I think it's serious."

"Who is... Sophie?"

Haltwhistle looked grim. "He met her at the crash scene, sir. She was one of the CAA examiners."

Colin fully expected the old man to blow his top, given the implication. Instead, Cartwright shrugged. "Then Mr. Montalban had better be careful. If he hurts her, McCleland will rip him apart."

"If he doesn't get found out first," Haltwhistle pointed out. "That really will be the end of him, especially if what I think's going to happen, does."

"And what might that be?" Black Jack eyed the Flight Lieutenant, then he understood what Colin was getting at. "If McCleland wants to get serious with the young lady, she will have to be vetted. That's down to you."

"What? Jim's missus? He'll love that!"

"Her background has to be checked thoroughly before I'll give permission for him to go with her." At the questioning look, Cartwright elaborated. "No AID agent can be in a long term relationship or marry without my expressed consent."

The white caps finished collecting the horde late in the afternoon, under Cartwright's supervision.

Once done and safely underway, he and Haltwhistle headed back to the camp.

"I think it's time to bring in Mr. Marinell and have a chat. It's long overdue," Colin said.

"I'm looking forward to going head to head with him," Cartwright agreed.

Haltwhistle harrumphed. "Oh he's a character, alright. He got mouthy with my esteemed partner and Jim lamped him."

Cartwright rolled his eyes. One was intelligent but hot tempered and the other was a loose cannon. Both were brilliant in their own ways and made up for the other's shortcomings. But there were times they made things difficult-hell, almost impossible for their long suffering boss.

The holes in the middle of the desert after their first mission together was testament to that.

"Then this should be interesting," was Black Jack's only statement.

"Do you want to get him rounded up, or should we handle it?" Colin asked.

The CO smiled. "Oh. I think this deserves some personal service, don't you?"

Colin smiled. "Yes sir."

Marinell was in the middle of dressing down an unfortunate leading aircraftsman for an unspecified mistake, as Colin and Cartwright with Irwin keeping a watching brief headed across the pan towards the direction of the tirade.

"Do you actually pay attention, or do you just turn up to work and hope for the best?" Marinell ranted. He was waving a screwdriver in the terrified technician's face. "If I were you I'd start filling out your dole papers because I'm going to get you out of here, son. Do you understand?"

Mid rant, the young man who was shaking at this point was even more perturbed by the sight of an approach of two officers, one wearing a white cap and the other wearing the braids of an Air Vice Marshal, and both striding towards where they were standing.

"Look at me when I'm talking to you!" Marinell bellowed.

"Sir, there's someone -"

"Shut up! You'll be a good man to pay attention -"

He was interrupted by a loud throat clearing from Cartwright. Marinell turned to see the formidable shape of Air Vice Marshal John Cartwright DSO DFC and Haltwhistle with his gloved hands crossed in front of him.

"Oh you've brought the heavy mob out, this time? Was that McCleland guy not hard enough?"

Marinell scoffed. He was not being as circumspect as he had been during the inspection, that's for sure.

"We'll have less of that, Mr. Marinell. Put your hands up against the wall and spread eagle,"

Colin said, with some glee as he got his handcuffs out of his pocket.

"You're under arrest for suspicion of murder, theft, and making threats of murder." Colin went through the usual speech and was halfway through putting the handcuffs on when Marinell elbowed Colin viciously in the stomach and kicked him for good measure, sending the Flt Lt sprawling in to Cartwright.

Marinell took off running, pulling a Glock 17 from his pocket.

"Get back! I'll shoot anyone who comes near me!" He ran off towards the hangar.

Colin, winded a bit, drew his Sig and took off after him, still clutching his ribs where Marinell had given him a good battering.

"You go around the back, I'll take the front," Haltwhistle shouted to Irwin.

Several people pointed in the direction of where Marinell had gone and Colin sprinted across the concrete, past a row of gleaming Typhoons which looked loaded and ready for action, but whose ground crews were working feverishly on.

The huge doors of the hangar were pulled back allowing the aircraft to be wheeled in and out of.

Colin slowed as he came up on the yawning opening, with the gun ready and he in classic cup and saucer hold stance.

A shot rang out from the shadows and Haltwhistle hit the deck. Quickly checking his person, he was relieved to find he wasn't hit.

The sound of laughter came from somewhere near the back of the hangar.

"Thought you had me, Haltwhistle? Guess what? Not happening. You can kiss my entire arse and like it!"

The sound of the voice was moving from left to right as Colin was looking along the back wall.

Too many shadows to see exactly where he was.

"Let's top kidding ourselves Marinell! You're finished!" Colin's voice echoed around the building.

"Then come and get me! I'll show you how finished I am! How would you like me to show you how finished I am?"

Colin bristled but Marinell just laughed. He worked out he was somewhere towards the back right corner of the hangar so he inched his way around the doorway and mindful that several hundred million pounds worth of combat aircraft were now also in the line of fire and a stray bullet could cause something catastrophic.

Another gunshot rang out and Haltwhistle dived into an arched doorway and fired back in the direction of the sound of the blast. There was a grunt of pain.

Clearly he had found his target. Haltwhistle made a mental note to thank Jim for the Sig. The accuracy it possessed compared to the Glock had made the difference.

Fortunately he had a clear shot and no aircraft would be hit. A movement in the shadows and a door opened and closed, followed by another gunshot.

Marinell must have been keeping Irwin at bay.

Colin slipped out though a side door, but noticed a couple of spots of blood on the floor and on the door handle. In a moment, he was barreling along the outside of the hangar.

He saw Marinell favoring his upper arm, sprinting for the vast warehouse store and went in through the main door.

Dammit! The biggest and best place to hide on the entire base.

He went in after him and with his gun ready, he knew he had to be careful where he went and which aisle to choose.

Wordlessly, he pointed at the far aisle. Irwin nodded and swept away.

Colin went down the left-hand row where the general spare parts such as door hinges and tools including spanners and hammers could be found. Crouching down, Haltwhistle looked at the floor, looking for feet or shadows. Nothing, but then the aisle was nearly a hundred meters long.

Above him a rumbling sound came and Colin looked up to see a shelving unit rocking back and forth. He ran as fast as he could as the contents of the shelves came raining down on to the concrete floor. Heavy metal piping and fitments for them.

"Beware of the unidentified flying objects!" Marinell's voice tormented him.

Colin went to the end of the aisle and slowly paced along the ends of them, hoping to get a glimpse of where Marinell was.

A heavy wrench came down with a whoosh and smashed in to the ground directly in front of him. Colin jumped backwards, the Sig slipping from his fingers as Marinell gave him the finger, laughed and sprinted off up the aisle.

"Useless wanker!" Marinell shouted as he ran, pushing a shelving unit, which wobbled, dropping it's wares from the top shelf on to Irwin below. He let out a yell of pain as his leg became trapped.

"Call in backup," Haltwhistle told him.

He retrieved his gun and set off after him. At the other end of the aisle, his target grabbed a one of the store workers, and flung him over, blocking the aisle just log enough to delay Colin getting out right behind him.

Back outside, Marinell was heading for the building which housed the canteen. With his ribs aching, Colin was straining to keep up with the fleeing figure, who stopped, turned, grinned and dove in to the canteen building.

The door was still closing as Colin jumped and kicked it open furiously, causing the door to swing back, breaking the overhead arm which controlled it's swing.

Plunging in to the dining hall, Marinell was waiting for him and fired four times. The Glock clicked empty.

"Shit!" Marinell cursed.

Colin chose that moment to pounce, pointing the Sig at the sergeant's heart.

"You wouldn't shoot an unarmed man would you?" Marinell tutted.

Jim would have just blown his sorry arse away. Colin instead closed in on him, leaping over tables and chairs to get at the errant man.

"Let's try this again," Haltwhistle said as casually as possible. Marinell swung for him and caught Colin in the ribs with a good punch, right where he had hit him before. Colin hammered down on Marinell's back as he had seen Jim do, which sent his assailant down on his knees.

Colin lashed out viciously, catching Marinell's jaw with the steel toe capped shoes, sending the sergeant backwards with a mouthful of blood.

Marinell kicked out in response, smashing Colin in the side of his right thigh. Haltwhistle punched him in arm where his bullet had nicked him. The sergeant howled in pain and Colin struck him in the face with the palm of his hand as he had seen Jim do.

"Fuck you, Haltwhistle!" Marinell roared as he lay on the ground, blood oozing from his mouth and nose.

Back on his feet, the white cap pointed the Sig at the sergeant's plaintive form.

"You are under arrest, you fucking pain in the arse."

Taken out of the canteen under guard, Marinell was bundled unceremoniously into the back of one of the squad cars by Flt. Lt. Irwin and taken to the cells for a stay overnight. Haltwhistle wanted to interview him straight away, but Cartwright talked him out of it.

"You're hot right now. You're too close to this. Go home and rest for the night, we'll talk tomorrow. That's an order," Black Jack told him.

Colin smiled. "Yes sir."

NINETEEN

Sophie was glad to be back at her desk. It gave some measure of comfort after spending, what she felt, was far too much time in Montalban's presence.

The report on the type of explosive was due back any time. It would be the final part of the file but whether it made any difference to the overall case, given Jim and Colin's involvement, was anyone's guess.

"I found a bit on our friends from the other day," said Phil. "I had to call in a few favors and asked friends of friends."

"Go on." Sophie was attentive to that.

"Well, this is all heresay. As you said, they're both RAF, but according to the records, both of them retired from the service."

That didn't make sense. "How can that be? They're both about 30? Were they medically retired?"

Jim most certainly didn't seem to be deficient in his health, she thought.

"It didn't say, so I put the feelers out and this is where it gets to be a bit of a guessing game." Phil thought for a minute. "There were rumors floating around that the ministry and the RAF got together to form a special squad. Nothing official and certainly not something I can get anything concrete on, but reading between the lines, this is some sort of agency that they send in when things look too dodgy for the likes of us and the police."

"Like a secret service?" Sophie's suspicions had been right all along, not that she was going to say anything.

"Pretty much." Phil looked at the carpet tiles for a moment.

"So they are above the law..." she murmured, without wishing to give away what she already knew.

Phil seemed a little on edge. He was playing with the collar of his shirt and fidgeting, rather akin to a schoolboy who had been caught in a devious act. He had certainly seemed to act unusually of late.

"I'm thinking they're beyond it. I've read about this sort of stuff, kind of like what the old S.O.E. was doing in the war," he went on. "These are the sort of people the government send in when shit gets real. They do the job and then disappear in to the woodwork. I'm talking licensed to kill."

"I think you've seen too many Bond films, Phil!" Sophie giggled, knowing full well her colleague was not too far from the truth.

"It wouldn't surprise me to find out it was this mob who decided to take the Vulcan for a spin a few weeks ago. That case has gone stone cold."

"You're not seeing this guy on the side, are you?" he finally asked.

"No, course not." Sophie did not like bending or withholding the truth, but her senses were on edge.

He looked over her briefly then smiled. "Fair enough."

The chime on the email inbox meant a new piece of correspondence had been received. Opening the message, it was the test results they had been waiting for.

"Tetryl?" Phil wondered aloud. He thumbed through a textbook, looking for the name and reasonably quickly got his answer. "An explosive found in military equipment."

That detail cemented in both of their minds they were now privy to a military operation. By rights, the case should be handed off.

"We need to report in," said Sophie.

***

Colin headed back to the mess a bit bruised, and with his countenance marked but he was happy to find Anna had cooked a delicious steak and kidney pudding. He walked through the door and the rich smell of home cooking filled the air.

"Hello love," he said. He was tired out. Satisfied but tired out. He was also rather the worse for wear after the day's action.

"What the hell happened to you?" Anna asked. She touched his forehead. "Have you been in a fight?"

He nodded. "Yes."

Anna became irritated. "Well, I can't blame Jim this time, so you'd better talk fast if you want to get me out of my bad mood!"

She fixed her battered husband with a fearsome glare.

"I'm sorry love." She was about to give him the 'Don't you love me' line but he beat her to it.

"But I got the man who called you the other night."

That brought her up short. "You got him?" she asked, wide eyed.

He didn't smile but he was pleased. "I'm pretty certain of it. I got him."

Anna hugged him. "Thank you," she sighed. The relief flowed from her. She looked at the kitchen. "I made you your favorite."

He held her tight to him. "Thank you." It was a treat he was certainly looking forward to.

Colin looked at his wife and beamed. "I may have a favorite for you too," he grinned despite the pain from his legs and ribs.

"Oh that sounds wonderful." She returned his big wide smile and gave him a sultry expression.

Anna always gave off the impression she was quite reserved and around the camps Colin had been posted to, people had treated her respectfully rather than leered at her. But Colin knew otherwise, having been married to her for a few years, he was sure that were was nothing that he didn't know about his other half.

"I just fancy a quiet night in. Just you and me," he said. "Let's watch a film and just relax. It's been a bad few days."

"That sounds like a wonderful plan to me," Anna replied. "You pick something. But no guns, no fights, no nothing."

Colin shook his head. "Oh, I've had quite enough of those for one day."

He was starving and tucked into his meal with gusto, wolfing it down in large mouthfuls. Anna simply smiled. Colin only did that when he had had a really tough day. She found her appetite had returned after the good news.

After supper, Colin chose a comedy for them both to enjoy. Anna curled up to him. He had forgotten about the more fruity scenes in the movie and he found his wife looking at him with a twinkle in her eye.

"Tonight," she winked.

***

Marinell sat across the interview room table from Haltwhistle and Cartwright. An armed guard stood to attention by the door just in case the sergeant tried another shunt like his outburst yesterday. From where Colin sat, there seemed to be little chance of that, this time.

Cartwright read through the man's personnel file and the incident reports had been filed concerning the previous day's near fatal chase.

"You don't seem to be a team player, a supporter of talent or a leader to look up to. Not exactly what we want in this service," Black Jack said coldly.

"I just do my job and go home. If someone doesn't measure up, get another job." Marinell showed absolutely no contrition.

"You're already in enough trouble Marinell. Resisting arrest, assault of an officer, we could throw attempted murder in to the bag. If I were you, I'd start helping yourself," Colin told him.

"Some people... skin as thin as tracing paper," was the uninterested reply.

The dismissive shake of his head meant Cartwright was not impressed in the slightest.

"Completely the wrong attitude. You don't deserve to wear that uniform if you make arbitrary decisions about lads' lives without thinking of them. You live this career, you don't just 'turn up and go home' as you put it."

For his part, Marinell folded his arms, a rather difficult proposition when his wrists were cuffed.

"Look pal, are you just going to berate me or is this going somewhere?"

"If you think that's a good attitude to have, you can waltz that fucker back!" Cartwright told him.

The lack of respect was shocking. Either whoever had trained this man had done a poor job, or somehow his personality had gone unnoticed by the selection board.

"Oh it's going somewhere, don't you worry about that," Haltwhistle said, glowering at the man on the other side of the table. He produced a stack of photographs of the stash of weapons and munitions they had found at his allotment.

"There were taken in the garage of your vegetable garden. All surplus weaponry and equipment.

My question for you is this. How did this little lot get on your allotment?"

Marinell looked at the pictures in a very desultory manner. "I have never seen it before. I haven't been over there in weeks!" he exclaimed.

"How, then, would you account for the vegetables you're growing then? Surely you tend to them?"

Cartwright demanded. Black Jack grew vegetables himself. He knew how much care they needed.

"Do you know how slowly that stuff grows? I haven't been there in maybe six weeks!" the suspect insisted.

"I do actually, son. So don't give me that crap," the Air Vice Marshal said icily.

"I'm telling you I haven't been there!" Marinell was adamant.

Haltwhistle leaned forward, unfolding his arms. He spoke in a low, slow and uncompromising tone.

"Well... someone has."

Producing a picture of the rifle, he placed it in front of the accused. "Ever seen that before?"

"Yeah. On a firing range," was the pithy response.

Colin slapped the table top. "Oh come off it! It says here you're a good shot with a rifle! So fill us in, did you cap Fliplugs?"

"No!" Marinell barked.

Haltwhistle tossed a picture of the Focus onto the table. "How about this car? Ever seen it before?"

Marinell simply gazed at it disinterestedly. "Yeah. It's Woodley's car. I saw it around."

"It was also found on your allotment. Let me guess," Colin grimaced. "You don't know how it ended up there either?" The vitriol was virtually dripping out of every pore Haltwhistle had.

"Is the correct answer for 10 points," Marinell replied, equally snide.

Cartwright drummed his fingers on the table. "I'm waiting, Mr. Marinell."

Marinell cocked an eyebrow. "For what, a bus?"

If Jim had been here, he would have simply decked him, thought Colin. But Cartwright's eyes were as cold as the Arctic.

"Are you finished? Are you done?' Black Jack was beyond unimpressed. 'Big... deal."

Haltwhistle produced another set of photos, spreading them across the table top in front of the uncooperative Marinell.

"How about this stuff? Never seen that before either? You must have myopia. I'd love to be able to say 'I've never seen something.' Amaze me, Marinell. Let me hear the sound of someone saying 'I've never seen that before'," said Colin, even more caustic.

But this time, Marinell sat in silence, looking at the pictures. Cartwright and Haltwhistle gave each other a sideways look. Clearly they had hit a nerve of some sort.

"I take it, from your reaction, you have indeed, seen that before and myopia isn't an issue for you?" Colin said lightly.

Finally, after an age, Marinell spoke. "Yes. It was for my retirement."

"What was the plan? Sell the stuff, make the money and disappear into the wild blue yonder?"

Marinell looked at him, for the first time, taking him seriously. "Your partner has rubbed off on you."

Colin blustered on. "Whatever he may have done is nowhere near as bad as what you appear to have, so I'd suggest you focus on this. So back to the matter at hand. Where did this little lot come from?"

Marinell appeared to be genuinely humbled.

"I... I did some things as a kid and.. put this away in case anything happened."

"So you stole this collection, is that what you're saying? Did you steal the weapons? And the Focus as well?"

Marinell became frustrated again. "No, I told you, I don't know anything about that!"

Colin finally lost his temper. "Then what do you know anything about? Come on, let's have a really good excuse! I'm all ears!" he bellowed in the sergeant's face. The same smug self- satisfied smile was back on the suspect's face.

"It was you who called my wife, wasn't it? Wasn't it? Do you know what you did to her? To my wife? Did it feel good?" Colin was nearly hoarse from the shouting. He was on his feet and bending over the table in fury.

Cartwright slowly, quietly said "Sit down, Haltwhistle."

There was a short silence while Colin recomposed himself. He was indeed too hot and too close to this. But he was also felt he was close to the solution.

"I'm telling you right now," Marinell banged his index finger on the desk to underline his point.

"I know fuck all about those bloody guns or car or bombs or whatever else was piled up there."

He sat back and glared at his two interrogators. "Happy? Are we done? Can I go now?"

"Not even close." Colin pointed at the picture of the rifle. "This gun we found is being checked right now. Convince me now you didn't have anything to do with Fliplugs's shooting." It was a bluff, because he knew the forensics hadn't got to the gun yet, but it may get a rise out of this man.

But no, Marinell stuck to being innocent.

"I've not fired a rifle in months! Check my records. So no, I've not been near it."

Cartwright, reading Marinell's file again noticed something. "It says here a note from your sergeant in basic. 'Shows aptitude for long distance shooting with rifle.'," Black Jack set the file down. "Anything to say about that?"

Marinell became defensive. "Just because I'm good with a gun doesn't mean I killed anyone!"

"It doesn't look good for you when a rifle was found on your property and you are apparently good with a gun, does it?" Haltwhistle pointed out.

"I hope you don't shoot the way you investigate," Marinell glowered. "Your wife would never be satisfied."

That hit a raw nerve.

Colin was about ready to explode. "I want to know. Right now, to my face. It was you who called Anna, wasn't it?"

Marinell looked straight at him. "No offense, but what the fuck are you talking about?"

Colin clenched his jaw. "Don't lie to me. Did you torment my wife on the phone the other night?"

The sergeant looked definitely confused. "No. I didn't."

Haltwhistle was fuming. His hands were balled up in to fists and he was like a coiled spring.

"Stand easy, Colin,' Cartwright warned.

But Marinell's body language said it all as regards to his innocence on that matter. Apparently satisfied, Colin seemed to calm down a little.

"Alright. If you didn't put the munitions in your allotment, who did?" Cartwright asked.

"The Invisible Man! Sooty and Sweep! Bodie and Doyle! I don't bloody know!" was the exasperated reply.

Black Jack rolled his eyes. "Alright, alright. Let's say you're correct. Who else would have access to your allotment? Wife? Girlfriend?"

Marinell looked down at the table. Finally he looked at his accusers. "Don't make me laugh," he said bitterly. "My missus left me."

"I'm very sorry to hear that," Colin did not sound sincere.

"I didn't think you would be. She shacked up with that arsehole in bomb disposal."

Haltwhistle was suddenly interested.

"Which arsehole in bomb disposal? Who are you talking about, man?"

Marinell looked sad. "I can't remember his name now. Big bastard. Broad. She fancied him because he had muscles."

No. She fancied him because he treats her right, Colin thought. He knew instantly who Marinell was referring to. He rolled his tongue in thought.

Cartwright could tell he was pondering something.

"Interview terminated. At 10:15am." He nodded to the armed guard. "Take him back to his cell."

TWENTY

That evening at the club, Jim and Sophie tucked in to another delicious and filling meal of chicken fajitas and rice for McCleland and a fish dish kept Sophie satisfied.

"I wonder why we're being wined and dined?" she wondered. "What's he got up his sleeve for us?"

"Probably something to do with that yarn I spun him about being a former pilot, and I'd left the service and was looking for a job," Jim guessed. "How do you soften someone up? Make them comfortable and then hit them with the demand."

Sophie set her glass down on the table. She was horrified. "I don't like this Jim!" she cried. A few of the other patrons looked over at them.

"Keep your voice down. If it's my only way in, I need to take it. I need to find out what is going on here!" he hissed.

She folded her arms and looked at him. Her eyes became watery. "This is getting out of hand," she said with iron in her voice. "You might be enjoying yourself but the more we get in to this the more danger we're in." She got closer to him and her voice hardened, almost as firm as he had been on the first night in his apartment. "I really, really like you Jim but I don't want to get killed for it. And I don't want to see you get hurt. I like you the way you are."

Jim reached over and touched her cheek. "It won't come to that. I can promise you." The look on his face told her he was serious.

She was quiet for a moment, then what he meant dawned on her. It was written all over him.

"Do you love me?" she asked.

He looked at her and nodded. "Yes. Yes I do."

Jim did not like to tell people his feelings and generally kept them to himself. Colin was a lot more expressive, hell he was happily married and he and Anna had a very special close, loving relationship which sometimes he found himself a little envious of. Yes, he had had girlfriends and his reputation was well earned, but this girl was different. Sophie was smart, funny, gentle and kind. And he wanted to be with her. For her part, she had known there were strong feelings for him too. Her ex-boyfriend had not been pleasant to her at all, but she had not told Jim all of the details, fearing given his macho, gung ho approach he would track Dom down and teach him a lesson or two.

It was still a surprise to hear something like this, as much as she liked it.

"But you've only known me for a week or so!" Sophie was a little taken aback.

Jim was deadly serious. "If you know, you know. And I know I can't let anyone hurt you. So no, I won't let you be in danger, not if I can help it." He met her eyes with his. "And yes, I love you."

Sophie sat in silence for a moment, taking it in. "Thank you." She reached across the table to him.

"Was there anyone else before me?" she asked in a small voice. She elaborated at his confusion. "That you loved?"

McCleland shook his head. "No." He was very definite about it.

She smiled a little. "That makes me feel special."

He stood up and gave her a hug. "Now. Let's see what Montalban has in store for us."

Jim held his arm out and Sophie took it. Her glittering black dress caught the lights in the restaurant and made it twinkle, the light shimmering off it as they glided over to where Montalban was sitting.

The charismatic wavy haired man was perched in his usual spot by the pool tables.

Dressed in a single-breasted dark blue suit, shoes gleamed in the light and a dress shirt. Jim had to hand it to the guy. He was immaculate.

"My friends. Did you enjoy your meals this evening?" he greeted them, getting up and clasping their hands.

"Yes. It was delicious," Jim assured him.

Montalban ushered them to sit down. They did so in a plushy appointed booth.

"I have invited you both here as I am entertaining some guests tonight. Important guests I would very much like for you to meet."

"How do we fit in?" Sophie asked, immediately on edge. Her inquiring mind and want to analyze a situation was already working overtime.

"All will be revealed in time, Miss Hawkesworth," he replied A little menacingly, Sophie thought.

Montalban served them both drinks again and sat with them.

"How long have you two been together?" Their host was interested in their personal history... for what reason? Again Sophie was intrigued by his sudden deep interest in them.

Jim and Sophie shared a look and she squeezed his hand. "Quite a while. We... well, we're very happy."

Montalban smiled faintly. "No doubt you are."

The main doors of the club opened and three men walked in, one with heavily gelled hair which swept back into a mullet. He sported several gold rings, a gold neck chain and designer label shoes with a matching suit. The second man was dressed casually, and the third? The third surveyed the room like it was a battlefield and he was the lone sniper out to pick off any survivors. Jim could have sworn he looked like one of those surveillance robots in sci-fi movies who was out to cause serious trouble.

McCleland did not recognize the first two gentleman, but the third he knew. A Dutchman.

Joest van der Graan.

Oh Christ, Jim thought.

Montalban went over to greet them personally. Sophie caught Jim's expression and moved close to his ear.

"Who's that?" she whispered.

Grim, stone faced, Jim turned to her and said in a low voice "You don't want to know."

She sighed. "Well apparently we're about to. So let me in on the secret."

"He's suspected of murder in a lot of countries. He controls almost all of the organized crime in Amsterdam. He's hardcore. His party piece is cutting people's hands off to send a message to people who try to fuck him over."

Sophie looked like she had been slapped. "And we're involved with these people? We can't just sit and pretend to be civil with them! We have got to do something!" she hissed.

Jim sat back, looking resigned. "I'm open to ideas, baby." Sophie looked like she wanted the ground to swallow her up. "Let's just play along for now and slip away when it goes quiet, alright?"

"I am really not feeling this," she said. "In fact, this is a terrible idea. I think we should just go, now."

Sophie was almost pleading with him. He held her hand, but she snatched it back. "No Jim. I'm scared. You should be too. This is not a game."

"Soph, listen to me," he insisted. She looked at him but her lip trembled. "I've been involved with things and done things I'm not proud of. I've got myself into some serious shit but always found a way out. I need to know what this is all about but I need your help to do it. Just trust me, okay? I'll not let him hurt you. I just told you I love you. So let me do that."

Sophie still looked less than happy but managed a thin line of a smile. "Alright. But if it gets too bad, I want out and you're coming with me. Deal?"

"Deal."

Just then, Montalban returned with his motley crew of friends. He made the introductions without being invited.

"These are my friends, Jim Neal and Sophie Hawkesworth. These are my colleagues, Joel Alondra, Gustav Metzler and Joest van der Graan."

These three were the biggest organized crime bosses in Western Europe. Metzler had links with the Russian mafia, Alondra controlled several cartels in France and van der Graan... well. He'd be in good company with Hannibal Lecter.

"How do you do?" Jim said simply. The various gangsters grunted their greetings but van der Graan eyed McCleland up suspiciously.

Jim felt like he was in the cross hairs of a killer's rifle. Outwardly, he maintained his light touch.

"Is there a problem?" he asked with a wry smile.

Van der Graan continued looking at him. Jim noticed he was completely ignoring Sophie at this point. She could feel the air turning cold. Finally, van der Graan cracked a smile.

"No. No problem," he said in a thick Dutch accent. "You just look a little familiar to me."

"Well next time I'm in the *Reader's Digest* I'll send you a copy," Jim grinned. Sophie was horrified at his insolence, seriously thinking at any moment, her boyfriend would be disemboweled.

She kicked him under the table, but the Dutchman just grinned.

"You have a sharp sense of humor, Mr. Neal."

Montalban with a wave of his hand towards Jim said "Jim here is a good pool player. How about a little game once this is all over?" he suggested.

There were nods of agreement from the others. Sophie looked around and noticed the gangster's minders had just come in to the club and were now helping themselves to the entertainments on offer.

She knew if she caused a fuss now it would blow Jim's cover and that would be an end to it for them both. Their chance to leave had gone, for now. Her only choice was to play along and hope to hell that Jim somehow got them out of this. Now that she knew definitively how he felt about her, Sophie knew he would protect her as best as he could. He had taught her some basic self- defense moves, but it had only been a cursory introduction rather than training her to be an arse- kicking queen, as he put it.

Montalban spoke to Jim. "I have some urgent business tomorrow evening I wish for you to be involved with. I will call on your services for a delicate matter that I need your help with. I shall contact you tomorrow afternoon. If that's convenient?" He looked back and forth between them.

"Yeah er... that's fine," McCleland said, a bit taken aback.

"Excellent. There will be a generous incentive for you as well. Let us enjoy our evening together."

Sitting down at a table near the largest pool table, she leaned in close.

"What urgent business is he talking about?" she muttered.

"I think it's something to do with a flight, if my Colin Haltwhistle senses are not playing up."

Sophie looked nervous. "Just be careful, okay?"

The gangsters milled around making small talk. Alondra and Metzler stood laughing while Montalban entertained van der Graan with one of the one arm bandit machines. Then, approaching the pool tables came Montalban's bully boy Wilsoncroft, who seemed to have a problem with the world in general. He glowered at Jim and Sophie and marched over to them.

"I don't see why you're here. If I had my way, you'd both be out on your arses," he rumbled.

"If you want to talk about arses, you're showing yours right now, pal," was Jim's offhand reply.

"Listen to me, wanker. You'd best not get cocky with me. Do you know what happens to people who get cocky with me?"

Jim tapped his finger on the table and had a really bored look on his face. "I have a feeling we're about to be let in on that fact."

Wilsoncroft loomed over him. "Are you starting something, prick?"

Jim stood up and met his look. "How about we sort this out like a couple of men?"

He went over to one of the pool tables which was beautifully presented just like everything else in this club. Noticing this table did not feature metal detailing around the edges, he guessed that it had not been tampered with in the same manner that the table he had played Montalban on had been. He threw Wilsoncroft a cue, and set up the balls.

"Here's how it goes, pal. I win, you fuck off. You win, I fuck off. Either way, someone is going to be leaving the table and out of here. Deal?" he asked Wilsoncroft, while holding his cue.

"You've got a deal. Now play!" the lug barked at him.

Magnanimously, Jim said "You break." At Wilsoncroft's suspicious glare. "Please, I insist."

Wilsoncroft made the break. Not a very good one, it had to be said. The pack was mostly still together and only a yellow and a red were loose. Jim took care of the red with a thunderous shot which got plenty of side spin, forcing the cue ball into the pack and breaking it up nicely. Three more reds went down in quick succession. At the side of the table, Wilsoncroft was getting visibly angry at being bested, but Montalban pacified him.

A couple of tricky angles on the next two reds. A double off the cushion got the first one into the right corner pocket and a long shot took care of the other, which didn't present too much of an issue. The final red was a simple push into the top left corner which left an angle on the black into the middle left pocket.

It went down leaving Jim's opponent without potting a single yellow.

Placing the cue onto the table, Jim faced Wilsoncroft.

"Now. Fuck off, prick," was his only comment.

Montalban laughed, relishing the easy victory and the pasting his go to thug had just been deservedly given. The other bosses were equally impressed with Jim's skill.

Sophie meanwhile, had watched the game unfold and was dreading what she could see about to happen, happening.

"I told you he could play," Montalban explained.

But Wilsoncroft was not about to let it go so easily. A roar of rage emanated from the top of his lungs and he leaped onto the pool table with a cue in his hand, swinging the wooden staff viciously at Jim.

McCleland leaped backwards, feeling the air being cut like a knife just in front of his nose.

Wilsoncroft jumped off the table and came down, aiming to attack the man who had just humiliated him. He twirled the cue above his head. Sophie ducked as Wilsoncroft grabbed at her, something Jim was not about to allow.

He grabbed his own cue from the table top, and in a deft move, cracked it over his knee and performed a jumping front kick into Wilsoncroft's ribs, sending him backwards. Jim withdrew to just be the gambling machines which Wilsoncroft smashed with his cue, as he tried and failed to hit Jim and beat him down.

"Piece of shit!" the attacker howled as he relentlessly tried to pound McCleland.

Jim ducked, rolled and struck Wilsoncroft several glancing blows with the two cue halves, now being brandished as makeshift kendo sticks. Skillfully pummeling his opponent, Jim managed to get him to drop the now very damaged and secondhand looking cue from his cracked fingers.

From the floor, Wilsoncroft yelled, grabbing Jim and forcing him backwards into a baccarat table, where the players, who had been standing by after being alerted by the fight breaking out now scattered as easily as the cards and chips now did as the table collapsed under the combined weight of the two opponents.

McCleland kicked out and blocked a punch a punch with his right forearm, then landed a haymaker with his left. A one arm bandit was smashed by Wilsoncroft's heavy body slamming into it at high speed.

Still, this lug would not go down.

Blood soaked, Montalban's bully boy tried one last desperate lunge at Jim, who simply stepped sideways out of the path of his lurching opponent's way. Jim spun on his heel and kicked his attacker in the back of the neck and shoulders. Down he tumbled, but this time he did not get up.

A pool of blood collected under his body where the spindle of the roulette wheel had ruptured him.

Jim dusted his suit off, picking bits of glass and plastic out of the stitching and pulled it's rumpled fabric straight.

Heading back over to where Montalban had been watching he looked rueful.

"I'm sorry about that," he said, sincerely apologetic.

Montalban clapped Jim's shoulder. "I assure you, it's not a problem. There is no need to be sorry."

He produced a large wad of notes from his pocket, and handed McCleland a bundle of £50 notes.

"Buy yourself a new suit and accept the rest as a token of my regret for how yours and Sophie's evening has been disrupted."

Jim's girlfriend came over, visibly shaken.

"He was going to kill you Jim," she said softly. "He was going to kill us both." She was shaking, clearly perturbed by what she had seen. Jim realized she had never seen a real fight or someone get killed in front of her eyes before. Definitely an unnerving experience for anyone.

Montalban gave her some money as well. "My sincere apologies, Miss Hawkesworth."

She reached out for Jim's hand and tugged at it.

"I'm going to take you home," Jim told her gently. He turned to Montalban. "Thank you." He felt genuinely appreciative this time for this man's understanding. He was a man of honor, even if he had a twisted way of going about his business.

"Very well. Have a pleasant evening." He did not seem to care about the thousands of pounds worth of damage done to his place, or even the bloody corpse now handily placed dangling from a roulette wheel, the legacy of someone who had played his round on the black and red and lost everything. Literally, in this case.

After Jim and Sophie left, the other gangsters gathered round Montalban as the cleaning and repair crew went into action to sort out the mess made by Wilsoncroft's ill advised attempt to get even with Jim.

"Where did you find that guy? He's perfect!" Alondra exclaimed.

"Yes," agreed Montalban. "He could prove to be a very useful commodity."

"Did you see the way he took that *arschloch* out? He's definitely someone I would want on my team," Metzler commented.

Montalban looked rather superior as he knew his plans were falling into place.

"If I told you he is also a pilot, then he fits into our field of fire perfectly," he smiled, taking a sip of tequila.

"You are joking, surely?" van der Graan spluttered, nearly dropping his cocktail.

"When have you ever known me to jest, Joest?" was the dry response.

He may not have known or even cared if he had, but Montalban had just placed Jim in mortal danger.

***

Sophie was quiet in the car as Jim drove her home. She barely said two words and simply gazed out of the car's window as the dusk gathered outside. She didn't speak fully until they reached the front door of her little house.

Opening the front door, she turned to her man. "He was going to kill us Jim," she said, repeating her earlier statement.

They went inside and she sat on the sofa, still clad in her beautiful shimmering black dress.

Sophie looked up at him, her troubled expression cut in to his heart.

"This is all too much for me. I don't... I can't," she was struggling to find the words. Jim sat with her and held her tight. Finally she was able to look at him. "I can't go back there anymore. I don't want to come home wondering if I'm going to be alone again tomorrow."

She started babbling. Some of the speech was intelligible but most of it was gobbledygook. She had never seen violence so in-the-face or seen anyone as willing to give it as Wilsoncroft had tonight. It had been very unsettling. Jim got up and went to the kitchen, making her a hot drink.

Once it was ready he brought it to her and she broke down in his arms.

"How can you live this life?" she asked him. He touched her face. She had always believed she was a strong person and independent but what she had experienced tonight was beyond anything Sophie had come up against before.

"It was all I was good at," he replied as gently as he could.

She sniffled a little and wiped her nose.

"All you were good at? Jim, you could do anything you wanted!" Sophie looked at him.

He considered that for a moment. It brought up some uncomfortable memories for him.

"Well, I could do some boring job in an office for years, or I could do what I do. I'm not the kind of person who could do the office thing. I'd be bored and waste away," he said.

"You'd be safe. You could come home to me in one piece! How do you know you'd be bored?"

Sophie took a sip of the coffee Jim had made.

"I tried it once." McCleland looked pained for a moment. Sophie was going to ask for more details but she got the impression he didn't want to talk about it so let it pass.

"You took that guy out like Jackie Chan on steroids," she commented instead. Despite what she had witnessed, it would be a lie if she said she wasn't impressed with his physical prowess, which she had experienced first-hand of course...

For Jim, it was something he'd enjoyed since he was a teenager. He was seriously thinking about introducing her to his *sifu*. Something in the back of his mind said she would acquit herself well.

"As you said, he was going to kill us. And Montalban... probably would have let him," Jim said. Then he remembered his duty.

"I need to put my call in to the old man," he said, reaching for the portable transmitter. Switching it on, he made the connection.

"Rapier 1 to Wren's Nest. Come in."

"Wren's Nest." It was Colin. "Are you OK mate?"

Jim looked at Sophie, who was still a bit shaken up. "We've been better but we're ok. What's going on over there?"

"We think we've got our man, he's all tucked up here. I'll tell you who when I see you. What's the sit rep?"

"I found ammunition wrapping and gun oil residue in Montalban's place this morning, but there wasn't anything at his club."

Sophie looked surprised. Jim threw the wax covered paper to her for a look. She would need a sample for her own work.

"Well, that's a breakthrough!" Haltwhistle was pleased by Jim's discovery. "I'll have to see if we can get a warrant and search the place. What else have you got?"

"I've been told to fly somewhere tomorrow night at 10, but I don't know where to or from where I'm taking off yet." Jim looked at Sophie. "Oh yeah, and I ended up having to do away with some nutjob who was threatening to kill me and Soph. Apart from that we're good."

Colin paused a moment. "Why doesn't that surprise me? Radio in tomorrow and report the locations for the flight. Hopefully we can get this wrapped up quickly. Good night mate. Wren's Nest out." He switched the unit off and put it away.

"Wren's Nest, Rapier 1? Why not just call yourselves Angel and Spike or Starfleet Command?"

She cuddled up to him tighter. Then she felt the wad in his inside pocket. The money Montalban had given him. She reached into his coat and took it out.

"I don't want this filthy blood money on my conscience." Sophie got up to throw it away.

Knowing the thick pile of notes was needed for something other than spending, Jim called out.

"Don't do that. It's evidence. I need to turn it in to Colin," he warned her. His serious tone got her attention.

She smiled, the first time she had managed a genuine smile all day.

"See? I was right. You are an honorable man. As well as dashing, handsome and completely uncouth!"

Jim hadn't the heart to tell her he had cashed the cheque for the hundred thousand that he had won.

"I do have a question though. It was you in that Vulcan over London wasn't it?" Sophie asked.

Jim looked around, looking like a naughty schoolboy.

"I'll take that as a yes," she snickered. "Phil was up in arms about that, and so was our boss. I thought it was brilliant!"

"Desperate times call for desperate measures," he admitted, satisfied with the idea of rubbing the CAA's nose in it.

He got up and took her face in his hands. "Let's go to bed."

"I love you too Jim," she said softly. At the quizzical look on his face she said "You told me you love me. I... I realized I feel the same."

She kissed him and led him upstairs.

TWENTY-ONE

Montalban led his cohorts into his tastefully appointed office above the club itself, and sat them down at the huge table which dominated the center of the room. Just as with the office part of the room, the walls were tastefully decorated in paintings and books with classical literature. Van der Graan clearly had no appreciation for such art as he dismissed it out of hand.

"You and this frilly crap, Inigo. Get something crazy and sexy in your life."

Montalban threw him a disgusted glance. "I did not bring you here to discuss interior design, Joest."

Van der Graan picked up some of the books from the shelf. "Moby Dick? Shakespeare? Milton?

Steinbeck? What is this, some sort of revenge and bad guy shrine?"

Montalban invited them to sit down at the long table. Metzler and van der Graan relaxed. The chairs were very comfortable.

"So what have you dragged us to dismal old England for, Inigo?" Alondra demanded.

Montalban threw a map of Europe on to the table in front of them.

"Gentlemen. We are all in a unique position in our respective countries. We have under our collective grasp a handle on all of our unique business opportunities, that the nations of France, Germany and the Netherlands offer. Our forefathers fought against each other in petty squabbles over land right. I plan to unite all of them under one co-operative network."

"We already have that. It's called the EU," Metzler commented.

"We know our history, Montalban, what's your point?" Alondra said in a bored voice.

"I propose a co-operation, the chance to bring each of our interests under one roof and closer and work together to enjoy larger profits."

There were looks exchanged around the room. Montalban smiled while they murmured among each other.

"What's in it for us?" Alondra asked.

"Mutual co-operation, the chance to bring each country closer together. Closer and more successful than anything some mutual loathing in Brussels could hope to get," Montalban enthused.

It was at this point his brother Hector raised his hand. "What about all of the other cartels and crime rings? They will not take kindly to being put out of business. They will want reprisals."

Montalban grinned broadly. "That, brother is why I arranged for some insurance. You yourself have picked the pieces up to courier, twice now."

Hector remembered the meeting from a few evenings before. "Yes. You told me not to look at any of it and just deliver it."

"Correct. Now you will see the fruits of that labor." Montalban went to wall mounted cupboard and opened it. He produced a sniper rifle, specifically a surplus RAF rifle.

"Holy shit," exclaimed Metzler.

"Quite," commented Montalban. "I have procured a supply of equipment which should deter anyone who disagrees with our… policies," he explained, showing off the rifle.

"Where the hell did you get that?" gasped Alondra.

Montalban chose his words carefully. "I have my ways."

Metzler was impressed by what he was looking at. Alondra was less enthused. In fact he looked horrified by what Montalban was proposing.

"How much more can you get?" Metzler said in his clipped Germanic brogue.

"I have been reliably informed that I have a good inventory available to us at any time. And not just this, but explosives, night vision equipment and radio scanners, among other things."

Montalban was very confident but there was no trace of smugness.

"My delivery did not arrive, any idea where it ended up?" Van der Graan gave a very dismissive aura off.

Montalban appeared sad for a second. "The news carried a story about it's destruction. It is most unfortunate."

Alondra shook his head. "You propose for us to form a union of crime essentially and knock over anyone who disagrees with us. Is that it?"

The reply was succinct. "And sell on the surplus weapons. Absolutely." Montalban was applying a suppressor to the rifle, but in a slow measured way to avert his guests from realizing what he was doing. "The British government sells arms all the time, all we are doing is making money for ourselves. I see nothing wrong with the arrangement."

"And who is going to run this... company?" was Alondra's next question.

The very wide smile was truly unsettling. "I will listen to all of your opinions. But I have the final say on all matters."

There was another uncertain exchange of looks around the table.

"Could we not take a vote on this and decide for ourselves if it's a viable proposition?" Alondra asked.

"How could it not be a viable proposition? We all make money and reap the benefits a mutually inclusive arrangement offers," Montalban replied, genuinely nonplussed.

But like Alondra, van der Graan was unswayed. "You mean an arrangement you are in charge of. What gives you the right to dictate to us?"

"I am perfectly capable of running my own affairs," Alondra agreed.

"Your attitude surprises me, Joest. Really it does. It is very... disappointing," Montalban told him, all hurt pride.

Then he walked around the room, peering over the shoulders of the other men. He came back to the head of the table. Placing his hands palm down on the table top, he took them all in with a cold stare.

"Perhaps I should show you in more detail what I intend to do?"

Alondra half expected the table top to flip over, revealing a battle map or some such. Instead Montalban went back to the sniper rifle.

Realizing Montalban was intending to use it, Metzler was prepared to hit the deck. Instead the Latino whipped the gun into arms, took aim directly at Alondra, and put his finger on the trigger before the Frenchman could protest.

"You're fired." The thunderous blast from the gun reduced Alondra and his men to pieces. Alondra himself was flung backward in his chair and crashed into the far wall at the end of the room. The Spaniard seemed delighted by what he had done as the others present looked on in horror. Montalban put the safety catch on and replaced the rifle back into it's cradle, which it sat prominently on, a nascent reminder to the others of what would happen if they questioned his proposal again.

"Yes, it appears I will be successful," he said turning and taking the others in. "Would any of you care to take a shot at leadership?"

Horrified by what they had just witnessed, the others sat in silence, seemingly afraid to say anything for fear of being gunned down in the same manner the unfortunate French godfather had been.

"What? Have you all lost the use of your tongues?" Montalban taunted them. He looked from man to man. "Then I can assume you are all in agreement with my proposal?"

Metzler, usually a rough-and-ready sort, was justifiably on edge. "I don't suppose there is any room for negotiation or you're up for compromising?"

Montalban thought about that for a moment, looked over at the rifle and back to the German.

"No." He looked over his colleagues. "All you care about is how much money is in your pockets. There is so much more to life than that.

Who's richest. The one with the money or the one with the power to get the money?"

The atmosphere in the room had become tense. Montalban retook his seat and looked around at the nervous faces.

"Come along. Smile, enjoy the evening!" he laughed. "Unless you have any other business to discuss, I offer you the hospitality of my establishment."

Apart from van der Graan, Metzler and Hector filed out, studiously giving Alondra's mangled body a wide berth as they departed.

Montalban would have him cleared away, just as he would the body of Wilsoncroft downstairs, who Neal had taken care of with efficiency. Neal was definitely someone he was interested in working with.

It was of Neal that van der Graan now spoke.

"Nice move by getting them onside. You certainly convinced me!" he grinned.

"I thought you took the role of objecting a bit too seriously. I really thought of ending your deal instead," was the chilling reply.

"Me? But we're in this together! Aren't we?"

Montalban's expression gave van der Graan decidedly mixed messages.

"Inigo?" was the concerned question.

For his part, Montalban merely clasped his hands behind his back. "Did you want to talk to me about something? I am a very busy man."

"Yes..." was the slow comment. "That Neal guy. I know him from somewhere. I can't think where."

Inigo inclined his head. "Perhaps your paths have crossed at one time or another?"

Van der Graan was unconvinced. "No. something... something recent."

Montalban looked at his partner in crime in a noncommittal manner.

"Unless you have something concrete to go on, then I cannot do anything about any nebulous situation you or may not be privy to. He came to the club three nights ago and beat me fair and square at a round of pool, and he and his charming lady friend were my guests earlier today. I find him agreeable... and useful company."

Montalban went to his desk, tidying his affairs, while van der Graan followed him.

"And you don't find it a coincidence a pilot would just show up out of the blue? I'm telling you, there's something wrong. I know him. As for that girl... I would not say no to her."

"I believe Mr. Neal would have something to say about that in the negative, judging by how he cleaned up Wilsoncroft tonight," was Montalban's offhand remark. "Unless there is anything else, may I suggest we retire downstairs and enjoy what remains of our evening. We have matters to attend to tomorrow."

***

The guns and equipment recovered from the scene of the crime had been analyzed and listed, just as Haltwhistle had ordered. He and Cartwright were in Sutton Donington's forensics laboratory, where the weapons were being checked for fingerprints and DNA.

One of the guns recovered had been a rifle, an AWL96A1, the weapon used to kill Fliplugs, but the light inside the allotment garage had been too low to get a proper visual inspection. Putting on a pair of latex gloves, Colin checked the weapon thoroughly.

The barrel was dirty, the smell of cordite in the muzzle was quite strong, proof that it had been recently fired and not cleaned.

Turning his attention to the chamber, Colin found it too was dirty and had a distinct smell of burned powder. Clearly whoever had fired it had not bothered to strip and clean the gun afterwards.

Removing the magazine, Colin found a full magazine of 7.62mm ammunition, but one round was missing, indicating it had fired one round.

While Cartwright watched, Haltwhistle tapped on the chief forensic examiner's door. The room was kept spotlessly clean and as sanitary as an operating room in a hospital.

"I'd like this rifle checked for prints and DNA next," he said, holding the gun out.

The offending weapon was bagged, tagged and taken to a laboratory.

"It may take some time to fully check this out," the examiner said apologetically.

Time. It all came back to time and how much of it was needed for this to be uncovered. Colin looked at his watch.

"How much time are we talking? A couple of days?" he pressed, getting impatient.

The examiner shook his head. "Oh no. Nothing that extreme. We should have an answer by the end of the day."

"Could you check over the other gear we found? And the car?"

"Give us a chance to breathe! Yes, we'll check it out."

They took their leave from the laboratory, the door closing in his wake. Colin looked at Cartwright, who was seated and nodded to the spot next to him. The Air Vice Marshal had a manner akin to a headmaster about to dress down a disobedient student.

Cartwright pulled a face. "Thank you for speaking for your commanding officer, Haltwhistle."

Colin turned pale. "I'm sorry sir. I just want to get this investigation done. I think I know who it is, but I just need the proof."

Black Jack, unimpressed, clasped his gloved hands together. "Fine. But next time you go over my head, I'll serve you yours on a gilded tray."

Colin became defensive. "You gave me the leeway to head this matter up sir. I don't see how-"

"When I arrived at the camp, yourself and McCleland continued as if you were in charge. Both of you should have come to me and requested if you were still leading the investigation, and you didn't. I would have thought assuming command of the station would have provided a big hint as to what you should have done but no, you both continued bulldozing your way through this."

"With all due respect, sir, why didn't you say anything?"

Black Jack scowled. "I didn't think I had to!" Colin didn't answer, and Cartwright continued.

"This whole thing has just been you and McCleland going in and leaving me to pick up the pieces of your bull in a china shop approach. Do you know how much trouble you have caused with that little stunt yesterday? Do you know how close you were to being thrown out of the service? You shot the place up, you risked lives and millions of pounds worth of equipment. You didn't wait for backup of any kind. Our policy is to protect lives, not risk them, that's my view on it."

Haltwhistle had to be very careful how he phrased this next statement.

"Well sir, when a dangerous and armed suspect is threatening my life and those of other personnel, and is a suspect in a crime, I take the prick out, that's my view on it." Colin looked grim and not about to give an inch. "You said yourself, we have to fight fire with fire sometimes."

The AVM simply folded his arms. He had come to the conclusion the white cap was as pigheaded as his partner.

"I don't think napalming the case is fighting fire with fire."

"Sir, he pulled a gun on me! He threatened people's lives!" Colin protested. "What did you want me to do? Point a water pistol at him?"

Cartwright let out a deep sigh, and Colin knew what that meant. The stark glare he was getting seemed to bore in to him.

"I would advise you to watch your tone, Haltwhistle. I am not debating this with you. I am telling you straight up. Even in AID we have rules to go by. We cannot endanger people ourselves, especially civilians and people in the service we swore to protect, no matter what our feelings are. Is that quite clear for you?"

Colin could feel himself getting angry. He controlled his ire enough to reply.

"Sir. With all due respect. We were responding to a threat situation. You were there. You saw what he did. I resolved the situation with equal force to what the assailant provided. Who knows what would have happened if we had not acted?" Colin was unswerving in his opinion and his actions, Cartwright had to give him that. And yes, he had to concede he had acted with equal force to the threat posed and neutralized it. Still...

"Well, just so you know. If it comes to light that any of the aircraft or equipment has been damaged because of your actions, it will be on you, Haltwhistle. And if you speak out of turn to me again, I will walk you out of the door personally. Clear?"

Haltwhistle looked more irritated than chastened. "I'll bear that in mind, sir."

"And next time you and McCleland decide to do your Starsky and Hutch act, can you just be a bit more subtle about it?" Black Jack hadn't finished and Haltwhistle knew not to interrupt.

"Generally, the villain will be tipped off you're on to him if you go speeding after him or cruising for a bruising."

Haltwhistle nodded. "Very good sir." He paused. "Jim called in, he reported he found gun wrapping and gun oil in Montalban's house. Do you think it's enough to enforce a search warrant?"

Cartwright shook his head. "On just that evidence? Fat chance. We'll have to hope something else comes up."

The two men sat in an awkward silence for some time, awaiting the results would hopefully come. After what seemed like a lifetime, Colin was twiddling his thumbs after exhausting things to look up on Google via his phone when he and Cartwright were called in to the laboratory.

Invited to put on static resistant smocks and footwear, they were brought to the work bench.

"Alright, we checked the rifle, compared to the round you found. It was fired from this gun," explained the examiner. "This is indeed the murder weapon."

"There's something else," Colin asked.

The examiner nodded. He pointed to the magazine and the breach of the rifle."

"You were right. The gun was not cleaned after it was used. Whoever fired it used gloves, so no fingerprints."

Colin looked visibly dejected. So close, yet so far.

"However," the examiner went on.

Haltwhistle eyed him. "However...? Don't keep me hanging. I'm not in the mood."

"There was a fingerprint on the stock. It matched the fingerprints on the other bullets in the magazine, and the other stuff you found in that haul you brought in."

The Flight Lieutenant looked into the microscope being offered to him where a copy of the fingerprint was being displayed. Yes, there it was.

Cartwright also took a look and stood up.

"I want you to run that fingerprint and compare it to the records of the entire personnel on this station. Get me a match," Black Jack said.

"That could also take some time, sir. We'll have to go through-" the examiner was interrupted by Colin, trying to hold his temper in check and failing dismally.

"Let it take time. Just find us the bloody answer."

He headed outside. He thought he knew what the answer was, but he wanted to see the man about something else.

"Where are you going?" Cartwright demanded.

"I want to talk to someone," was the cryptic response. Cartwright followed him outside, being once again dragged into something without his subordinate asking for permission first.

"What did I just say about the bull in the china shop?" he commented.

Colin stopped and realized his mistake. "I'm sorry sir."

"I suppose you may as well finish what you started." Black Jack was resigned. "But this heading off on a whim is going to stop. Do I make myself understood?"

Contrite, Haltwhistle took the dressing down with grace. "Yes sir."

They headed outside the building and headed over to the simple white house on the barracks where he had been previously.

Getting out of the car, he went up to the door. It was a Sunday, so no doubt everyone would be off duty today.

Knocking on the door, Colin waited. Finally Kevin Johnson answered the door.

"Sir! How can I help you this fine Sunday?" He noticed Cartwright behind Haltwhistle and noticed the Air Vice Marshal braids on his cuffs. "Hello sir, I haven't had the pleasure?"

"You're about to," was Black Jack's dark reply. Johnson's face fell.

"I need to talk to you. Can we come in?" It was more of an order than a request, and Short Fuse picked up on that.

"Er, sure of course. Come on in," he said, opening the door wide.

Colin let himself in to the living room and took a seat before being invited. Johnson stood close by, waiting for whatever the white cap had to say. Cartwright meanwhile stood in the doorway, watching.

"If I may, sir?" Colin asked to Cartwright.

A surprised look from the CO and a quiet, "By all means, Haltwhistle."

"Why didn't you tell me your wife used to go out with Tim Marinell? You must have known him to be with his ex," Haltwhistle looked at Johnson with an unimpressed expression. He wasn't in the mood for pleasantries.

"I did. I didn't want to cause trouble for Gemma. She's already been through a lot."

Colin steepled his fingers, and rubbed his hands together, considering how he would phrase his next statement.

"You lied to me Johnson. When I asked you if you knew Marinell, you said you'd only met him a couple of times but you must have met him more than if she left him. He is not the sort of person to take that quietly. I want to know right now, what's the full story?"

Johnson looked down at his fireplace. Finally he turned to face the two officers.

"You're right. He treated her bad. I sorted him out when we got together, and we never had anything to do with him since." Johnson looked angry. "She didn't want anything to do with him. I hope I can make her not be treated bad anymore."

"That's all very noble," Colin interjected. "It doesn't make misleading us right. I have a good mind to bust you for obstruction of justice."

He thought about what Marinell had said before. The key to the allotment. If it was here...

"Did Gemma have the key to the garage on Marinell's allotment?"

Johnson was thoughtful. "I don't think so."

"Is she in?" Cartwright asked, armed folded and lacking patience.

"Yeah, she's upstairs." He went to the stairs. "Gemma? Come down."

She appeared at the top of the stairs. Having heard the whole thing, she came down looking rather ashen.

"Young lady, I'm Air Vice Marshal Cartwright," said Black Jack. "This is very serious and I require an honest answer. Did you have a key to Marinell's allotment?"

She nodded. "Yes, but I gave it away."

Colin and Cartwright looked at each other.

"To who? When?" Colin demanded.

She was mumbling and looking like she didn't know where she was.

"It was ages ago. I can't remember his name. He said he had to give it back to Tim and knew I had it. We were together at the time," she explained.

"And you're absolutely positive you don't have the key?" Cartwright said.

Gemma nodded. "Positive, sir. When we were looking through the camp, I half expected to find it, but nothing."

"Either way, I'm going to have these quarters searched," Black Jack said firmly.

A thorough search by a team of NCO's did indeed turn up nothing. If they had found the key, Haltwhistle would have definitely brought both Johnson and Gemma up on charges, but he let it go.

"Until we say otherwise you are suspects in the murder or Fliplugs and the theft of the weapons. I'm confining you both to this house,"

Haltwhistle told them. "We'll have the house checked over again, just in case."

He was content they were innocent. Unless the fingerprint was his, then the shit would hit the fan.

"Let's get back to the office," Black Jack said softly.

Once Cartwright was seated in his office chair, his expression was unreadable.

"Is something wrong sir?" Colin asked.

"I'll tell you later," was the pacific answer. Cartwright folded his arms across his chest, giving the impression any further questions or conversation was unnecessary.

Picking up on this, Colin simply replied "Very good sir."

TWENTY-TWO

Sophie had left the house for the office at about 7:30. She was still feeling a bit out of it after the events of the previous night but she also knew deep down she was happy. Jim had come into her life less than two weeks before and had literally swept her off her feet.

Her parents had always warned her about rough edged guys, preferring her to date a lawyer or a banker, but she had always preferred a man with a bit of fire in his stomach, and Jim certainly had that. Colin was a different kettle of fish, he was more thoughtful and quieter. A bit more bookish, and Anna was lovely, with a wicked sense of humour. They had both made her feel welcome, but their lifestyle seemed rather dangerous and led them into adventure and trouble and equal measure.

Sophie liked that.

She put the iPod onto shuffle and it played some random 80s big hair songs. Dios, Guns'n'Roses (Jim hated them, to her amusement), AC/DC.

The little MG turned at the junction and headed onto the main road towards London. What Sophie hadn't noticed was the silver Mercedes two cars behind her which had been pacing her since she had left the house. Now it made it's presence known.

At the traffic light just before the M25 crossing, the silver car stopped next to her, then swerved in front of her car and three armed men got out, each holding what appeared to be machine guns. Gesturing for her to get out of the car, Sophie, terrified, did as they demanded. Colin had told her if anything like this happened, to do as whoever it was said. The chances of getting out alive would increase dramatically.

Ushered in to the back of the Mercedes, she watched out of the windows as the car shot off and on to the London orbital.

"Where are we going?" Sophie demanded.

The man in the front passenger seat turned around and pointed a gun at her. Hector Montalban.

"I would advise you to keep quiet, Miss Hawkesworth."

***

Jim awoke to find Sophie had gone to work, a quickly scribbled note with kisses and hearts she had written told him so. He had to get the money that Montalban had plied him with over to the base and have it bagged up. Getting dressed, he went downstairs and headed out of the front door. The wheelie bins positioned by the roadside told him he should take the trash out, which he did. He was about to head back up the driveway when a screech of tyres brought a big BMW 7 Series to a halt. Two masked men jumped out and grabbed McCleland. The first thug went down thanks to a good palm strike to the unfortunate man's jaw which felled him with a grunt of pain.

The other was a touch smarter and stood by, clubbing Jim over the head and into unconsciousness.

To any of the neighbors who may have been watching, Jim was shoved into the back of the car and it roared off.

When McCleland came around, he found van der Graan and Montalban leering at him. He was in a hangar, a well-lit one with the doors open and a smart looking red and white Beechcraft Super King Air twin prop aircraft sitting in front of him. Hector Montalban stood watching, puffing on a cigarette.

"I am glad to see you are awake, Mr. McCleland," said Montalban. Jim opened his mouth to reply, but Montalban waved his hand at him. "Please don't persist in insulting my intelligence by pretending to be Mr. Neal. I find it demeaning."

Montalban rose from his seat and circled around Jim, clearly enjoying the situation. Hector, as ever was by his side.

"I informed you I appreciate honesty and integrity. Two things you apparently do not have an ounce of. Hector here decided to do a thorough check on you after your dispatching of Wilsoncroft, and what he found made very interesting reading. The fact our contact managed to identify your Ford Mustang while you were pursuing him helped. When the same car was seen at the scene of the plane crash, the pieces fell in to place."

A couple of thugs were holding Jim up from behind, who he presumed to be the ones who had jumped him outside of Sophie's house.

Sophie. Was she alright?

Van der Graan was clearly aching to give Jim a work over.

"This piece of shit blew up $20 million of my dope! I told you I recognized him!" He looked down at their prisoner with disgust.

"That's funny, I'm looking at a $20 million dope right now," Jim shot back.

Van der Graan balled his hands into fists. Montalban looked at his colleague and made a motion for him to back off. He turned back to Jim.

"Of course, Mr. McCleland, by all means cast your aspersions and crude comments while you can enjoy them. As you can see, my colleague has an issue with you. I told him he is free to do whatever he wants to you once the task has been completed. But what we all is more important."

Montalban gestured to the Beechcraft. "At the appointed time this evening, you will fly this aircraft to Amsterdam. Once that has been done you will be taken to a place of... entertainment."

Jim, already thinking of ways to escape, continued cracking jokes. "Well, Amsterdam is full of strip joints so I'll be right at home!"

A swift punch to his sternum left Jim winded. He was hauled up straight again.

"I would advise you to not make cheap jokes, Mr. McCleland."

Jim looked at the two lugs. Neither presented a huge threat but van der Graan had a firearm on his person, so if he tried anything he'd be shot instantly.

"And if I tell you to take that plane and stick it up your arse sideways?"

Montalban looked over towards Metzler in the corner of the hangar and nodded. He disappeared behind a pile of plastic covered packing crates and reappeared with a bound and gagged Sophie at gunpoint. Jim started.

"You bastards...! If you've hurt her-"

"If you do not agree with my demands, your lady friend will die. The choice is yours, Mr. McCleland," Montalban informed him with a smug look on his face. He was holding Jim's revolver and merrily playing with it from hand to hand. If he killed her with his gun and made it look like Jim had done it which was easy to do...

"Yes, Squadron Leader James McCleland of the Airborne Intelligence Division, you are presented with an untenable problem. Save the woman you love and ferry high grade contraband weapons for which you will be jailed for the rest of your life, unless my colleague here disposes of you first, or see this young lady perish because of your stubborn refusal to co-operate and disregard for her safety. I would not wish to be in your position at this moment in time." Montalban was positively gleeful.

"If you've hurt her in any way Montalban... I'll kill you," Jim spat viciously.

The criminal looked absolutely satisfied and at peace with himself.

"You are in a position to threaten no one, Mr. McCleland. I however am in a position to demand anything I feel appropriate." was the blunt reply. "You will fly the aircraft or this young lady, who you involved in your mission because of your own hubris, may I remind you, will come to an unfortunate end. If you have anyone to blame, McCleland, it is yourself. Your arrogance brought about this entire situation."

Jim had to give Montalban that one. It had been a stupid idea to bring Soph into this, and even Cartwright had seen trouble coming.

"Do not feel too bad, though. I find it useful to have an insurance policy." The Spaniard turned and the head of the CAA, Fernest, was standing close by. It was obvious now what had happened. As the overseer of investigations, he had access to all of the information. It was lucky his friend had in fact, removed the evidence before it mysteriously disappeared and the case was swept under the carpet.

There was a grunt of pain and the other crash scene officer, Phil was hauled forward. Bloodied and bruised, he was thrown to the cold hangar floor.

"My friend was able to inform me of who had been sent from the military to check things over. And Phil was able to tell us some other details. It was a simple case of identifying you once Joest had seen you at the club. You even gave your business card to your good lady, and she in turn handed it over. In effect, you led us straight to you. A look at your apartment filled in the rest of the story."

"Oh, so you went down the George Orwell road of looking me up. Two plus two does not equal five, Winston," McCleland spat.

"As for her..." Fernest was pointing at Sophie. "She didn't suspect a thing. I got her and her partner to do all the legwork while I sat back and watched, and she never noticed the reports were doctored or that shit had been messed with." He chortled. "Stupid cow."

Inigo cocked the hammer of Jim's revolver and shot Phil dead, the gun blasts reverberating around the concrete space. Sophie visibly recoiled at the sight.

"Very poor show, McCleland. You've just killed a CAA official." Montalban looked from Jim to Sophie and back. "I am curious. What does she matter to you anyway? A man with your reputation for attracting women which you use either for pleasure or to further your mission's objectives should not care what happens to her."

If Jim could have got his hands on Montalban's neck, he would have throttled the life out of him where he stood. He also had Metzler and the redoubtable van der Graan to contend with. He would come up with a plan.

"I asked you a question. What is it about her that is so important?" Montalban pressed.

Jim looked at Sophie. "I love her," was the simple reply.

The gangster laughed harshly. "My heart is awash with joy for you both." The insincerity was palpable. Malevolence practically personified him at this moment. "I am awaiting your acceptance or rejection, Mr. McCleland."

The pilot sighed and rolled his eyes. "Alright, Montalban. I'll fly your fucking plane for you," he acquiesced. "But I want Sophie in the cockpit with me."

Montalban gazed at him with an almost awestruck respect. His deep brown eyes seemed amused.

"As I pointed out, you are not in a position to make threats or any sort of demand at all, Mr. McCleland." He looked at Sophie and back to Jim. "But as you seem to have strong feelings and care so much about this young lady, I will agree to your terms."

Your first mistake, you fucking bellend, thought Jim.

"I have foreseen every move you make, Mr. McCleland. So do not think that you can outwit me."

"Like you magnetized your pool table?" Jim allowed himself a cheeky smile. His foe may be smart but he wasn't infallible. He had to concede his carelessness had landed him in the situation that he was in now. "Even a broken clock is right twice a day!"

Montalban's smile disappeared for a moment, understanding how Jim had outsmarted him. Then he shook his head.

"*Touche,* Mr. McCleland. I will also be in the cockpit, just to make sure you do not try anything clever again. We will take off at 10 pm this evening."

He indicated to Metzler and the two goons to haul Jim and Sophie away.

A storeroom door was flung open and they were both thrown into the tiny, dank room full of cleaning utensils, bleach and assorted cleansing products. Jim took it all in with a glance and then untied Sophie. She grabbed him and hugged him tight.

"What happened to you?" he said stroking her hair and face.

Sophie began shouting. She was angry more than anything else. "I was on my way to work. I stopped at the traffic lights and a car pulled up all these men appeared and pointed guns at me!"

She stamped her foot in frustration. "Jim, what the hell is going on here? This is more than some work to find out what was going on in that club."

She looked at him with a fire in her eyes he hadn't seen before. She was furious, much more so than when she had confronted him in his apartment.

"I want to know what's going on, right now! What was all that about weapons that he was going on about?" she demanded, fuming. "I've had guns pointed at me, been tied up and thrown into a strange car! What's this about drugs that you blew up? Why does he want to kill you? What's this Air Intelligence Division?"

Jim opened his mouth but for the second time today was interrupted before he could get any words out.

"Don't fob me off, McCleland. Tell me! Phil said he did some asking and your team, agency, whatever it is, gets sent in to straighten the mess out?"

Presumably calling him by his surname was something that was going to become a thing when she was annoyed with him.

Assuming she stuck around after all of this. He wouldn't blame her for dropping him like a hot rock if they made it out of this mess alive.

"I suppose I should tell you now. Yeah. Colin and I were brought in about a year ago to this new department. We didn't know what we were getting into at the time."

He filled Sophie in on the plane crash, the fallout from it at the camp, Colin was working on things at that end. He left out the matter of Fliplugs being murdered, he reckoned she was upset enough as it was without mentioning that unpleasant little factoid. When he had finished, her eyes were as big as saucers.

"This is incredible! It sounds like one of your dumb action movies or something! So you work for the secret service? I knew it the second I saw you and Colin." Sophie found a crate to sit herself on.

"Not exactly. We deal with threats from the air rather than Jack Bauer stuff," he admitted.

"No wonder you wanted me out of the way that day," she managed a little joke amid the chaos.

"Yeah. Not the best way to get acquainted with the girl I love," was his glib reply.

She gave him the look to show she wasn't amused.

"I'm glad I did!" Jim assured her. "What about Fernest?"

Her eyes flashed. "I'm gonna kill him!" She took a breath. She was still trying to make sense of this insane day so far. "The weapons make sense now. We got the report back on the findings of the crash. There were traces of aged explosives. Tetryl. I knew the Cessna was carrying something unstable, no wonder it went down. When you mentioned the gun oil, I re-read the reports. There were traces of the same type of oil on board."

"Did your dickhead boss read it?"

She winked. "No. I sent off the findings before he could read and change anything. I got the feeling something wasn't right when he started working late in the office and didn't want anyone around."

He hugged her. "Nice one!"

Sophie looked at him. "Now. Why does that other bastard want to kill you? What did you do to him?"

McCleland took a deep breath and sat on a packing box. "Mine and Colin's first mission together, we went behind enemy lines to find a traitor and at one point we had to get some guns and equipment. What we didn't know was the man we were buying them from was in with a bunch of opium dealers." He let out a bitter laugh. "Shit got real and it went up in smoke. Part of the shipment must have been meant for him." He nodded towards the door and to van der Graan.

She looked incredulous. "You do get yourselves into some trouble, don't you?" She bit her lip and giggled at the mischievous idea in her head. "You should have asked Montalban for some guns!"

Jim guffawed. "That is so not right!"

That joke was worthy of him and his demented outlook. Either he was rubbing off on her or she had the same attitude but kept it well hidden.

Jim looked thoughtful. "If we get out of this, I'm going to marry you."

Sophie took a step back, shocked. "You want to marry me?"

Jim fixed her with a sincere look.

"Hey, a girl who sticks by you through this nonsense is a definite keeper," was the explanation.

Sophie looked faintly offended but quickly laughed. "Jim you are a character!" Then she understood he was serious. "That's possibly the least romantic proposal in the history of the world!"

Jim shrugged. "Well, I thought it was better than saying 'Hey baby, let's get hitched' ."

There was a good point made there, but at the moment there were more pressing matters to take care of.

"First things first. Can you get us out of here?" she asked seriously.

"I escaped from a Russian bunker in the middle of Afghanistan, I can get us out of Southend," Jim told her confidently.

"It'd be a first. Everyone in Southend has tried to get out of Southend!"

He looked at the door, then at the bleach and cleaners. In a corner sat a bottle of hydrogen peroxide among the other chemicals stored. couple of gas canisters were sat in the same corner. He considered smashing the lightbulb overhead and using the filaments to pick the lock.

"I read somewhere bleach and hydrogen peroxide explode if they come into contact," Sophie saw what Jim was looking at and understood.

He looked at her and broke into a ghoulish smile. *Yes I know*, he thought. "That's not what I was gonna do. I'm game if you are."

He went to the gas canisters and picked them up. One was empty but the other was full. Perfect.

"Are you sure this will work?" she asked him. "I don't fancy getting fried!"

Jim shook the gas canister, making sure of its contents, then looked at the bleach, which Sophie had pointed out. Her idea was sound, but it was 50/50 if the liquid would go up as she imagined.

He had had a mess around with chemicals during a science lesson in school. The results were a loud explosion, a lot of smoke and a two-day suspension from school, which he had thoroughly enjoyed, but those were potassium, sulfur and other ingredients.

Deciding on his course of action, he placed the gas canister, bottom up near the door.

"Yeah, I can get us out of here. Get down on the floor, wrap your face up and cover your ears," he told her. He omitted the 'That's an order' part in case she punched him, with the mood she was in.

"Can you, just for once, do something that's not stupidly dangerous?"

"Well, there was one time I had to do a gear-up landing because the hydraulics went. That was interesting!"

He ripped the protective nozzle from the gas canister and set the bottom up on a box. Realizing what her boyfriend was intending to do, the girl was horrified. This would not just blow the door off, it would do a lot more damage than that.

"I need something to make a spark," he said, looking around.

"Where did you learn all this stuff? Surely not basic training?" Sophie looked a touch worried.

Was he a secret anarchist on top of everything else?

"I just messed around a lot as a kid." The look his father had given him when the headmaster had told him what a young James had done with the chemicals to make them explode and smash the windows of the science lab was still in his mind. He decided not to admit he'd read *The Anarchist Cookbook.*

Sophie found a box of matches on a shelf close to hand, and gave them to him.

"Fire in the hole," he warned her.

He struck a couple of matches, placing them near the nozzle which was now emitting propane and they took cover behind a pile of cardboard boxes crammed into the back of the room.

The gas ignited and blasted the canister through the door with a thunderous roar which ripped the wooden construct clean off. On the other side of the door, the man who was guarding the two prisoners inside had been amused by their apparent adoration for each other and was wondering what they would do in there when his afternoon was interrupted by a tremendous eruption within the room behind him. That was the last thing he was aware of.

TWENTY-THREE

It took what seemed like an age to get the match, but the following morning, there it was. The forensic examiner knocked at the office door.

"Come in!" was Cartwright's brisk answer.

In he came with paperwork in hand, handed it to Colin and quickly departed. With details in hand, he showed it to Cartwright, who quickly scanned over it.

"What are your orders, sir?"

Cartwright gave him a deadly look. "Let's get him." He rose from the desk and took from the top right drawer his Colt 1911. Checking the magazine and the breech, he holstered it. "Call for backup. Just in case. Have we heard from Jim this morning?"

"No sir. He didn't answer the call," Haltwhistle admitted.

"No doubt he'll ring in his own good time," was the brisk comment as they strode across the camp's grounds. Heading over to the barracks, Haltwhistle drew his own weapon. He and Cartwright arrived at the door with their guns drawn, a pair of white cap SIB officers in their wake.

Giving the door a brisk rap with his gloved hand, Colin stepped back. The door opened and framing the doorway was the slight silhouetted form of a young man in his early 20s. He had a scar over his left eye.

"Hello sir, can I help you?" he greeted them, then he noticed the drawn weapons and knew. He started backing up and Colin went in the doorway, his trusty Sig P226 he wished he had thanked Jim for giving to him, in his hand.

"I trust we can come in?" he said. Cartwright, Woodley and the corporal's commanding officer hot on his heels.

"Erm... sure. What can I help you with?" was the plaintive question.

"What do you know about surplus weapons?" Colin looked around the cramped ground floor rooms, almost disinterestedly. Cartwright and Woodley eyes the young man with a mixture of disappointment and outright anger. Colin found the Focus's car keys in the kid's jacket.

"I would be very careful what you say because anything you do can and will be used in a court of law," Woodley spat.

The corporal blanched and became defensive. "What am I being accused of?"

Colin produced his handcuffs. "Corporal Andrew Jones. You are under arrest for the murder of Joseph Smith, the manslaughter of Christopher Woodley, theft of government property, illegal use of a motor vehicle and conspiracy to distribute contraband weapons without the correct paperwork or licenses."

Knowing the game was up, Jones bared his wrists and Haltwhistle applied the handcuffs. He was led out by Woodley and Cartwright and put in the back of one of the RAF Focuses. A team went into the rooms and began searching them for any more clues, which in short order produced the key to Marinell's allotment and a pair of mud-stained hiking boots, which were quickly bagged up.

Watching the car pull off from the barracks' outer door, Cartwright's pale blue eyes glinted in the sunlight.

"I want a signed full confession, and I want to know what else he knows," Black Jack ordered.

"Yes sir." Haltwhistle helped his boss into his Mondeo and then Woodley climbed into the back.

"I want to know how he got my son involved," was his comment from the rear seat.

Colin drove back over to the main administration building where his and McCleland's office was set up.

Flanking Jones as they went inside, Haltwhistle noticed how dark it was becoming outside. It had been a quick day.

Sitting the young man down opposite his desk, The Flight Lieutenant ushered Cartwright into the seat while he set up all of the evidence that had been collected. Woodley meanwhile took up position by the windows, his entire being shaking with fury.

Colin checked the hiking boot against the footprint. The thick treads matched perfectly. They had been cleaned somewhat but mud still stuck to parts of the heel and around the soles.

Cartwright did not wait to go in gently at all. "Why did you kill Joe Smith?"

Jones was quiet and looked down at the floor and the desk. Colin remembered reading something about finding a guilty person he had come across in a textbook he had read while studying psychology as part of his police training. If the suspect is on the edge, stressed and restless then that person will be the innocent party. The guilty person is going to be calm and collected, knowing the game has been played and he or she has lost.

And here was a young man who was acting quiet, calm and in control. His record stated a crack shot with a rifle and he had won several shooting competitions. He could have easily made the shot that killed Fliplugs. If he hadn't been so careless handling his weapon, he would have got away scot free.

"I thought he knew more about what was going on. He was going to blab on Marinell. That could have opened the door to..." Jones looked up at his three interrogators. "Well, it did anyway."

"It got opened when that plane went down the other week," Colin told him.

Jones went quiet again, considering that comeback. Before he could reply, Cartwright fired another question at him.

"Why Marinell's lockup? Why not someone else's?"

Jones smiled a little. "He was my sergeant. And a prick. He bullied people. When he finished with that girl I was hoping to make a move on her, but she went with that guy from bomb disposal. I knew he had a garden or something off base, and I learned she still had a key from talking to her, so I came up with a story to get it from her."

"Let me see if I have this straight. You framed a man of something he was innocent of?" Colin summed it up succinctly. Jones nodded. Marinell may be a thoroughly unpleasant person and guilty of his own crimes, but he was set up in this case, and with his reputation, it would have been easy to make mud stick.

"How did my son get involved with you?" Woodley demanded from the side of the room. Colin should be asking the questions, while Cartwright understood the man's anger, he still looked at him unwavering. The Group Captain backed off.

"I got talking to him. He was in debt. I offered him an out. When he told me he could fly..."

Jones' voice tailed off.

"You promised him the world if he'd fly something for someone, didn't you?" Colin asked.

"Hector Montalban?"

There was no answer. Haltwhistle kicked the chair under Jones' person.

"*Who?*" Woodley yelled at the top of his lungs. It caused Jones to jump out of his seat.

"You're right. Montalban. Hector and Inigo Montalban. And Chris Fernest."

Jim... And Sophie... Every swear word he could think of was now going through Colin's mind.

"How did you meet Montalban?" was the politest question he could muster.

Jones pressed his hands together and fidgeted with his fingers. "I knew him before I joined up. I never got involved with his businesses but we were friends. I thought I'd lost that Mustang, when I met him in the restaurant but clearly, I didn't."

Colin stepped from behind the desk to face the killer.

"Fernest… he wouldn't be an air crash investigator would he?" His mind was already going over the implications.

"Yes sir. For the CAA."

Shit! Haltwhistle thought. "How do the weapons come into it? What were you stockpiling them for?"

"I couldn't move them all at once, so I used the car to deliver them in dribs and drabs. When that Mustang was chasing me, I knew it was that McCleland guy because I'd seen him get out of it when he arrived at the base."

"That 'McCleland guy' as you put it, is a Squadron Leader, an accomplished pilot and a very brave man indeed," Cartwright informed him. "His life is now at serious risk because of your little criminal escapade."

Colin couldn't believe Black Jack was publicly defending Jim like this. But yet, here he was.

"Well, Squadron Leader McCleland then. Anyway, it doesn't matter. I met with Montalban's brother and handed the stuff to him then got the fuck out of there," said Jones in a fluster.

"'It doesn't matter'? My son is dead because of you!" shouted Woodley. Cartwright held his hand up to interrupt, then turned back to the pathetic form of Jones and sat back.

"What about the missing paperwork from the stores?" Colin demanded. "The goods out papers?"

"I got Fliplugs to show me around the stores one day and he pointed out where they were kept. I snuck in one evening when no one was looking and… you know…"

"Tried to cover your tracks by destroying it." Cartwright finished. He was disgusted. "I suppose you wiped the computers and the disc drives too."

Jones nodded slowly. "With the electromagnet. And… I didn't want to kill Fliplugs but he would have talked at some point."

Colin had to hand it to him. He had thought of everything. It was just as well he had been so messy in the execution of his little scheme otherwise Jones would have escaped.

"How did you get off the base when it was locked down?" Haltwhistle folded his arms. No stone being left unturned now.

"I rolled under the fence on the far side of the base. There's a bit of a gap there. There's a line of bushes and you just go through those and under the fence." The kid was slender enough to pull that off.

"How convenient. But I have one last question." Colin did not want to be fenced with. "It was you who rang my wife and frightened her, wasn't it? Don't try to deny it, your fingerprints were on the call jammer we found."

Jones looked up at him. "Yes sir. I just wanted to give myself a bit of breathing space."

"You're lucky you're breathing at all!" Woodley snapped.

It had been simmering for a while but now Colin was going in for the kill. He grabbed Jones, lifting him up from his seat and shoved him backward against the wall by the throat.

"My wife may need to see a psychiatrist because of that little stunt you pulled!" Haltwhistle exploded furiously. This time it was Cartwright and Woodley who pulled Colin back.

"Stand down, Haltwhistle!" Black Jack snapped.

The white cap released his hold on Jones and stepped away. The killer choked and spluttered; Haltwhistle had taken hold of his larynx. Satisfied his man was calmer, Black Jack regarded the corporal with contempt.

"Do you realize what you have done, young man?" Cartwright said quietly. "You have brought the service into disrepute. You risked good people's lives. You have had a direct hand in two people's deaths, one of them murder. You're involved in gun running, which is a capital offense. What have you got to say for yourself?"

Jones was contrite but he didn't have much to say for himself. "I don't know... Sorry."

Woodley was almost beside himself with incandescent fury and this time Colin had to drag him back from physically assaulting the young man.

"Calm down, sir!"

Woodley had turned a bright red color and he was shouting at the top of his lungs. "'Calm down'? This bastard killed my son and one of my men! Don't fucking tell me to calm down!"

"Woodley, you're dismissed," barked Cartwright angrily. He had had enough of explosive tempers.

Colin escorted him out of the room and once the door was closed sat the group captain down outside.

"This isn't over," Haltwhistle told him. "We need you to be objective. As the base commander, I'm asking you to stay calm. Please, sir."

"That's ironic, coming from someone who just lost it himself." Woodley was pacified but he was far from happy, understandably so. "Well, you got the man but this will not go down easily. As far as I know, no one has ever been murdered on a base before. This is a grave disgrace. And it's my fault."

"No sir. don't think that." Colin tried to placate him, but they both knew the regulations.

"As commander, I am responsible for the conduct and actions of my men," Woodley said sadly.

"I've failed in my duty as an officer." He looked at Haltwhistle. "I assure you Flight Lieutenant Glover was posted on because he wanted a fresh challenge. He's in Goose Bay."

"I know, sir. I checked his file." Despite his hotheaded temperament, Haltwhistle's shrewd mind was still searching for answers. "Wait here, we need to find out just one more thing."

He went back into the room. Cartwright was waiting for him while Jones sat quiet and morose in his chair.

"What are Montalban and Fernest planning to do with the weapons they have?" Colin asked, retaking his seat.

"They're gonna sell them on in Europe. Make some big money," was the simple explanation.

Don't we do that all the time? They're just cutting out the middleman. Colin mused. He kept the thought to himself. A bollocking was the last thing he wanted right now.

"To who? Come on Jones, don't make this harder for yourself than it already is." Cartwright said, leaning forward across the desk with an intent look in his eye.

"I don't know. All I know is that it's set for tonight. I was supposed to meet him tonight with a bigger shipment."

Tired of playing games, Haltwhistle rose. "Where?" he demanded.

Jones went quiet again. He looked down at the table. He truly believed he had planned everything out perfectly, and here he was, beaten by a better opponent.

"I would advise you to tell us before things get a lot worse for everyone." Black Jack was looking at the killer over the top of his spectacles.

Jones knew he had no more cards to play and would have to fold. His game was over.

"Southend Airport. 10 pm."

Cartwright and Colin looked at the clock on the wall and exchanged a look. Both were on their feet, sprinting out of the room at a dead run. It was at times like this that Colin wished he had Jim's Mustang to hand.

"Have all units converge on Southend Airport, now!" Black Jack shouted at Woodley as they rushed out of the room. The base commander glowered at Jones and indicated for the white cap waiting at the door to take care of him. He stalked off towards his office to make the calls.

Cartwright and Haltwhistle reached the waiting police car. Once behind the wheel, Colin briskly started the engine.

"We could take his Focus, sir. It'd be a real Trojan Horse for Montalban if you get my meaning."

Understanding what Haltwhistle had in mind, Black Jack dismissed the notion. "I like your thinking, but it'd also put us in Montalban's grubby paws. No, we move in as a unit."

Haltwhistle nodded and pulled off in a screech of blue rubber smoke.

The AVM shook his head. "Just like your dad."

"Sir?" Colin asked as he fed the wheel through his hands and skidded out of the base's main gate.

"I'll tell you another time. Let's get there."

TWENTY-FOUR

Before the smoke had cleared, Jim was already heading for the doorway. The remains of the door itself hung on the hinges and in pieces littering the floor.

"Let's go," he shouted, grabbing Sophie's hand. Looking down for a second, he skated sideways away from the remains of the guard. Despite herself, Sophie shuddered at the sight.

"Come on," Jim insisted, pulling her along behind him.

A startled goon who was recovering his senses after feeling the effects of the explosion was leveling a Beretta at them. Jim gave him a good swing on the jaw while Sophie kicked him in the crotch for good measure. McCleland scooped up his gun and ran on, with a deafened Metzler after them brandishing his own handgun and trying to take aim.

Jim pulled Sophie behind him into an alcove on the wall of the hangar and unloaded eleven rounds into the German, putting him down permanently. Sophie looked horrified at the sudden violence Jim was capable of. The remaining five rounds in the gun he used to dispatch one of the lugs who had been holding him down. Three down, but who knew how many more guys Montalban had?

The Beretta now out of ammunition, he threw it away. The goon's machine gun, which Jim saw was MoD issue was primed and fully loaded. Snatching it from beside the dead man, he and Sophie carried on. Rounding the pile of packing crates, six people who he recognized as people who worked at Montalban's club were running toward him and Sophie.

Jim opened fire, cutting them down before they could get off any shots towards them. The girl covered her ears, not quite wanting to see what was happening before her eyes. She winced and crouched down to make herself as small a target as possible as McCleland easily mowed down his opponents. He was justified in his actions. The six men flew backward as bullets riddled them.

Looking up, Sophie spotted a man with a sniper rifle. She pulled Jim's shoulder. In an instant, he saw the figure and noticed above him an air-conditioning vent. A blast of hot lead loosened the metal grating which fell on the unfortunate gunman, who was flattened by the heavy object with a sickening crunch of bones.

They ran along the inside wall of the hangar as several more hoods who Jim identified as some of the other gangster's men from the club appeared, all carrying pistols.

Wasting no time, McCleland picked them off with a furious hail of fire as they cut loose with their own weapons at him and Sophie. They fell where they had stood and he grabbed his girlfriend's hand, hustling her along.

"Are you sure you don't have a license to kill?" she asked.

"I won't say if you don't!"

The result of the devastation Jim was dishing out was littered in their wake. The machine gun clicked empty. He had been tempted to shoot the Beechcraft's engines out, but the aircraft may be fully fueled and was a risk not worth taking. He didn't fancy getting himself or Sophie immolated.

Searching one of the slain club workers, who he noticed was one of the lugs who had put him in the storeroom, Jim found two Glock 17s, doubtless more surplus. Not his choice of weapon, they were a bit too light for his liking, but they would do for the time being.

Jesus, these guys were seriously tooled up, he thought. A combat knife in a nylon scabbard would come in useful too. With Glocks held akimbo, one in each hand, another man appeared and Jim opened up with both pistols hammering his person with round after round which reduced him to the floor as well.

McCleland pulled Sophie outside through an unlocked door. From the surroundings, he reckoned they were at Southend Airport given the Vulcan bomber XL426's presence, whose nose was poking out of the hangar on the far side of the airfield. Its classic lines and threatening stance was something Jim had always loved. But now was not the time to admire such a beautiful relic.

There was no time to waste. With Sophie behind him, she was struggling to keep up. Her insistence on wearing high heels was costing her. Unzipping the ankle boots, she cast them aside.

Ahead of them, a guard holding a machine gun stood waiting but crucially had his back to them.

Holstering the pistols and keeping quiet, Jim drew the combat knife. With the vicious blade ready he advanced as quietly as he could on the guard. Sophie could not bear to watch and screwed her eyes shut, having no wish to witness the grisly outcome of his intentions.

Expertly, Jim clamped his hand over the guard's mouth and plunged the knife into the small of his back, twisting the blade as he did. The unfortunate guard gave a muffled gurgling sound and dropped to the concrete floor, his jacket stained with a pool of red.

Footsteps could be heard coming from the blind side of the hangar. Jim pressed himself against the wall as Sophie did the same. The barrel of a gun poked hopefully around the edge of the concrete.

Fernest.

Sophie lashed out, hitting her manager with all of her strength. The gun fell from his hands.

She kicked him in the back of the knee, causing him to collapse to the ground, yelping in pain.

"You wanker!" she shouted. All of her pent-up anger was now being directed at her boss, as she kicked repeatedly into his softer areas.

"Get off me, you bitch!" he snarled, trying to protect his more sensitive regions.

She kicked him again, uncoordinated but enough to have him in a position where Jim could finish the job.

McCleland's muscular arms were around his neck in an instant, and the weasly man was in a choke-hold. Sophie glowered at him, half enjoying seeing his plight, half repulsed with the skill with which her boyfriend could dispatch people. Fernest gasped for air, but Jim kept his mighty hold of him. In a few moments, the older man stopped struggling and slumped to the floor, his face blue-gray.

Jim grimaced and looked at Sophie.

"I hope you took care of your ex like that! Are you okay?"

She nodded. As they rounded the corner of the hangar, Montalban, Hector and van der Graan were waiting for them. Jim took aim with his Glocks.

"I will give you your due, Mr. McCleland. You are a tenacious man. But tenacity must be balanced with intelligence to prosper."

Three more of the gangster's people appeared and pointed their guns at the two escapees.

"Put down the guns. I believe your farcical show of defiance is at an end."

"I love how you talk in fucking riddles, Montalban," Jim sighed. "Can't you just say 'You're fucked' like everyone else?"

Montalban exchanged a look with his brother and shook his head. These British lacked the intellectual and linguistic finesse that the language they had created gave them. How sad.

"Very well, if you wish me to be as crass as you seem to appreciate, you're fucked Mr. McCleland, and so is Miss Hawkesworth there," the Latin criminal replied. "Now. Put down the guns."

Jim placed the pistols down and he and Sophie were once again frog-marched into the hangar where they were forced down into chairs and bound.

"So much for getting out of Southend!"

"Silence!" shouted van der Graan.

"This is a bit hard to take coming from someone who thinks *Top Gear* is something you jack up your arm!" Jim chuckled.

Inigo and Hector looked pityingly at their captives.

"Now you will be where I can keep a good eye on both of you," said Montalban. He stopped and looked at Jim. "I believe thanks are in order."

Jim was a bit confused. What could this prick possibly want to thank him for? "I can't wait to hear this."

"I am thankful, Mr. McCleland because you have removed an obstacle that was between myself and my ultimate goal."

"And what might that be? Are you trying to pop your cherry?"

Montalban smiled thinly. "You are quite idiotic, Mr. McCleland. It will be your downfall. You are merely a pawn to a corrupt government. If this was one of those action films you so enjoy, it would be at this point that I would outline my entire plan to you while you are at my mercy. But this is not a movie so I will let you draw your own conclusions. It does appear that we will do very well for ourselves, thanks to your actions. I believe your partner Mr. Haltwhistle would have resolved this long ago, if it was he who was in your place."

Montalban stood over McCleland.

"It is a great shame it is you and not he who is here. Haltwhistle would have presented a far greater challenge than you present. You played the game and lost, McCleland." Montalban knelt so they were face to face. "And soon you will die alongside this young woman."

Jim was putting the pieces together. The presence of the crime lords, along with what Montalban had just said added up to one thing.

"You and Mr. Nutjob over there are out to take over all the crime rackets in Europe."

Montalban clapped his hands condescendingly. "Congratulations. You see while your parents were killed in a car crash, mine gave me ambition and the ability to follow through on my ideas."

It was an attempt to get under his skin, he realized, and he'd be damned if Montalban's knowledge of him would unsettle things.

"Evidently, our friend here is an educated man," Jim said to Sophie. "We're in the presence of genius!"

She picked up on what he meant and managed a smile.

"I intend to keep a very good eyes on her," van der Graan leered at Sophie. He stood over Jim and glowered down at him. "And as for this... fucking piece of shit, I'm going to open him up. Slowly."

Jim half expected the crazed Dutchman to produce a carving knife and set to work, but Montalban raised a hand.

"Save it for a better time, once we're out of the country."

The disappointment on van der Graan's face was clearly evident. Their jocularity was interrupted by a pair of men who strode across the tarmac towards the hangar and for them.

The airport manager and the head of security, surely, Jim thought. Montalban went to greet them, the Ruger clasped behind his back.

"What the hell is going on here?" the manager demanded. "What was all of that gunfire? I have the police on –"

His protestations were cut off by a gunshot to the face and his associate was dealt with in the same way.

"I sincerely hope they are more efficient than you." The Latin looked at the Ruger and then at Jim. "This could prove useful."

He had the ideal way to set McCleland up for the murder of the man and get away Scot free.

Montalban merely smiled and went back to the glass cubicle-type office in the corner of the hangar.

Jim sat in silence, his face set in stone. He was seething at having his private business discussed openly when Montalban should not even know anything in that regard. Whatever lines of inquiry he had, they were good.

Next to him Sophie, looked at her boyfriend. "I'm sorry about your mum and dad," she said softly.

"It was a long time ago," was his bitter reply.

***

Colin gunned the Focus as fast as he could while his CO sat alongside, disgusted. They were traveling at far more than the speed limit while the sirens blared.

"The chief CAA examiner in with this scam?" Cartwright was mulling over what they had discovered.

"RAF surplus weapons and all the big criminals in Europe," Haltwhistle offered. "What the hell have we got ourselves in to here?"

"Something far worse if we hadn't found out!"

The police radio cracked in the police car as Colin and Cartwright made their way towards the Essex seaside town.

"Reports of shots fired at Southend Airport. SO19 armed response unit required immediately," the dispatcher called.

"Jim. It must be," Colin said.

Cartwright picked up the radio's microphone. "This is Air Vice Marshal Cartwright, Ministry of Defence. Do not, repeat do not move on Southend Airport without my instruction. This is a military priority. All calls should be routed to me on this channel. Out." He replaced the mike.

"We may not be in time to stop Montalban and help Jim, sir," Haltwhistle pointed out. "It may be a good move to have them go in."

"I don't want the boys in blue getting involved in this. Do you want to come up with a cover story? We'll be there in a few minutes," was his CO's reply.

Without taking his right hand off the wheel, Colin unscrewed the cap of his drink and took a large gulp of it, while Cartwright looked at him and shook his head. He picked up the radio mike again. "We need some specialist help," he said darkly.

TWENTY-FIVE

Darkness was falling in the April sky and a large wall clock read 8:45 pm. Montalban appeared holding McCleland's Ruger.

"It is time to start up. Fortunately, the aircraft is already loaded."

It's a good job I didn't blast the damn thing, Jim thought. He took a quick look at the cargo. The weapons and explosives were loaded in ice boxes. Montalban was trying to stabilize the mines by keeping them refrigerated. Risky, but it could work. If it didn't, then there would have been a very big hole where Southend Airport used to be.

"I'll need to go through pre-flight checks before we even turn on an engine," Jim told him.

"I believe you are stalling for time, Mr. McCleland. Speed is of the essence, or perhaps you are expecting your colleagues to appear at any moment. Perhaps Mr. Cartwright and Mr. Haltwhistle?"

But Jim was correct. "You clearly know absolutely sweet fuck all about flying." Despite being surrounded by the goons who wanted to damage him, McCleland was resolute. "First, I have to check the fuel for water, then I have to check the drainage holes are clear and make sure the control surfaces are working properly. Once that's done, then I might be able to start the engines, after I check the instruments of course."

Van der Graan was hopping from foot to foot. "Let me do something to him, Inigo, I'm sick to death of his mouth." He looked at the girl hungrily. "And then I'm going to do something to this little lady here."

Sophie recoiled as the Dutchman neared her.

"You even look at her funny and I'll take one of those guns over there and stick it up where the sun doesn't shine," Jim warned him.

Van der Graan punched Jim in the mouth. "You shut up, you fucker!"

"Leave him alone!" Sophie pleaded.

Jim spat a gob of blood out and checked his teeth. No, they were all still there. He glowered up at van der Graan, who pulled a large, evil-looking steel-bladed knife with a brown wooden handle from his jacket. He ran the blade dangerously up Jim's exposed wrists.

McCleland simply looked at his tormentor coldly. "Let's see you do that if I'm untied."

Van der Grann faced him. "You are not scared of me, are you? Perhaps I shouldn't harm you. Perhaps..."

He started turning the knife over in his hands and looked at Sophie.

Montalban had remained calm throughout this entire affair, and he was now. "Stand down, Joest. I'm going by the theory Mr. McCleland, as a trained pilot, needs the time to make sure the aircraft is safe." He looked at the Beechcraft. "Alright, you have the time for your checks. But try anything, and there will be... consequences."

Jim stood up and waved towards the Twin Air. He turned. "Sophie comes too," he said. "Or this plane does not leave the tarmac and then where will you be?"

"Interesting," Montalban observed. "An unrepentant womanizer has met someone who had turned his attitude.' He seemed to be both disgusted and impressed. "However, I agreed to her being in the cockpit. That is as far as my agreement to your demand goes, Mr. McCleland. Now. Go about your checks."

Throughout all of this, Hector had stood by, silent and watching. Jim was tempted to speculate he was the more dangerous one of the two brothers, given his propensity to take everything in rather than react.

"What time is he meant to get here?" Jim heard Hector say to his brother.

"Ten. Then, we will be gone."

"What about our delivery boy?"

Inigo gave his brother a dark stare. "He will have fulfilled his usefulness."

McCleland took his time to go through the external inspections. Usually, it took twenty to thirty minutes but he was still hoping that Col would somehow miraculously appear. There was no way he was going to let van der Graan get his filthy paws on Sophie, even if it cost him his life. He felt her watching him and she dared to move close to him.

"Couldn't you mess with the plane?" she whispered.

He'd considered and dismissed the idea. "If it goes tech, we'll be capped for sure."

"But couldn't you damage the flaps or something?"

He saw the merit of the idea, but Montalban would know instantly what they had done.

"I can't *MacGyver* it, babe. But I can pull a Murdock." He realized what he had said and in the process had lost all credibility of not being a geek, just like her.

Despite the situation, she gave him a big grin. "You won't live that one down, mister! You are a crazy fool though!"

He grinned and then caught sight of Montalban glowering at them.

McCleland looked at his girlfriend. "I'll come up with something. It'll have to be when we're in the air. Trust me."

Once he was satisfied there was no water in the fuel or lubricants, Jim went up into the cockpit while Sophie made herself comfortable in the co-pilot's seat. Sitting himself in the left-hand chair, he placed his feet on the pedals and checked the flaps and rudders, moving the control stick back and forth to check the movement. Everything felt normal.

Sophie watched him work with interest. Jim was thoroughly professional and knew exactly what he was doing. He also seemed to be the most relaxed doing this. Even more relaxed than when he was with his friends or with her.

And all that despite working with a gun to his head.

Montalban was also watching McCleland doing his routine, with an interest more in his behavior than what he was doing. Clearly, the Anglo-Spaniard was taking no chances in case Jim came up with yet another plan to escape and cause trouble.

"Are you satisfied everything is as it should be?" Montalban demanded impatiently, looking at his watch.

"I'm getting there," Jim replied, going over his route on a map strapped to his leg just above the knee."This takes time. You can't just get in and go like in a car, pal."

"I would advise you to make haste, Mr. McCleland. For both your sakes."

Jim looked up from his map. "I thought you were waiting for someone to turn up? If you're waiting, then what's the hurry?"

Montalban loomed over his reluctant pilot. "You will mind your place, Mr. McCleland! That is of no concern of yours!"

Jim, unphased replied "It is actually. if you overload the plane, the extra weight will mean we can't take off easily. So you might want to be careful how much you load the damn thing. You see where I'm coming from?"

But Montalban was equally unflustered by Jim's observation. "If you had put as much effort into your subterfuge as you do your aviation, you would not be sitting here, at my mercy. I would thank you to bear that in mind."

Montalban stepped out of the aircraft.

"Fucking twat," Jim said.

Montalban was waiting for Jones to appear, but repeated checking of his watch and attempts to contact him bore no result.

"Something's wrong. He's bottled out on us!" Hector spat.

"It is of no consequence. We have more than enough on board and in Madrid to support our cause."

They boarded the Beechcraft and strapped in. Montalban, leaning into the cockpit and holding Jim's revolver to make sure he remained cooperative, made his presence known.

"It is time, Mr. McCleland. Get us airborne."

Jim was satisfied all was well and in the right spot on the map. He reached for the engine startup controls. He briefly winked at Sophie. Nothing untoward was going to happen.

Yet.

He started the port engine first and once the Pratt and Whitney was spun up and humming, Jim started the starboard engine.

Checking the revs on each dial, the Beechcraft taxied out of the hangar and into the evening air.

Then something to his right caught his eye. Flashing blue lights which were getting closer and the faint wail of sirens could be heard even over the roar of the engines.

Overhead, the outline of an Augusta Merlin helicopter appeared from over the hangar roofs to the left.

Montalban, peering out of the cockpit windows saw the trap had been sprung.

"Take off! Take off!" he yelled, pointing the Ruger at Jim and Sophie.

Jim opened the throttles a little and taxied onto the runway. Through his headset, he could hear the air traffic controller frantically telling him they did not have permission to move or take off.

Montalban simply smashed the radio with the butt of the big revolver.

"Do it, or I shoot you both!"

"And if you do, who is going to fly the plane, dumbshit?" Jim shot back. Not for the first time, Sophie couldn't believe how brash Jim was acting in the face of certain death and didn't seem to care about it. She was reminded of something she had heard her dad say:

"Only when you're close to death do you really feel alive."

Well, Jim apparently felt lively.

Montalban cocked the gun and pointed it at Sophie's head.

"Do it now!"

Jim opened the throttles and waited for the feel and the ground speed to match before he rotated, pulling back on the control column. The Beechcraft clawed its way into the sky and withdrew its undercarriage as the aircraft gained altitude, he went over his instruments and adjusted the flaps.

Satisfied with his readings, Jim turned towards the coast.

"Now I'm gonna need to know where we're going, Winston," Jim said.

"Our friends are waiting at the airfield at Stadtlohn-Vreden. A nice, quiet place near the border of Holland and Germany," said Montalban.

"That's nice. From the ugly club around here, sounds like you've got a whole load of psychos to meet up with and go on a crime spree," Jim replied. "Using the weapons that were nicked from Sutton Donington. And Woodley was carrying some of that stuff when his plane went down, and now you want me to deliver the goods. I assume that Soph and me will be fed to sharks or piranha fish or some shit after that."

"Your imagination is really a work of art. No, your fates will be much simpler." Montalban paused and smiled almost with pity. "Perhaps you are not as stupid as you look, McCleland."

Van der Grann glowered at Jim while Montalban merely looked on at at his prisoners.

"I find it to be better than looking less stupid than you are," McCleland winked.

The Merlin, Jim noticed was keeping a discreet distance but following them. If they made it out to sea, a lot of legal wrangling would inevitably ensue. He had to get this aeroplane down again as quickly as possible.

He could turn the Beechcraft and pretend the flaps had failed, but violent maneuvering could make whatever was on board have the same result as what happened to Woodley, and that was not an option.

The lights of towns on the coast could be seen below and beyond them the inky black expanse of the English Channel beckoned.

Thinking over a course of action, Jim considered dumping the fuel. The idea of ditching in the channel itself occurred but the landing would more than likely cause the aircraft to explode.

Then one of those wonderful coincidences that only someone with the luck of the Irish seems to have occurred. The Beechcraft was touched by an air pocket. It bounced in the turbulent atmosphere. For a moment, he thought it would set off the explosives, but they remained intact.

McCleland took advantage of it, and put the aircraft in a steep dive to starboard. He pulled the control column hard over and the aeroplane plunged toward the ground. Applying some rudder control and opening the throttles, Jim rolled out and then swung the yoke the other way to the left. The ground was spiraling towards them but he had complete control. The Beechcraft bucked and rolled and Montalban was knocked off balance for an instant.

That instant was enough.

McCleland elbowed him viciously in the ribs and the criminal dropped the Ruger. Before Hector or van der Graan could react, Sophie sprang and picked it up. She had never held a firearm before and despite her misgivings about such things, she was making the best of it, pointing it at them to ward them off.

Montalban roared and struck downward, catching McCleland in the ribs. Winded, Jim recoiled as the aircraft bucked to one side as the control column was jarred. One more violent movement could be the end of the whole thing.

The stocky Latino punched his opponent repeatedly, bringing blood to Jim's lips, but the AID agent slugged his attacker in the solar plexus. Montalban groaned as McCleland grabbed the yoke and pulled it the opposite way. The sudden movement threw the Spaniard back and Jim kicked out with the side of his foot.

The level flight indicator pulled back to normal as Jim had Montalban on his knees and was now smashing his face repeatedly into the cockpit's dashboard. The instrument panel squeaked and cracked under the relentless pummeling and several of the dials' glass covers and LCD readouts broke apart as the man's head was forcibly introduced to the unyielding plastic.

Hector Montalban, with his own weapon drawn was at the cockpit door, but Sophie still had McCleland's revolver trained on him. Her petite hands and fingers barely reached the trigger.

One brother pulled the other back, Inigo's face a bloody mess and nose broken.

"You...!" Hector was aiming his pistol at the back of Jim's head but Sophie, despite her hand shaking squeezed the trigger of the .357 which barked a furious rasp. The loud crack filled the cabin and when she opened her eyes, the evil sibling was lying dead on the cabin floor, a large bloody wound in his chest.

The three remaining members of Montalban's team and van der Graan were clustered around but Sophie had five rounds left.

"Back off!" she warned, her voice trembling. She kept the gun trained on them as Jim turned the Beechcraft back towards Southend Airport.

"Good girl," Jim told her gently. But Sophie didn't feel good at all.

She could not believe what she had done. She had killed someone. Yes, it was in self-defense, but it was still a horrific thing to do. Sophie was in shock and Jim put his free hand on her knee and squeezed her gently, seeing how shattered she was.

"It's ok," he nodded back toward their remaining passengers. "Keep an eye on them."

Despite herself, and although she didn't need to, Sophie cocked the revolver's hammer and kept it trained on the remaining criminals. Without the radio, and with most of his instruments broken, Jim had to land the aircraft by visual navigation only, and at night that was an extremely difficult proposition.

With the Merlin still watching from close behind, Jim extended the wheels and throttled back, adjusting the flaps and using the airfield's runway lights as a guide. He felt the wheels touch the tarmac harder than he would have liked and lowered the nose. Once he was sure they were down, he throttled back and taxied as far away from the rest of the airfield as he could and shut down the engines. The aircraft was still full of fuel and with a load of highly unstable munitions aboard, it was a potent cocktail of destruction in the offing.

Jim ripped off the headset and grabbed the Ruger from Sophie's unsteady fingers. The remaining goons were warily looking at McCleland and considering their options while the pilot and would be co-pilot advanced on them, the gun still ready for any action.

Van der Graan broke the stalemate. "You... vile, slimy son of a bitch!"

"My mum wouldn't like that, shithead," Jim told him, smashing his free fist into the Dutchman's mouth and sent him reeling. McCleland kicked van der Graan hard in the face. He tumbled backward into a seat and onto the floor.

"Fucking prick." Jim was hoping for more action than that, but van der Graan was like all bullies: a coward when confronted. He was out for the count and not offering any sort of comeback.

Just in case any of the others tried something brave, McCleland pointed the gun at them.

"Get the fuck back! Now!" he barked.

He stepped over Montalban's unconscious form and avoided his brother's body as he made his way to the back of the aircraft where the loading door was. One of them was heading for it, but the other seemed to want to fancy his chances.

"Don't even think about it, unless you want to sound like Sam Smith. I'll blow your bollocks off," Jim warned him, the Ruger's business end pointed at his groin.

"You're packing a sniper rifle?" Sophie asked with a grin.

He wisely backed off and went down the steps as Colin arrived on the scene with several squad cars. The first man was immediately manhandled to the ground and roughly searched by the white caps on hand.

"Jim! Are you alright?" Haltwhistle shouted.

"Col, get these people back! Get everyone back!" Jim waved his friend away. "Get Sophie away from here!"

Colin helped Sophie down the steps and put her in the car. Jim was intending to follow them but from behind him, Montalban stirred.

His face felt sticky. He was laying in the cockpit doorway and the engines were not running.

They must be back on the ground. He pulled himself up. Behind him, Hector lay dead and Sophie was leaving the aircraft with McCleland right behind her.

McCleland.

All pretenses of being a civilized man were gone. He intended to get the man who had foiled his plans and kill him. And Sophie.

Montalban got himself to his feet and steadied himself. He had been defeated. Not just that, but he had been cheated not just once, but twice.

"*McCleland!*" he uttered in a primal scream of Jim's name. Despite being almost blind, he viciously swung out at Jim, who blocked the incoming blows in the tight confines of the cabin.

But Montalban was frenzied and continued his attack on the man who had foiled his plans.

The crazed criminal pummeled Jim, punching him in the stomach and ribs repeatedly, his big meaty fists forcing the air from Jim's lungs. For his part, his opponent rallied and punched his attacker in the face and floating ribs with a couple of well-placed jabs to each.

"I'm going to kill you!" Inigo roared, continuing to attack his target.

Jim had to admit, Montalban was quite a fighter. They traded heavy blows before Jim front kicked him away fiercely, sending the Anglo-Spaniard tumbling into the cockpit and against the throttle controls, which jammed and caused the Beechcraft to buck violently under the sudden movement.

Something did not feel right. The weight had shifted in the luggage compartment. Knowing what had happened, Jim scrambled for the doorway, aiming to barrel down the steps.

"Oh fuck!" He exclaimed as he reached the door.

Just as Colin had ordered, the squad cars had retreated to a safe distance.

"What's going on? Is McCleland out of there?" came Cartwright's voice over the squad car's radio.

With no immediate answer, he barked "Will someone tell me what the hell is going on?"

Cartwright's demand for information was drowned out by the enormous explosion of the dingbat mines had indeed been onboard and deemed time degraded while in storage. The Beechcraft was completely engulfed by explosive fire. The handsome aircraft was utterly destroyed by the blast and the fireball consumed everything and everyone which had been on board. The night sky was lit up brightly by the immense conflagration of explosives and aviation fuel mixing uncontrollably. The sound of the blast was deafening, terrifying. The heat from the eruption carried across the airfield.

Shocked, Colin watched as the column of flame climbed into the sky. A single word escaped his lips.

"Jim..."

In the rear seat, Sophie sat transfixed. Unable to speak, she saw the billowing cloud as well. The last thing she remembered was Jim hustling her down the steps, then someone shouted his name and he had gone back. If he had gone back to take care of something. If...

The thought was too much to bear. She felt herself breaking down. The idea of him gone was unbearable. Jim was so full of life, so energetic, so fun...

Sophie wept uncontrollably.

The fire engines and emergency crews went into action, the wail of their sirens cut through the night air as sharply as the explosion had.

"Get us over there, now!" Colin ordered. The patrol car set off again, with Cartwright's car just behind. Arriving at the scene, Colin leaped out, sprinting towards the blaze but was stopped by the fire chief.

"No! No further. Too much risk of another explosion!"

Haltwhistle was livid, desperately clawing toward the flaming debris.

"My friend is in there!" he shouted, trying to scramble towards the inferno while he was held back by two burly firemen.

The fire chief looked sad. "There's no way he would survive that. If he was in there, he's gone."

Colin stopped and looked at the chief, disbelieving. Behind him Sophie, her cheeks wet and streaked pulled Haltwhistle close to her. Cartwright's formidable form appeared, looking ashen.

"Is there any chance he could have made it out?" Black Jack asked.

Colin's stony silence and the fire chief's slow shake of his head gave him all the confirmation he needed. Sophie told him of what Jim had done immediately after he had got her away from the plane. She felt numb.

If only he hadn't gone back...

"He clearly thought a lot of you to put your life so far above his, Miss Hawkesworth," Black Jack said gently.

"He'd say that was part of the job when we joined up," Colin pointed out, broken.

"He loved me," she whispered. She was overcome and sobbed into Colin's jacket as he looked on at the blazing wreckage, himself blinking back tears.

Cartwright, his face drawn and grim, put his hand on Colin's shoulder and led them both away.

The task of writing *that* letter did not hold great appeal to him.

But it seemed there was nothing else to be done.

TWENTY-SIX

In a ditch one hundred yards away, Jim, soot-blackened and bleeding from a cut on his forehead stirred.

The last thing he remembered was sprinting away from the Beechcraft and diving into the ditch as the aeroplane exploded. His head and ribs ached and he felt dizzy. The explosion was still ringing in his ears. The last time he had felt this deaf, he had seen Motorhead live in concert and made the mistake of standing near the stage.

McCleland dragged himself up. He could see the blazing aircraft ahead of him and the dark figures of Sophie, Colin and Cartwright watching the fire being brought under control. Getting to his feet, he stumbled forward, half deafened by the blast and groggy. He could hear them talking about him as if he was dead. Colin was hugging Sophie.

Jim came up behind them, almost falling over. His bedraggled form must have looked pretty disastrous for anyone else watching. He pulled his jacket down and tried to straighten his hair in an attempt to make himself look presentable, considering his commanding officer was here.

They had not heard or seen his approach and still had their backs to him. They were starting to turn away. Looking at the destroyed plane, his sense of humor shone through.

"That party went with a bang!"

Sophie slowly turned at the familiar voice, as did Haltwhistle and Cartwright. Colin was shocked to say the least, partly at the fact his friend was still alive but mostly at his battered appearance.

He had really been through the wringer today.

But Sophie was suddenly angry.

Furious.

She saw Jim. Her eyes widened in joy and shock and she slapped him across the face, hard.

"You fucking bastard! How dare you not be dead!" she shouted. She slapped patter cake style around her boyfriend's face and head, crying and finally collapsed against him. Jim held her tight.

"Nice to see you're alright too, baby," he mumbled. He looked at her and wiped her face.

"Bloody hell, it's ugly," Colin teased, relieved to see his friend.

With a bit of the usual machismo, the reply was succinct. "Fuck off, you cheeky bastard."

Despite his CO being present, he kissed her with relief. Jim looked at her, then at the burning remains of the Beechcraft.

"I can think of one good thing for you." He looked at her with a mischievous smile.

"What's that?" Sophie asked, a bit puzzled.

His lips twisted into a pouting smile. "You've got a hell of an air crash to investigate!"

"You're a tosser!" she scalded.

"You're not quite turned out to my liking, McCleland," Cartwright observed, looking at his tattered garments and smudged, bloody countenance. After all this, the old man was worried about how well pressed his clothes were?

Jim nodded and forced some decorum. "Yes sir. Sorry sir."

Black Jack smiled a little. "We'll skip the court martial this time. Good work. Was there anyone on board?"

"Montalban, his brother and van der Graan, sir." Jim and Sophie looked at the blazing aircraft which the fire crews were still trying to bring under control.

"There's a bunch of nutters at an airfield at Stadtlohn-Vreden, sir. They're waiting for me to land, the boys at Interpol or GSG9 could pick them up, but they'll need to be packing serious heat," McCleland warned.

"I'll send the order," Cartwright assured him.

"Jesus Christ, man, what the hell did you do here?" Colin gasped, surveying the devastation.

Beyond the flaming remains of the Beechcraft, there was the unfortunate carnage in the hangar.

Jim wiped his face on his sleeve. The soot and blood smeared on his shirt into an unsightly mess.

He looked at his friend. "I told you, there's no such thing as a no-win situation."

"I told you not to turn this into the Gunfight at the OK Corral!" Cartwright chided good naturedly. He knew that, given the circumstances, the use of deadly force had been necessary.

"Indeed, sir," McCleland said. "The strain was more than they could bear."

Despite herself, Sophie bit her lip to keep from smiling.

"It's funny. Our friend was killed by the thing he wanted the most. Kind of ironic," said Colin.

"Well, if I was going to borrow a line from our former friend Montalban, he existed outside of the social contract. If you go there, don't be surprised when someone follows you there and forces you to fulfill that contract," Jim replied, stroking Sophie's arm.

Cartwright looked at his agent with a surprised look on his face. "Jesus, that almost sounded philosophical!" At the same time, he was wondering how the hell he was going to explain all of this or cover it up.

Irwin, ever-present throughout the investigation took charge of the scene, knowing all evidence was vital now he knew the full story of what had happened.

The emergency crews were bringing the blaze under control as the four of them made their way over to the hangar which housed the

Vulcan. It was the safest place on the airfield. Under the shadow of the huge bomber, they were joined by the helicopter pilot of the recently landed Augusta Merlin. Colin and Jim both reacted in surprise as they immediately recognized him.

"Mel! What the hell are you doing here?" Haltwhistle grinned broadly.

"Do you think I was going to be left out of this little get-together?" Mel Waters laughed.

Looking at McCleland's disheveled state, he commented "Jesus Jim, you've been in the wars, haven't you?"

He looked around the airfield which was now swarming with emergency services. "Looking at this lot you caused a war as well!"

Noticing the still oozing gash on Jim's forehead, Cartwright nodded to Jim. "Are you sure you're alright?"

McCleland wiped his forehead again. The bleeding had eased but he still came back with a fair bit of blood on his fingertips. "Yeah. I'm fine. I'm more concerned about this lovely lady."

Sophie stood quietly by Jim, coming to terms with the day's events. "I'm alright," she said softly. She managed a smile, but she was obviously troubled.

"With your permission sir, I'd like to take her home and get her settled," he said.

"Don't you think you should get patched up first?" Colin joked.

"Nah." Jim looked at his girlfriend and wiped her face. "You're more important."

Colin, Mel and Cartwright looked at each other. Jim? Watching out for a lady? Sophie looked at him.

He looked like hell, but he had come through it all and stopped Montalban's evil scheme. Most importantly from her point of view, they were both still alive.

"I'm very sorry you've been caught up in this, Miss Hawkesworth," Cartwright said. "I assure you, I will handle this officer myself. He put you at grave and unnecessary risk."

She looked at the middle-aged, somewhat fearsome-looking man with his shock of steel gray hair.

"You will do nothing of the sort, Mr… Cartwright. I agreed to go with him no matter what happened." Then Sophie regarded Jim. "The answer is yes," she said at the confused looks from Jim's colleagues.

"Yes to what, sweetie?" Jim looked confused.

Sophie quirked an eyebrow. "You must have had a sharp crack on the head!" She snuggled up to him. "Yes. I will marry you."

Colin and Cartwright looked shocked. If Haltwhistle's jaw had been an inch lower it would have hit the hangar floor.

"With your permission sir?" Jim stopped and turned to his boss.

Cartwright nodded. "By all means."

They looked on as Jim led Sophie away. He and Colin watched as McCleland clasped his hand around his fiancé's as they disappeared.

"Well, there's a turn-up for the books!" quipped Mel, watching them go.

EPILOGUE

A few days later, Anna and Sophie joined Jim, Colin, Cartwright and Waters for a drink to formally close the case in the Sutton Donington Officers' Mess. McCleland, plaster on his forehead and reddish-purple bruise forming on his left cheek had been cleaned up and a nice gold ring sat on Sophie's left ring finger.

The ribbon of the Queen's Commendation for Bravery in the Air was sewn onto the left breast of Jim's jacket, beneath his wings. The award was not just for his recent actions, but for his entire RAF service thus far. His piloting prowess was renowned, but it had taken some convincing from Cartwright to accept it.

"I'd much rather have a pay rise, sir," McCleland had complained.

"Just take it with good grace, Jim," Black Jack had replied.

"Jones will be away for a very long time. As for Marinell, his career is over as well," Cartwright said, setting his dark ale down. "And with those mobsters in custody, we can certainly say this operation was a success. Your... impromptu flight will be explained away, Jim. I suggest that it doesn't make it into your log book."

"Yes sir."

Sophie raised an eyebrow. "Isn't that an offense?" she asked.

"In cases like these, it's best not to reveal the full facts," was Cartwright's cryptic reply. "There will be no CAA investigation either.

It wouldn't do to find out the chief examiner was a gangster and running guns."

"What about Woodley, sir? Will he remain in charge?" Haltwhistle asked. It had not escaped everyone's notice he was wearing Squadron Leader's braid on the cuffs of his blues, a well- earned promotion being his reward for solving the mystery.

Black Jack pursed his lips. He had had a big hand in the matter and based on his recommendations, action had been taken.

"No, he was relieved of command by the man at the top. The base will be thoroughly investigated and reviewed."

Jim curled his lip. He had visions of having to plow through years of questionable decisions and dodgy dealings. Apparently, his expression gave away what he was thinking.

Cartwright gave him the good news.

"Don't worry, McCleland. That is something I argued was not an AID priority. You can be safe in the knowledge, you won't have to go trawling through years of records."

"Thank fuck for that!" There was an audible sigh of relief.

"That place is a den of iniquity. My dad would have had a fit to see an RAF station like that.

Hopefully, Irwin'll do a good job," Colin said. "He has a good head on his shoulders. I still say it's funny how his predecessor was shuttled out. It makes you wonder what else was going on behind the scenes."

"A lot of fingers in a lot of pies, I think," Jim told him. "Poor Fliplugs. At least we got who did it." He held up his glass to toast a fallen comrade.

"You made a pretty good fact finder," Colin grinned nodding towards his partner.

Jim shook his head. "I've got to say it was interesting, doing the Hercule Poirot stuff. But it's not my thing."

"Let me guess. Dropping a bomb is?" Haltwhistle needled him gently.

McCleland looked at Sophie. "No. That's too easy. Caring for someone is harder but it's so worth it."

She smiled, knowing what he meant. A warm feeling filled her heart.

Anna took a sip of her lemon and lime. "So, more grounded and now with a good lady at your side. I'm impressed, Jim. It's long past time you settled down."

Waters pretended to faint. "Good God. Martin James McCleland is in love. Wonders will never cease!"

Sophie leaned close to him. "Martin McCleland? Your name is actually Martin?"

"Tell anyone, I'll shoot you. I prefer Jim." He immediately felt guilty and touched her hand, but Sophie laughed it off.

"It's alright. Martin's a nice name too." She smiled. "Can I call you that?"

Jim's eyes narrowed. "My mum used it to get my attention. I'd... rather you didn't."

"Then I will when I want you to listen to me!" she teased. At his pained expression, she touched his elbow. "Just kidding."

Colin finished his glass of lager. "One thing we never cleared up was what caused that mine to explode? On the Cessna I mean."

Sophie brightened. "Yes. The explosive had aged to where it was unstable. A good knock or an electrical spark would be enough to set it off."

"It had sat in storage for years, which'd explain how it aged," Jim offered.

"And there was a thunderstorm that night," Sophie finished. "With all the lightning and the thing thrown about, it was inevitable."

"A tragic accident," Cartwright observed. "I wouldn't like to think about what would have happened if it had gone off on base!"

"I'll say," Waters commented. "Well, I'm glad I was able to help you all out again." Then he looked at Jim. "I was under orders to shoot you down if you had crossed the coast."

Sophie looked alarmed. If that had indeed been the case, it had been rather too much of a close call.

"I'm rather glad you didn't get the chance," McCleland grinned. He turned to his fiancé. "Are you sure you want to do this, considering this lot who I work with and everything?"

She put her face in his. "Yes!"

Cartwright smiled. He was glad to see Jim growing up at last. "Good luck to you both. And you'll be pleased to know..." Black Jack pulled a V5 registration document from his inside pocket. "The Trans Am is yours as well. Alf says it's a bit too much of a handful for him, so, you can have it."

Jim grinned broadly while Sophie put her head in her hands. "Oh, God! That thing is a pimpmobile!" she groaned.

At that piece of news, Jim pulled the Mustang's keys from his pocket and handed them to his partner.

"She's all yours."

Colin took the keys. "But... you love the Mustang!"

"Hey, it's about time you had a decent set of wheels," Jim told him. "It beats that shitbox Mondeo of yours."

Anna took another sip of her lemon and lime. "What about those gangsters?"

"He took care of them as only he can!" Sophie told her, pointing a thumb at her man. Anna merely made an Ohhh expression and the two ladies clinked their glasses.

"I dunno. You gave as good as you got. You saved my life as well," Jim told her. She smiled and rubbed his elbow, but the experience of taking a life still weighed heavily on Sophie and it would take a while for the unease to subside. Jim stroked her fingers in return.

He produced a bottle of Mountain Dew and handed it to his friend. "Here. You look like you need it."

Surprisingly, Haltwhistle threw it in a bin. "I think I've had my share." And he wasn't just referring to the drink.

"Just between you and me, mate... You really need to learn to fight!" McCleland teased.

"I think you need to take the self-defense course again, Haltwhistle," Cartwright agreed, eyeing the bruises on him.

"Alright! I'll come to the bloody Kung Fu club!" he said, much to Jim's amusement.

"I'd be up for that too," Sophie agreed.

"I was gonna invite you along anyway," McCleland said, squeezing her hand.

"I'll still want a written report of everything that happened in the club and on that plane, McCleland," Cartwright told him. "And not your usual half-arsed two-sentence effort. A full report."

He inclined his head toward his CO. "Yes sir."

Cartwright produced another letter, a handwritten note on a crumpled piece of paper. "I also got this, which may interest you." He put his glasses on. "'Dear sir, I am writing to complain about the conduct of one the officers at your air base. On the night of the 18th April, a Ford Mustang was driven dangerously quickly blah blah blah.' It goes on to say. 'The officer was rude to me and told me to Get lost Grandad. I do not feel this is appropriate behavior for a member of the Royal Air Force. I believe him to be a pervert, as he was using binoculars spy on people's business, etcetera, etcetera.'"

Jim and Colin were chuckling like naughty schoolboys. McCleland knew who had composed the note and was not at all conciliatory. Sophie slapped his arm playfully.

"It's stuff like this that tells me you're doing your jobs," the AVM said, screwing the letter into a ball. "If we didn't put noses out of joint, then we wouldn't be needed. I do take exception to the 'Get lost Grandad,' McCleland. You'd better not refer to me that way!"

Anna finished her drink. "Colin and I have something to tell everyone."

Haltwhistle went quiet. He had hoped to inform his commanding officer personally and in private.

"You're both turning into me?" Jim quipped. Colin gave him a not-impressed-with-that look.

"No. Well, yes I suppose we are, but not that," said Mrs. Haltwhistle. She looked at her husband and then at the group. "I'm pregnant."

Sophie grabbed her friend and hugged her tight. Jim followed suit and felt a lump in his inside coat pocket. He pulled it out.

The money Montalban had given him to compensate Sophie and himself. He could think of no better use for it. He handed it to Anna.

"You'll probably be needing this then. Put it to good use."

Sophie looked at it and smiled. The money would certainly come in useful, and it was not an inconsequential amount either. Anna quickly counted the cash which amounted to around £2000.

Cartwright looked at the roll of bank notes, which was clearly got through means he'd rather not be privy to. He hadn't been told about this and he didn't know where the money had come from.

All things considered, he was prepared to let this one slide for a good cause.

Anna quickly put the money into her bag and looked at Jim. "Thank you."

It was indeed a day to celebrate and enjoy each other's company.

THE END

ABOUT THE AUTHOR

Barrie Taylor was born in the UK in 1982. Raised in a military environment, he emigrated to the USA in 2016. Enjoying writing from childhood, Barrie progressed from short stories to full length manuscripts. He lives with his family in Missouri. *Blind Corner* is his second novel.

OTHER TITLES BY BARRIE TAYLOR

NOTE FROM BARRIE TAYLOR

Word-of-mouth is crucial for any author to succeed. If you enjoyed *Blind Corner*, please leave a review online—anywhere you are able. Even if it's just a sentence or two. It would make all the difference and would be very much appreciated.

Thanks!
Barrie Taylor

We hope you enjoyed reading this title from:

www.blackrosewriting.com

Subscribe to our mailing list – *The Rosevine* – and receive **FREE** books, daily deals, and stay current with news about upcoming releases and our hottest authors.
Scan the QR code below to sign up.

Already a subscriber? Please accept a sincere thank you for being a fan of Black Rose Writing authors.

View other Black Rose Writing titles at www.blackrosewriting.com/books and use promo code **PRINT** to receive a **20% discount** when purchasing.